THE
KILLING
DOLL

Also available in Large Print
by Ruth Rendell:

Death Notes
A Sleeping Life
Master of the Moor

THE KILLING DOLL

Ruth Rendell

G.K.HALL&CO.
Boston, Massachusetts
1984

Published in Large Print by arrangement with Pantheon Books, a division of Random House, Inc.

Set in 16 pt Times Roman.

Library of Congress Cataloging in Publication Data

Rendell, Ruth, 1930–
  The killing doll.

  ''Published in large print by arrangement with Pantheon Books''—Verso t.p.
  1. Large type books. I. Title.
[PR6068.E63K5 1984b]   823'.914   84–10954
ISBN 0–8161–3720–X (lg. print)

For Simon

THE
KILLING
DOLL

1

The winter before he was sixteen, Pup sold his soul to the devil. It was the beginning of December and dark before five. About two hours after that, Pup collected the things he wanted and went down on to the old railway line. Dolly had gone to the hospital — there was visiting between seven and eight — and Harold was nowhere about. Possibly he had gone to the hospital too; he sometimes did.

Pup carried a cycle lamp. He went out of the gate in the fence at the end of the garden and climbed down the slope through the trees and bushes. Here the old railway line lay in a valley so that the gardens looked down on to it, though in other places the grass path where the lines and sleepers had once been ran along a raised embankment. It ran over bridges and under bridges, four or five miles of it, so overgrown in the summertime that, from the air, it must have looked like a strip of woodland. Now, in the winter, the birches and buddleias were bare, the grass thin and damp, clogged with rubbish, sodden paper, and rusty tins. Between the clouds a misty moon glowed, a sponge floating in soapy water.

To the left of him rose the brick arch over which Mistley Avenue passed. It was more than a bridge and less than a tunnel, a damp, dark hole through which a light or two could vaguely be seen glimmering. In the middle of it, someone had once dumped a feather mattress from which the down was still leaking. There were always feathers everywhere inside the Mistley tunnel, stuck to the bricks or ground in the mud or floating like white insects in the dark air. Pup shone his torch and its beam showed him the tunnel's greenish walls, running with wetness. He squatted down among the feathers and lit the candle he had brought with him. He had also brought a small kitchen knife and a cup. His soul, he had thought, must take some visible, tangible form for him to hand over. The knife was quite sharp and needed only a touch to the ball of his thumb to bring the blood welling. A drop of blood, two or three in fact, fell into the cup, and Pup contemplated them by the light of his candle. Now he had gone so far, he hardly knew what words to speak.

Up in a tall chestnut tree in one of the back

gardens an owl cried. It was no hoot that it made, still less a tu-whit-tu-woo, but a cold unearthly cry. Pup listened as it was repeated, that keening eldritch sound, and then he saw the owl, a big, dark, flapping shape silhouetted for a moment against the inky reddish sky at the tunnel's mouth. He was suddenly aware that he was cold. His blood was flowing in single sluggish drops down the shiny white inside of the cup. He stood up and held out the cup and said:

"Devil, O Devil, this is my soul. If you'll give me everything I ask for, you can have my soul and keep it forever. Take it now. In exchange you've got to make me happy." He paused and listened to the utter silence. A feather floated down from the roof and was caught and burned in the candle flame. Pup wondered if it was a sign that his soul had been received. He decided to take immediate advantage of it. "Make me grow," he said.

It was two weeks before he told Dolly about it and then he told only part of it.

"You what?" said Dolly.

He was doing Marlowe's *Faustus* for "O" level. "It's in a play we're doing at school. I thought I might as well try it. After all, my soul's not much use to me, is it? You can't see it or feel it or do anything with it, so I thought I'd sell it to the devil."

"Sell it for what?"

"Well," said Pup vaguely, "just good things to have. Everything I want really. I asked him for things."

"You might have asked him to stop Mother dying," said Dolly as if she were talking of someone offering up prayers.

"I don't think that's the kind of thing he does," said Pup thoughtfully, taking a second chocolate éclair. Already, a little prematurely assuming maternal care of him, she was feeding Pup up on rich cakes and encouraging him to take plenty of sugar in his tea. Building him up, she called it.

Harold, in front of whom any conversation, however private, could be conducted with impunity because he never heard a word when he was reading, had his book propped up against the pot of Tiptree pineapple jam. He was eating sliced tomatoes and egg-and-bacon pie with a fork, American fashion, putting down the fork to lift his cup, keeping his left hand free for turning the pages. Dolly never drank tea. When the visit was over, up in her own room, she would have her nightly ration of two glasses of wine.

"You going to come with me, Dad?" she said. He gave no sign of having heard, so she tapped on the back cover of *The Queen That Never Was,* a life of Sophia Dorothea of Celle. "I said, are you coming with me?"

"It's a very painful thing, going to that hospital," said Harold.

4

"She likes to see you."

"I don't know about that," said Harold, using a favorite phrase of his. "She wouldn't if she knew how painful it was."

There was no chance of his going. She went on her own as usual. After she had gone and Harold had departed for what he called the breakfast room, though no one within living memory had ever eaten breakfast in it, to spend the evening with Sophia Dorothea, Pup went up to the first floor where his bedroom was. There were three floors but they hardly used the top one. Pup's room was at the back, looking out on to the old railway line, the backs of the gray stucco houses in Wrayfield Road, Mrs. Brewer's garden next door and the Buxtons' garden next door on the other side. He drew the curtains. These were made of very old pink and fawn folkweave and had belonged to Harold's mother when this house had been hers. On the bedroom wall Pup had marked out, with the aid of one of Dolly's tape measures, a column six feet high, divided on one side into centimeters (because he had learnt the metric system at school) and inches on the other because feet and inches were still more familiar to him when referring to a person's height.

He took off his shoes. It was a month since he had measured himself. He had last measured himself on 18 November and then he had still been four feet eleven. For months

5

and months he had been four feet eleven, and now as he stood up against the gradated column, tension pulled at his stomach. He shut his eyes. What was he going to do if he stayed four feet eleven for the rest of his life?

"Devil, O Devil . . ." prayed Pup.

He marked where the top of his head reached. He turned round and looked. Four feet eleven and a half. Was he deluding himself? He didn't think so. If anything, he hadn't stretched his knees the way he usually did and his hair was flatter than usual, it had just been cut. The new mark was beyond a doubt half an inch higher than the last mark. Four feet eleven and a half. Anyone weak enough or vain enough to stretch a bit would have made it five feet. Had the devil done this for him? On the whole Pup thought it unlikely — it was mere coincidence.

All the Yearmans tended to shortness. Harold was a small, spare man, thin as a boy at fifty-two, a just respectable five feet six. Let me be a just respectable five feet six, prayed Pup, looking at himself in Grandma Yearman's spotted mirror. Six-and-a-half inches, please, Devil. Faustus had not asked for — or been offered — personal beauty. Perhaps he was handsome enough and tall enough already. Pup had the long Yearman face, domed forehead, long straight nose, wide mouth, the Yearman yellow-brown hair and the Yearmans' yellow eyes, which those

6

who were kind called hazel. Neither he nor Dolly had inherited Edith's red hair, Edith's pale bright blue eyes, a redhead's pink freckled, tender skin. He would be happy enough with his appearance, he thought, if he could grow six-and-a-half inches.

Dolly would never be happy with hers. Dolly's appearance was something else altogether, though she never spoke of how she felt about it to anyone, not to Pup, not even to Edith. She had not written the letter to the magazine, though it might have come from her. "Disfigured, Stockport" seemed to have precisely what she had. Coming home from the hospital — they had told her they doubted her mother would live to see the New Year — she sat on the bus reading the magazine with her right cheek against the dark window. On buses she always sat on the right-hand side for that reason and if there was no right-hand seat vacant she waited for the next bus. Of course she seldom went on buses. It was not as if she had ever gone out to work.

"Being attractive to the opposite sex does not depend on being pretty in a physical sense, you know. Think how many plain women seem to have a host of admirers. Their secret is self-confidence. Cultivate your personality, make yourself an interesting, lively person to be with, try to get out and meet people as much as you can and you will soon have forgotten all about your birthmark in the excitement of making new friends."

Dolly had no friends. Edith had sheltered her and now she wondered what she was going to do without Edith. As soon as she was sixteen, Edith had got her to leave school. There was no question of her having a job. She stayed at home, helping her mother, in the way girls did years ago when Grandma Yearman was young. They used to go out shopping together and Edith got Dolly to take her arm.

"You're not helping that girl, treating her like an invalid, Edith," Mrs. Buxton had said. "There's girls with worse disfigurements than hers get married and lead normal lives. There's a girl I often see about when I go to my daughter's in Finsbury Park, she's got a mark all over the lower half of her face, not just the cheek like Dolly, and I see her about with her baby in its pram. Lovely baby and not a mark on it."

"We took her to one specialist after another," said Edith. "There was nothing to be done. Harold spent a fortune."

Dolly never said a word. She sat at the sewing machine, learning to be a dressmaker under Edith's instruction. They never went anywhere but they were always dressed as if about to be taken out to lunch, trim home-made dresses, sheer tights, polished shoes, their hair shampooed and set, Dolly's, of course, carefully combed so that a curtain of

8

it hung across the cheek. The high spot of their day was Pup coming home to tea.

For seven years it had gone on like that. Dolly was twenty-three.

"It's just as well I never went out to work, if you ask me," she said to Pup. "At any rate I learned how to look after you and run this place."

It was a big house, furnished much as Grandma Yearman had left it. Most of the others like it in Manningtree Grove had been divided up into flats. The Yearmans' house was shabby and rather dark. Squares of old carpet were islanded on its floors in seas of linoleum or stained boards. The plumbing was antique and the wiring unreliable. Harold and Dolly and Pup were not interested in home-making or housekeeping. They did almost nothing about celebrating Christmas. Pup put up some paper chains in the dining room but no one bothered to take them down and they were still there in March when Edith died. There was snow on the ground and it lay untrodden, virgin, a gleaming white avenue of it, on the old railway line. Dolly fed the birds with cake crumbs that she put on an old bookcase outside the kitchen window and threw a brick at Mrs. Brewer's cat when it came after them. She didn't hit it but would one day; she hated that cat, all cats, and one day she would get that one.

Mrs. Buxton came in, wearing Wellington

boots that had to be cut at the tops, her legs were so fat.

"I just wanted to say how sorry I am about your mother, dear. I know what she meant to you, she was more than a mother if that's possible. And your poor little brother, I feel for him. Fancy, you've still got paper chains up in March."

Pup had been sixteen in February but you felt he was younger than he was because he was so small. He was quiet and kind and polite and made no demur when Dolly got him to kiss her before he went off to school and kiss her again when he came in. The mantle of Edith's maternity had slipped on to her shoulders and she was suddenly more maternal than Edith had ever been. She worried over him, wondering why he was so contained and reserved.

He had measured himself on 18 January and 18 February and each time he had grown a little. On 18 March he was five feet one inch tall. He bought himself a paperback he saw on a stand about how to do magic. Faustus had been able to make gold, conjure apparitions, perform feats of trickery. More and more these days he was identifying with Faustus, though a healthy skepticism went on telling him his new growth was just chance.

"I shall never get over it," Harold said after Edith's funeral at Golders Green. "She was all the world to me. I shall never get over it."

Dolly got him a new biography of the last Tsarina out of the library but it was twenty-four hours before he felt able to start on it. He refused to sleep in the bedroom he and Edith had shared but moved into the other first-floor front one and said he was going to have *her* room kept exactly as it was. This was what Queen Victoria had done for Prince Albert when he died. Dolly had to make the bed up and turn down the sheet and drape one of Edith's nightdresses across it, although Edith herself had never lived like this, had rolled her nightdress up under the pillow and often hadn't made the bed at all.

Mrs. Collins, for whom Dolly was finishing a dress Edith had started before she went into hospital, said it brought tears to your eyes to see him. Entering the house, she had surprised Harold going off upstairs with a book about the Almanach de Gotha, had supposed it was the Bible and his destination his late wife's room. Mrs. Collins was religious in a curious sort of way, a member, indeed a leading light, of the Adonai Church of God Spiritists at Mount Pleasant Green.

"He ought to come to us," said Mrs. Collins. "She's bound to want to come through to him from the Other Side."

"She's more likely to want *me*," said Dolly through a mouthful of pins, going round Mrs. Collins's hem on her knees. "You ought to ask me."

"We do ask you, dear," Mrs. Collins said. "We invite all human souls," as if Dolly were some kind of freak who could just lay claim to that definition.

Pup got off the bus at Highgate tube station and walked home along the old railway line. In one hand he carried his school briefcase, in the other a plastic carrier containing the paper and paints and drawing pins and Blu-tak he had bought in Muswell Hill. It was July 18, a fine summer's day. Pup wore clean blue jeans, a clean white shirt and a lightweight gray zipper jacket. Dolly would have liked him to wear gray flannels but Pup, who was easy about most things, insisted on jeans. Nor would he let her make them for him. Levi's, they had to be like others wore, or F letter Us or Wranglers. He had come this way because he liked the old railway line but also to avoid the company of his friend Dilip Raj and certain others who went to his school and also lived in Manningtree Grove or its environs.

There were a lot of people on the line this afternoon, mostly children sitting on the parapets of bridges, but grown-ups as well: a young man who walked along kicking a can, finally kicking it over the parapet at Northwood Road and down into the street below, and women walking dogs. Pup paused to stroke the noble head of a Pyrenean mountain dog being walked from Milton Park to Stanhope Road and back. The sun shone in a bland, hazy sky and all the buddleia bushes were in flower, a mass of long purple spires on which here and there alighted a peacock or small tortoiseshell butterfly. They were getting rare, those butterflies now, but sometimes you saw them up on the old line when the bushes were in bloom.

Just before the Mistley tunnel he climbed up the bank through the long grass and hawthorn seedlings, the yellow flowering ragwort and the pink flowering campion and the paper Coke cans. He let himself in by the garden gate. Dolly was waiting for him, like a mother or a wife, holding out the unmarked cheek for a kiss. He kissed her. He would have kissed the other cheek, for he felt no revulsion. Dolly picked up a stone from the heap she kept on the window sill and hurled it at Mrs. Brewer's cat.

"You ought to throw earth," said Pup. "You might hurt it."

"It walks all over my plants," said Dolly, though there were no plants in the garden worth mentioning, only Solomon's seal and enchanter's nightshade and, in their season, some anemic Michaelmas daisies. "What did you do at school today?" Dolly often asked him this, believing it a mother's duty to ask and forgetting he was sixteen.

"Differential calculus," said Pup gravely.

He had very little idea what this was but hearing that sort of thing made Dolly happy. He had begun, half-consciously, half-unconsciously, on a course of keeping Dolly happy.

"It sounds difficult. Is that what your homework is?"

"That and Finno-Ugrian languages," said Pup, applying himself to salami, Cornish pasty, piccalilli, coleslaw and Battenburg cake.

Bags in hand again, he was going down the cavernous hall (the walls painted dark green to the halfway mark and pale green at the top like an old-fashioned hospital or even workhouse, the floor quarry-tiled in red and black) when his father let himself in at the front door. All the years of his marriage, the first thing Harold ever said when he came in was that he was worn out. Pup greeted him in his usual polite, friendly way.

"Hello, Dad. Had a good day?"

"I don't know about good," said Harold. "I know I'm worn out."

Pup went upstairs to his room. It was hot and stuffy and he opened the window. He took off his shoes. Today he felt no very great trepidation, for he could tell by the shortness of his jeans that he had grown, but even he had not hoped for five feet three. Five feet three. He was really growing and was no longer the shortest boy of his year. Dilip Raj and Christopher Theofanou were both shorter than him.

He put his shoes on again and took the drawing materials out of the bag. With the magic book open before him at a page of diagrams, he began to outline a crescent shape on one of the sheets of cartridge paper. He had four sheets of paper, one for each of the four elements, one to go on each wall of the room on the top floor he had marked out for his temple.

He was going to be a magician.

2

"Will you make me a robe?" Pup said.

"D'you mean a bathrobe?"

Pup shook his head. "Come upstairs. I want to show you something."

"I see," said Dolly like a cross mother. "I suppose it's that room you won't let me go in. I know you locked the door and took away the key. Now his lordship thinks it's time to open up, does he?" She tossed her head. "I don't know if I can spare the time."

Pup gave her his sweet smile. "Yes, you can, dear." Sometimes he called her dear and she loved it. The caressing word melted her. "You know you'll come. You'll like it."

"Oh, all right."

They seldom went up there. Or rather, Dolly corrected herself as they climbed the last flight, *she* seldom went up there. Once these top rooms had been servants'

16

bedrooms, or so Edith had told her, but had anyone in Crouch End ever had servants? It was Dark Ages stuff to Dolly. There were five rooms, low-ceilinged, the walls all papered in strange faded patterns (bunches of pallid sweet peas of spotty mauve, daisies tied with blue ribbon on yellowish stripes), the floors lino'd, pink or fawn or blue, odd bits of furniture standing about, a bed, a pier-glass, a wardrobe on legs with an oval mirror. She ran a mop over the floors twice a year, flicked a duster. That was how she knew he had locked the door of one of the rooms at the back. It was strange having these empty, scarcely known rooms in one's own house, as if it wasn't one's own. A shadow crossed Dolly's mind. Sometimes she had these premonitions.

Pup unlocked the door of the back room. Dolly gasped. The daisies on the yellow stripes were gone. Pup had painted over them in matt black. The ceiling was red. Under the window Dolly recognized from its shape an old bamboo card table that had been in the sweet pea room, but Pup had covered it with a black cloth. Each of the four black walls had pinned to it a sheet of paper with a design on it. On the north wall was a yellow square for earth, on the east a blue circle for air, on the south a red equilateral triangle, apex upwards, for fire, and on the west a silver crescent for water.

17

"They are *tattwas,*" said Pup. "They are the symbols of the four elements. I'm going to do magic." He could tell by her face what she was thinking. "Not conjuring tricks, I don't mean that, not rabbits out of hats." One by one, he took his books off the table and showed them to her: Eliphas Levi, A. E. Waite, Crowley. "It's a kind of science," he said, knowing that would get her. "It takes years of study. I think I might have a gift for it."

Dolly said nothing. She had opened one of the books at random and was reading the words of an incantation so esoteric and abstruse, so protracted and complex, that it seemed to her a person would have to be an intellectual giant to comprehend it.

"You can forget it if you don't want to know," said Pup. "You don't have to be in on it."

"Oh, I want to be in on it," Dolly said hastily. "If it takes years of study, d'you have to go to college?" She was ambitious for him; she didn't want him to go into the business with Harold. This might be the answer. "What can you *be* when you've done it?"

Pup nearly laughed. "It's not what you'll be, it's what you can do. You can get yourself what you want, anything you want." Doubt and hope were mingled in Dolly's expression. "So will you make me a robe? I want a golden robe with a black sun and moon and stars sort of stuck on it.''

''Appliquéd,'' said Dolly. She suddenly realized he was taller than she. It must have happened very recently. She felt a tender pride in him. ''Let's go down and see what I've got. I've got a dress length of gold poly-ester I got in John Lewis's sale that might do.''

Dolly was at the machine in the front-room window, stitching the side seams of the golden robe, when she saw Myra Brewer walking along the pavement on the other side of the privet hedge. Myra was going to visit her mother as she always did on Thursday evenings. Passing under the overhanging branches of the two ginkgo trees which grew in the Yearmans' garden, she put up her hand and plucked off a handful of the maidenhair fern-shaped leaves. Myra was one of those people who are unable to walk under over-hanging leaves without snatching at a bunch of them. Those Brewers, Dolly thought, including the cat among ''those Brewers,'' were always damaging her property. She banged on the window but Myra had already gone by. No one had hair that red, not even Edith's had been that red, Myra must put henna on it. Dolly heard the next-door door slam as Myra let herself in.

''I thought you were never coming,'' said Mrs. Brewer as her daughter made a pot of

19

tea she wouldn't put herself out to make.

"You always say that. You always say, 'Aren't you late?' or 'I thought you were never coming.' "

"If I say it, it's because it's true. You always are late except when he brings you in his car. Where is he tonight? Home with wifey, I suppose."

Myra could have cried when her mother talked to her like that. It was all true. He was at home with wifey and she was thirty-seven and her hair looked awful if she didn't put henna on it. She had been in the ladies' loo at West End Green on the way here and there had been this graffito on the wall that said: "The quietest thing on earth is the sound of hair going gray."

"It's no good looking like that," said Mrs. Brewer, putting cream in her tea the way she had done when a girl in Devonshire. "It's no good getting down in the mouth. You can talk all you like about the second half of the twentieth century and all that but human nature doesn't change. You should have seen the writing on the wall when his boys went to boarding school and he didn't divorce her then."

Myra said nothing. She had had enough writing on walls for one day.

"There's that little bitch with the birthmark throwing stones at Fluffy again," said Mrs. Brewer.

Fluffy was a long-coated tabby that Mrs. Brewer called a Persian. Sometimes he sat on the post between the Yearmans' front fence and the house next door. Mrs. Brewer had the ground-floor flat and the people on the next floor and the people on the top floor all had cats, though only Fluffy sat on the post. Dolly said there were more cats in Crouch End than in all the rest of London put together.

"Well, there are more mice in London than people," said Pup who knew about things like that.

Edith used to tidy up the front garden in the autumn, cut down the Michaelmas daisies, pull out the enchanter's nightshade and sweep up the leaves. Dolly supposed she would have to do it now. Wearing the cotton gloves that had been her mother's, using Edith's secateurs and Edith's small red-and-silver painted trowel, brought her mother most forcefully back to her. She could almost see her when she closed her eyes, that thin, pinched face, that fiery red hair, and smell the lemon verbena toilet water she used. The tears came into her eyes. She began furiously digging out weeds.

Fluffy came tightrope-walking along the fence, did his claw-scraping act up the side of the post and then sat on top of it. Dolly looked up at him while he was scraping and again when he settled down. Manningtree

Grove was long and straight and fairly wide in spite of the cars parked nose-to-tail along it, and motorists used it as a through route between Crouch End Hill and Stroud Green. Cars went down it very fast, especially the ones driven by boys of seventeen and eighteen. Dolly heard a car coming as it bounded over the hump where Mistley Avenue went across. She knew what she was doing and yet she did not quite know; her intention was half-fantasy. She leapt to her feet, clapped her hands and shouted out. Fluffy jumped off the post and fled across the road.

Dolly heard the car roar by, without a pause, with no sound of brakes. It had been going very fast; they thought nothing of driving at fifty down there. She waited for Fluffy to come back, to scrape the post and then sit on it. She even selected a stone to throw at him. After a little while she laid down the trowel and got up and went down the path, through the gate, out on to the pavement and looked. Fluffy lay near the gutter on the opposite side of the street beween the front bumper of a red Datsun and the rear bumper of a green Volvo. Dolly went across the road. He was dead, limp, though still very warm. A little blood was coming from the corner of his mouth but otherwise he was unmarked. The impact had killed him and flung him there. Dolly felt rather sick. She went back indoors and washed her hands.

Mrs. Brewer had been out at the time. She found the corpse during the evening and sat down and cried. She tried to get Myra on the phone but Myra was out somewhere with the married man. Dolly, who seldom drank before the evening, not before 5:30 anyway, had to have a glass of wine and then another after the Fluffy incident. An Indian woman called Mrs. Das who lived in the flat above Mrs. Buxton had heard Dolly yell and seen Fluffy flee and she told Mrs. Brewer about it. This was not because she liked cats — indeed, where she came from they outlawed cats, believing their bodies to be inhabited by the spirits of dead witches — but because Mrs. Brewer was one of the few people in the neighborhood, apart from other Indians, who condescended to speak to her. Dolly never spoke and Mrs. Das wasn't to know Dolly hardly ever spoke to anyone.

There was no way of proving it and nothing overt Mrs. Brewer could do. But she told everybody she knew.

"Her mother was as nice a woman as you'd meet," said Mrs. Buxton. "Your Myra reminds me of her in a way."

Myra had never seen Edith Yearman. She had already been ill before Mrs. Brewer came to live there. "In *what* way?"

"The hair for a start. The eyes. Of course Myra's a lot heavier built, she'd need to fine down a bit."

"Charming," said Myra to her mother. "That's the pot calling the kettle black."

Mrs. Brewer took no notice. "She must be sick in her mind, murdering a person's pet."

It seemed to Pup that he had probably stopped growing for good. He had been seventeen in February and five feet seven and he was still five feet seven. No Yearman, as far as he knew, had ever been so tall and he was satisfied. In the golden robe, appliquéd with sun, moon and stars, he made quite a commanding figure.

According to Eliphas Levi, author of *The Doctrine and Ritual of Transcendental Magic*, the magician may buy a knife for use as his dagger, providing he uses this knife to manufacture his other elemental weapons. Pup bought a knife in the big iron-mongers in Muswell Hill and painted the hilt of it with the name Lucifer and also with the archangelic name of fire. He could use the knife to make his wand and perhaps his pentacle but he was doubtful about carving a cup.

On the old railway line, the bushes and the branches of the trees were still bare. It had been a cold spring. Harold had had the flu and Dolly had had it mildly and it had swept through Pup's school and now Mrs. Brewer had it. Mrs. Brewer was fat and aging and her flu turned to bronchitis. Myra came to stay. She kept on with her job as part-time receptionist to a dentist in Camden Town, but she was there in the evenings and overnight. It was years since she had worked full-time. The afternoons were the best times for the married man to get away.

"He won't miss you," said Mrs. Brewer, wheezing. "He'll have a chance to catch up on things with wifey."

"I don't know why you're so cruel to me after all I do for you," said Myra.

"There's a saying in the Bible about being cruel only to be kind. You've got nothing, d'you realize that? Not even a roof over your head. That little bitch with the birthmark that murdered Fluffy has got more than you have and she's half your age. At least that's her father's house."

"He owns that great place? All of it?"

"All of it, miss. And a nice little business in the Broadway. Hodge and Yearman, Typewriters and Instant Print. I'm surprised you haven't noticed it when you've been passing through in *his* car."

"All right, Mother, for Christ's sake. Now you've started yourself off coughing."

Very early in the morning Pup and Dolly went together down on to the old railway line to find a tree branch for Pup's magic wand. Eliphas Levi, said Pup, suggested that the wand should be a perfectly straight branch of almond or hazel, cut at a single blow with the magical pruning knife or golden sickle, before the rising of the sun, at that moment when the tree is ready to blossom. He had with him his dagger with the painted hilt, ready for cutting the wand from the tree.

It was a cool clear London morning and the old railway line was as green as a country lane. The grass and the budding trees were drenched with bright, cold, glistening dew. Dolly had hardly ever seen the dawn but she guessed that, just as the sky is flooded with gold after the sun has set, so it may be before the sun rises. Between bars of darkish cloud, the sky was livid. Birds had been singing, a concentrated, unmusical twittering, since long before they climbed down the embankment.

Pup knew when the sun would rise, he had a sense about these things. Neither of them was entirely sure they could tell an almond or a hazel tree when they saw one, though Pup said it was faith and love which counted more than accuracy. They walked through the Mistley tunnel and along the channel between the weed-grown platforms which were all that now remained of a station that had once been there — Mount Pleasant Green. They had plenty of time and they walked nearly all the way to Tollington Road, over bridges and through tunnels, on the dewy turf, before they found a tree Pup said must be a hazel. From this tree, as the yellow of the sky began to brighten, he cut with a bold sweep of his arm a slender wand hung with golden catkins.

They walked back the way they had come. The air was not yet tainted with the fumes that would soon come drifting from the traffic passing under and passing over. Along the old railway line you could smell pale green tree flowers breaking into blossom, you could smell the new grass and the cow parsley that sprang up to cover the rank wet newspaper, the empty cans, the broken bottles, the feathers and the cigarette ends. It was cool and fresh, the sun blazing now but cold as midwinter.

Dolly wore her lion's mane hair in a style designed half to cover her face. She had a tweed suit on and a red wool jersey, both homemade (though few would have guessed it), and sensible brown hide walking shoes. From time to time she glanced at Pup, who carried his wand like a pilgrim's staff, with love and pride and hope. He had the same lion hair as her but he wore it just to the tips of his ears and this gave him a look of earnest innocence. His face was a long oval and he had the long straight nose and full lips of a saint or perhaps merely a bystander in certain medieval paintings. He was very thin and light on his feet. Although he wore jeans and a sweater and a jacket he somehow gave the impression, so contained and neatly made as he was, of being dressed much more formally.

It was just after half-past seven when they turned the corner into Manningtree Grove.

Dolly had not wanted to risk her tights on the embankment again, so they had got off the old railway line by going up the steps in Mount Pleasant Gardens. Harold must have come out to take the milk in, for he stood on the front garden path, a milk bottle cradled like a child in each arm, like twin babies, talking over the fence to Myra Brewer.

With an instinctive gesture that was almost a reflex, Dolly drew the curtain of hair across her cheek. She looked but said nothing. Myra Brewer was wearing a bright green blouse and a green-and-navy check skirt and her gold watch and some gold chains and had on her full panoply of make-up, enough, in fact, for going on a television talk show under powerful lights.

"Good morning, Myra," said Pup who had never been introduced to her but who happened to know what her first name was.

Myra said hello. Pup smiled gently at his father, gave Dolly the hazel wand to hold, and took the milk bottles out of Harold's arms as if they were too heavy a load for him or an impediment to his continued conversation. Later that day, after school, he stripped the catkins and the leaf buds from the hazel branch and painted it yellow. He painted a black spiral round it and inscribed upon it the name of Lucifer. Dolly gave him a glass tumbler, the last remaining one of a crystal water set, and he used this for the cup, painting the name of Lucifer on it and the archangelic name for the element of water. The pentacle was more difficult. At last he found a shop in Hornsey where the man agreed to cut him a plywood circle. Pup told him he wanted it for backing a mirror.

Dolly was invited to attend the ceremony of the consecration of the elemental weapons. At his request, she brought him a glass of red wine, a slice of bread and a saucerful of salt. He needed a rose too but they had none in the garden, so Dolly waited till it was dark and stuck her hand through the fence and picked a bud from Mrs. Buxton's *Rose gaujard* which was just coming out. Pup made his own holy water. Facing towards the north, standing to the south of his altar, he extended his hand over the saucer of salt and chanted:

"May wisdom abide in this salt and may it preserve my mind and body from all corruption. May all phantoms depart from it so that it may become a heavenly salt, salt of earth and earth of salt. May it feed the threshing ox and strengthen my hope with the horns of the winged bull! So mote it be."

He had got it out of a book but he had learned it by heart. Mixing the salt and some joss-stick ash into the water made it holy. Dolly sat on a cushion on the floor, watching him, feeling a deep thrill of excitement. Pup walked round in a circle with the glass of holy water, sprinkling it to the four quarters of the temple. He lit a joss stick and walked round again, saying:

"And when after all the phantoms are vanished, thou shalt see the holy formless fire, that fire which darts and flashes through the hidden depths of the universe, hear, thou Voice of Fire."

There was a great deal more. It went on for two hours and Dolly loved every minute of it. As he raised his arms and the golden sleeves hung like pennants, Pup's face was rapt, his eyes glowing with hieratic fervour. He was obsessed with magic these days, he admitted it himself. He read nothing but books on magic, which might have accounted for his failure to get more than three poorish "O" levels and made it seem unlikely that his "A" levels would be much better, always supposing he stayed on long enough to do them. The word "magician" had a frivolous or even charlatanish ring to it, so Pup called himself a geomancer.

"Can you be a geomancer without 'A' levels?" asked Dolly, who seemed to think it was something like going into computers or being a physicist.

Pup did not disillusion her. He was beginning to see that by Edith's death he had lost a cook and housekeeper and gained a mother. It seemed a long time ago now that he had cut his thumb and parted with his soul to the devil, a very long time since he had asked for anything. Wearing the robe, holding the dagger in his hands, he stood before his altar and asked for his own version of what Faustus had desired: a successful career, magical powers, wealth, Helen of Troy — but a Helen many times multiplied and to have, not merely to see and snatch at in vain.

3

*I*n a house at the Stroud Green end of Mount Pleasant Gardens, facing what remained of the old green and opposite the meeting place of the Adonai Church of God Spiritists, Diarmit Bawne sat in his room on the top floor. It was a so-called double room because it contained two beds, though it was no more than ten feet by fifteen. The other bed had been occupied by a kind of family connection of Diarmit's called Conal Moore, and when Conal had gone away he had promised to come back, but he had still not come back after three weeks and Diarmit was waiting for him anxiously. Diarmit had no work and no home but this room and knew hardly anyone in London. Fortunately, there was the Department of Health and Social Security to keep him and pay the rent of the room.

These days Diarmit spent a lot of time sitting at the window looking down into the street and at Mount Pleasant Green, across which he expected Conal Moore to come because that was the direction in which Crouch Hill station was. The green was deserted and had been for some time except for the pigeons, and the Dalmatian and the mongrel collie that half-heartedly chased the pigeons and scavenged from the litter bins. Diarmit made himself a cup of tea in a mug with a teabag and powdered milk. Conal had left two large tins of powdered milk in the room and three large boxes of teabags and some noodles and curry stuff you added hot water to to make a meal but he had left nothing else of his, not even any of his clothes. Diarmit wished he would come back because he was growing more and more frightened of being alone. He knew no one in the house and it was several days since he had spoken a word to anyone or anyone had spoken to him. He sat in the window and drank his tea, watching the Dalmatian and the collie, watching the chestnut leaves falling on to the wet green grass.

He was twenty-four, the youngest of twelve children. When he was nine in County Armagh, his mother had been killed by a bomb intended for a Member of Parliament whose house she cleaned. Diarmit saw the bomb go off and he saw what happened to his mother, though he was not injured, or not apparently injured, himself. His father, long before, had gone to America "to see what it was like," had seen and never come back. Diarmit's brothers and sisters were scattered about the British Isles. First he went to his eldest sister in Dublin but she had seven children of her own and an extra one was too much for her, so he was passed on to divide his time between his two sisters in Liverpool.

He had a brother in Belfast, a butcher with his own shop, the most successful and well-to-do of the Bawnes. When he was sixteen, Diarmit was sent back to Belfast to live with his brother and learn his trade. He was there two years. Then the whole street, including the shop, was bombed one day and the opposite side reduced to rubble. Neither the butcher nor Diarmit was hurt but Diarmit vanished and was found some days later, wandering in the countryside twenty miles away, having lost the power of speech and his memory.

After that he spent nearly a year in a mental hospital, though he was never certified. He came out, returned to Liverpool and resumed the existence of moving from one sister to the other. Neither wanted him. Family conferences were held to discuss the big question of what was to be done with Diarmit, what permanent job could be got for him, where was he permanently to live. The army was considered as a possibility, work on the land, bus driving, security officer, traffic warden. His mental history was against him; there was that black-out, that year in the hospital, that loss of speech that had afflicted him on several later occasions. He lived more or less always on the dole. Sometimes he had doubts as to whether he actually existed at all, and these were particularly strong when his speech failed him or when his sisters, exasperated, ignored his presence or their children acted as if any room in which he was was an empty room.

Conal Moore was his sister Mary's brother-in-law. He lived in London and worked for Budgen's on the delicatessen counter. Everybody in the family and everybody connected with the family was rooting for something for Diarmit, just to get him off Mary's back, so it was welcome news to hear from Conal, though it was no great surprise. Conal said he could get Diarmit a job on the butchery counter, after all that was Diarmit's line, and if he liked to come down he could share his place for a bit till he found somewhere.

Diarmit had come to Mount Pleasant Gardens and found a note waiting for him and the key to the room. The note and the key were on the table in the downstairs hall where all the tenants' correspondence was put. Diarmit could read his own name on the note but nothing else. He was better with print, for instance he could make out a lot of what was in a newspaper, but handwriting defeated him. He had let himself into the room and ever since then he had been waiting for Conal to come back and he had been wondering what was in the note.

The note was in his pocket. He carried it about with him. He had a sister living in London. Her name was Kathleen, she was married and she lived in Kilburn. Every day Diarmit meant to go and see Kathleen so that she could read Conal's note to him and so that he might have someone to talk to and be with. But every day it became harder and harder for him to do this, a now nearly impossible feat of effort and endurance. He had been to Kilburn, it was easy to get there from Mount Pleasant Green, you took the train from Crouch Hill to Brondesbury, it was easy to get there and he had got as far as walking along the road where Kathleen lived but he had not gone up to the house to knock at the door. He was too afraid. Sometimes he thought it would be better if he walked there instead, it would not be so quick and sudden as going by train.

When he had finished his tea he put on his jacket and went downstairs and out of the house. He walked across the green towards Crouch End. There was a Budgen's super-market at Crouch End and another at Muswell Hill but neither had a butchery counter. Perhaps there were others he didn't know about, he couldn't ask, he didn't know what to ask or how to frame the words.

It was a coldish, dull, negative sort of day in autumn. He went into Budgen's and bought a single item, a loaf of bread. It puzzled him that there was no butchery counter, only a section where pre-packed cuts of meat were on sale. He said thank you to the girl at the check-out but she said nothing to him. He wondered if she could see him or hear him, and he thought of giving a sudden loud shout but he was too afraid to do that. Never before had he been alone like this, but somehow always involved, for good or ill, with his large family.

He came out once more into the raw gray afternoon. There were a lot of people in Crouch End Broadway, slouching along or scurrying or marching fast, regardless of the small and timid in their path. Their faces were sullen and hostile or indifferent. Now he had bought the loaf he knew he wouldn't go to Kathleen's, he would go back to Mount Pleasant Gardens and wait for Conal Moore.

A woman in a fur coat walking ahead of him dropped a plastic carrier bag into the litter bin attached to a lamp-post. Diarmit turned his head this way and that to see if anyone was looking and then he took the carrier bag out again and put his loaf in it. It was a shiny olive-green bag with the name "Harrods" written on it in gold. He walked back across the green, carrying a small, sliced, wrapped white loaf in a Harrods bag, and the pigeons flapped and scuttered out of his way.

4

At the end of the autumn term, Pup left school. He left on a Thursday and on the Monday set off with Harold in the morning to work at Hodge and Yearman. Jimmy Hodge, who Harold had been in business with for thirty years, had just retired.

Dolly was cross about it and disappointed. She wanted him to get his "A" levels and go to a university. He had read so many books and learned so much and spent so much time in the temple and now it would all go to waste.

"It won't go to waste," said Pup. "I shall do it in my spare time, I shall do it in the evenings."

While he was at work, Dolly borrowed some of his books and tried to read them. The subject was immense and her brain reeled. The Philosopher's Stone, the Ancient Mysteries, the Qabala, Dr. Dee and Helena

Blavatsky, Magnetism and the Golden Flower — from all this she was able only to isolate and establish that the adept, the magus, once he had learned it all, might achieve anything he desired and have anything he wished. It was a science right enough, thought Dolly, to whom this signified a study that required protracted concentration and the learning of thousands of facts. What other science could be so complicated and so taxing to the mind? Dolly read about the magical Order of the Golden Dawn, that group or circle of magicians, founded in 1888, to which, it seemed, all the great names that figured in this pile of books had belonged. She imagined him one day as another Waite or Regardie, world-famous as the author of some such weighty textbook as one of these.

Pup himself was as keen as any student might be, embarking on the long training for a professional career. He and Harold came home from work together, sometimes calling in at the Haringey Central Library to change Harold's books; they had their tea and then, when Harold retreated to the breakfast room with the memoirs of a princess of Thurn und Taxis or went out on one of his mysterious trips, presumably to a pub, Pup would go up to the temple. He was obsessed with magic, it was an all-absorbing craze with him as football was to some of his contemporaries. The occult had him in its grip. He could hardly wait to get into the golden robe and begin an incantation or make divinations with the tarot cards or settle down to the study of etheric projection.

He cast horoscopes and he made talismans. He went back to the shop where the man had cut him the plywood for the pentacle and got him to cut out in metal two small polygonal shapes and pierce a hole in each. Dolly was a Venusian subject, so her talisman was a seven-sided pendant which he painted green and the letters on it red as was correct. For this, he had to use "virgin" instruments, unused before, bought new for the purpose, the brush, the paint, the thong.

"And I'm a virgin," said Pup.

Dolly nodded her head vigorously. That was how it should be. The magical powers were enhanced by virginity. Time after time, instructions in the books for performing a certain evocation or banishing ritual stressed that the magician should be chaste. It made Dolly happy that Pup never looked at a girl. He had friends of his own sex, sometimes he went to their homes, he went out for a drink occasionally with Chris Theofanou, but he had no eyes for girls. Carefully, almost reverently, she hung the talisman he had made her round her neck. It would keep away harm, he said, it would protect her from evil powers.

Quite often he invited her into the temple to watch him perform a particular rite. She covered some cushions in scarlet and gold and black material and on these she sat, watching him with awe and admiration. But he didn't always want her there and she never invited herself, she wouldn't put herself forward. It was enough for her to know he was making progress, that he was not like so many other boys of his age but was up there, quietly applying himself to his studies.

Sitting downstairs in the front room, pinning on a pattern or working the sewing machine, Dolly thought how proud their mother would have been if she could have seen him and known what he was doing. Perhaps she could see and did know. It was missing her mother that made Dolly go to the Adonai Church of God Spiritists.

Mrs. Brewer had a new cat, a ginger and white kitten that was too wise ever to go near the road or even into the front garden. It stayed in the back, prowling across conservatory roofs and hunting on the old railway line. Dolly kept a pile of stones on the old bookcase outside the kitchen window to hurl at it when it came into her garden, just as she had done in the days of Fluffy.

She wore her talisman for her first visit to Mount Pleasant Hall. Although she knew by sight many of the people who attended and could see that not one of them had any claim to elegance or style, she dressed herself with care. Dolly felt that if she could only be well enough dressed, well enough groomed, there must come a point where people would observe this alone and the nevus pass unnoticed. She wore the dress and coat she had just finished making for herself in tweed of a smart olive-drab shade. At the neck she tied a little vermilion silk scarf and hung on the pendant so that it showed between the lapels of the coat. She had chosen the tweed and the scarf particularly to complement the talisman.

No one in Manningtree Grove and its environs dressed as well as her except perhaps some of the young black girls going off to catch trains in the mornings. And yet, as she seldom went out, all this elegance was wasted on shopping in Crouch End Broadway or down the Holloway Road. This was the first time she had been out in the evening for she didn't know how long.

Before leaving she had drunk a tumblerful of wine to give her courage but, even so, being out alone at this hour filled her with unease. She had those agoraphobic sensations not uncommon in housebound, withdrawn people. She felt exposed and vulnerable and threatened. The people who were about in the evening were a different set from those she encountered shopping in the mornings and they seemed to her to have more curious eyes and less guarded expressions. Dolly had no friends. Pup didn't count, he was her child. Her mother had been her friend and her mother was dead. She wondered how she would feel when, in the next hour or so perhaps, she heard her mother's voice.

But in the event it was very different. No more than a dozen pepole came for the seance and that included Mrs. Collins and her daughter Wendy and the medium. The hall was a not very large room with a small curtained-off stage at one end. There were green roller blinds at the windows and coconut matting on the floor. Mrs. Collins was wearing the navy blue suit she called a costume that Dolly had made her. She smiled in a way Dolly knew that wearing it was meant as a compliment to her. Wendy was fat and long-chinned and well over thirty but she had no birthmark on her right cheek.

They all sat in a row on rush-bottomed tip-up chairs. Mrs. Collins switched off the uncompromising, high-wattage overhead light and turned on the table lamp she had brought, plugged in on yards of lead to somewhere at the back of the stage. The medium was an old woman, fatter even than Wendy, and had a somewhat more comfortable chair in which, as soon as everyone was seated, she went promptly into a trance.

After a while, people began to come through with messages: an old friend for Wendy Collins, an aunt for a Miss Finlay.

They spoke through the medium's lips in strangled whispers. It was not frightening, not exciting, not even *believable*. Edith's voice didn't sound like Edith. It was too soft and lugubrious.

"Dear daughter, I am always near you, I watch you taking care of Peter and my beloved husband . . ."

Edith had never spoken like that. Dolly felt indignant that the medium should be such a fraud, callously deluding people, and then, simultaneously with that thought, there came to her a breath of perfume, of lemon verbena. She almost cried out, so powerful for a brief moment was this scent of her dead mother.

It was gone in an instant, the medium was waking and the Adonai Spiritists were preparing to leave. Dolly was trembling from the shock that scent had given her. It seemed to prove the truth of what she had read in Pup's books.

During the seance it had grown dark outside. The yellow and white street lamps were on and a single white lamp shone in the center of Mount Pleasant Green. It would not have occurred to her to feel frightened to walk home in the dark on her own. But in the little vestibule where the notice boards were between the inner glass doors and the outer doors, a woman touched her sleeve, said she was Miss Finlay and might they walk home together? Dolly nodded and followed her out.

At the touch she had smelt lemon verbena again. It was Miss Finlay's scent, that was all, it was Miss Finlay's lemon scent that she had smelt all the time.

Miss Finlay scurried along as if pursued and Dolly had to take long strides to keep up with her. As they walked Dolly thought about that scent and about her mother's voice sounding so soft and low-pitched and Miss Finlay talked about how wonderful the seance had been and how amazing the medium.

"It must be marvelous to have powers."

Dolly felt affronted. "My brother has *real* powers. He does magic."

"What, like sticking pins in a wax image?"

"Of course not, nothing like that. He's a geomancer, it's scientific."

Miss Finlay giggled. Dolly was very offended and when Miss Finlay said she was looking for a dressmaker, she wanted a velvet skirt made, she merely shrugged and said she was in the phone book. They were outside the Yearmans' house and Dolly pushed the gate open. Nervous Miss Finlay had another half mile to walk up to Crescent Road all on her own. Dolly said good night absently. This was not the companion she was looking for, the friend that would make her forget her birthmark in the excitement of their meeting.

Pup must be in the temple. The landing light on the top floor was on. Dolly let herself into the house and without taking her coat off, went straight to the kitchen. There was an open bottle of Soave in the larder and she needed a glass of it. The second shock of the evening was when she opened the door and found the light on and Harold sitting at the table with Myra Brewer, two cans of Double Diamond and two bags of crisps between them.

Harold gave Dolly a sheepish grin.

"Tell her our news, Hal," said Myra.

He did so. Dolly listened to the halting, embarrassed, rather shamefaced announcement in silence. She was going to say she didn't believe it but that wasn't true; she found she had no difficulty at all in believing it. Still without speaking, she went back into the hall and closed the kitchen door.

Then, having taken a deep breath and clenched her fists, she ran upstairs to tell Pup.

5

*T*he top floor," Myra said, "would make quite a nice flat for Peter and Doreen."

Harold was unused to hearing his children called by their given names and he almost had to think who it was she meant. They were walking about the house, thinking what changes would have to be made when they were married. Or Myra was thinking of these things. Harold had supposed he and she would simply go along to some register office, presumably the Wood Green one, and get through the requisite very few words after which he would be a married man again. He was used to being married, found it difficult to sleep without a woman in his bed and hoped to resume the state with the minimum of upheaval. He considered what Myra had said and it seemed to him a tremendous step, comparable to changing one's trade or emigrating.

"I don't know about that," he said. When he used this phrase he meant not that he was ignorant on the subject but that he had doubts of its wisdom or feasibility.

"It seems so peculiar, a grown-up son and daughter living at home."

"I lived at home till I got married." And after, he might have added.

"Well, in those days . . ." Harold was fifteen years older than her, and she thought of herself as a girl; "He's a widower, he's got children practically my age," she was inclined to say when speaking of her future husband. "They could have a bedroom each and the front room for a lounge. I don't see why we shouldn't put in a kitchen, a sink and water heater really, that's all that's needed. I don't mind paying, I'll use my Unit Trusts."

"You'll have to tell them. I can't."

Harold avoided everything disagreeable. It was to this negative aim that he devoted his energies. Walking half a mile to work, poking about in the shop all day (he knew a great deal about typewriters), going home again — he did not object to any of that. He liked having a big house to spread himself in, though he never spread himself much, mooching between the kitchen, the breakfast room and the once-sacred bedroom. He liked living in the house in which he had been born, the only place he had ever lived in. His leisure he devoted to reading what he called "history books," biographies of the more colorful characters in history such as Mary Queen of Scots, Nell Gwynn, and the Prince Regent (never Cromwell, Robespierre, or Palmerston) and the memoirs of princelings and princesslings of nineteenth-century European minor royal houses. As a result of this, he was actually an authority, not, as he believed, on history itself, but on the myth and legend of history.

In the end he had to tell them. Myra wasn't there to do it. She was packing up in West Hampstead, telling the married man she had had a better offer, thank you very much, and when he had gone, crying herself to sleep.

Dreading it, loathing the idea of it, working himself up to a pitch of fear and shame, which was the exaggerated state he always got into if he had to exert himself or be candid, Harold falteringly told his daughter that Myra wanted her and Pup to move upstairs. As is generally so in these cases, Dolly took it much better than had been expected. She didn't scream or cry or attack him but was merely haughty.

"I wouldn't want to live in the same place as her anyway. I'd rather go up there. At least we'll be on our own, we'll be independent. I don't want to associate with her more than's strictly necessary."

"Don't be like that, Dolly," said Harold feebly.

"I will be like it. You said you'd never get over Mother, that's what you said."

"We'll be all right on our own," said Pup when he got home from work. "It'll be nice."

"Yes, it will. It'll be lovely, just you and me. We'll be all right, won't we, Pup? We'll be happy, just the two of us."

"Of course we will, dear," said Pup.

Dolly wasted no time. Next morning she lugged up to the top floor everything she wanted, chairs and tables and mirrors and a cabinet and a desk, table linen and bed linen and china and glass as well as Edith's sewing machine. Harold scarcely noticed. He never required more than a chair to sit on and a bed to lie on. Myra didn't care, she was going to get new anyway. Mrs. Brewer had not been accurate when she said Myra had nothing; she had her Unit Trusts and her National Savings, getting on for 1,500 pounds, the way it had mounted up over the years.

They were married in March. Harold came back from his honeymoon in Newquay to find Pup and Dolly moved upstairs and the house so silent as to give a false idea that it was occupied solely by his wife and himself. Myra made real coffee in the filter pot she had bought in St. Ives and open sandwiches with hard-boiled egg and tuna. Harold would have preferred Wall's pork pies and tomatoes and a pot of tea but he was not a man who complained. He sat quietly reading the

51

memoirs of Princess Marie-Louise for the third or fourth time.

Next day father and son met in the shop just before 9:30. Pup was as kindly and polite as ever. He had run the business in his father's absence and had run it efficiently, even keeping the books for the sales tax. Harold was teaching him how to service and repair typewriters and when he knew enough he said he was going to do outside servicing, visiting homes and offices. No other company in the vicinity was willing to do that and it was just the fillip they needed in this recession.

They went home together. On the way they called at the library and Pup carried Harold's books home inside his coat because it had started to rain. Myra ran from the kitchen to kiss Harold in the manner of a brand-new wife. There was a spicy smell of something made with peppers and curry that was as new to the house as Myra was. Not yet back at her job, she had had all day in which to cook and to beautify the place and herself, beginning as soon as Harold had left with a fresh application of henna to her hair.

During their long affair, the married man had given Myra a lot of fairly good jewelry. She hung it on herself liberally and, when she was dressed up, without restraint. She was wearing the navy blue acrylic blouse and emerald-and-navy-and-white check skirt which formed part of what she called her

52

"trousseau," and round her neck, half-a-dozen gold chains from which were suspended a gold wishbone, a gold four-leaved clover, a gold and ivory dice and other such toys. She had her best gold watch on and her charm bracelet and her former lover's ring with the fire opal that quite eclipsed Harold's wedding band.

Pup stood in front of her, smiling first at his father and then at her, as if giving them his blessing in a paternal way. Myra wondered if he was quite right in the head. He put out his hand and lifted the gold chains which hung over the large well-braced promontory of Myra's bosom. She jumped at Pup's touch; she couldn't help it. Pup gave her another smile, reassuring this time. He examined the wishbone, the four-leaved clover and the dice as if they interested him greatly, and he lifted Myra's hand and looked at the charms on her bracelet. Myra began to feel nervous and uncomfortable and she nearly said something sharp, when a diversion was created by the workmen descending the stairs. These were the men she had got in to install a sink and a water heater in the smallest of the five rooms on the top floor. She snatched her hand away from Pup and the gold chains flew about, jangling.

"That's the lot of them," the plumber said. "I'll pop in in the morning and check your taps."

"I was thinking," Myra said in the rather shrill way she had when she was not at ease, "while you're here, why don't we go the whole hog and have a bathroom put in for Peter and Doreen?"

"I don't know about that," said Harold.

"It's not very civilized, is it? To be perfectly honest, it's not ideal, is it, having just the one bathroom in a house this size?"

"Planning permission'd have to be got," said the plumber. "Planning permission is essential prior to the installation of your water closet."

"All right. Why not? How d'you go about it?"

The only possible convertible room was his temple. Pup said in his gentle way, in his soft, low voice, "Dolly and I don't need our own bathroom, thank you very much. For such a short time —" he smiled at Myra "— it would be a waste of money." He said, "Excuse me," to the workmen and walked past them up the stairs.

"What do you think Peter meant by 'such a short time,' Hal?" said Myra, dishing up stuffed peppers. She called her husband Hal because no one else had ever done so and it had a dashing ring, rather out of keeping with Harold's appearance. Pup's remark had made her think. In fact, he had only meant by it that he intended to share a house with her for no longer than he could help, and as soon as

54

his ship came in, he would move out.

"Ask me another," said Harold. He took the plate and said, "I thang you!" after the manner of Arthur Askey, which he thought and believed Myra would think a witty and sparkling rejoinder.

"You don't suppose he's thinking of getting married himself?" said Myra, asking him another.

"Don't make my laugh. He's only eighteen."

"It would be the best thing really for all of us, though I don't suppose there's much chance for poor Doreen."

Harold said nothing for a moment. He was still overcome at the conversion of the horrible, dark, dirty, old dining room into a reasonable place to eat in. The looping up of the port-wine-colored velvet curtains with lengths of red ribbon and the provision of a few blue scyllas in a Denbyware honeypot, which would have struck most people as pathetic, seemed to him only awesome. He had never before tasted green peppers and he didn't think he liked them much. There was a napkin with a bit of lace in one corner but he felt it would be going rather far to wipe his mouth on it.

"Dolly?" he said. "I don't know about that." Harold wanted to impress his wife with his wit but the only way he knew how to do this was by being facetious or coarse. From some old stock of such phrases he dredged up a metaphor: "You don't look at the mantelpiece when you're poking the fire."

"What an awful thing to say," said Myra coldly. "Does that go for your own married life, too?"

Harold nearly said he didn't know about that. Hastily he brought out instead something about her being too young and pretty for him really, people would call him a cradle snatcher. The truth was that while embracing Myra on the previous night, not in the Newquay hotel but for the first time in the matrimonial bed in the sacred bedroom, her resemblance to his dead wife, at first so seemingly attractive, had unnerved him. The room was dark but not absolutely dark, for the light from a yellow street lamp penetrated the olive-colored curtains, shedding a pale green luminosity. Myra's face had looked glaucous and gaunt while her red hair spread out over the pillow just as Edith's had. A certain amount of guilt had been affecting him — not much but a little — over his failure to visit his dying wife during her last days. He could imagine how she must have looked, though. With Myra he had been unwise enough to look at the mantelpiece while he poked the fire and he had had the horrible notion he was making love to a corpse. Much more of that and he wouldn't be able to do it at all.

"Can I give you some charlotte russe?" said

Myra.

Dolly had made no fuss about moving upstairs because anything was preferable to sharing living space with Myra. At first she was stunned by what had happened and happened so quickly. In spite of the reassuring things she had said to Pup, the things a dispossessed mother says, she had felt helpless. She had felt lost or as if all her security had been knocked from under her feet and left her floating towards danger and want. It was now that she needed that friend to confide in and consult for advice. Wendy Collins might have been that friend, for a day or two Dolly thought she could be, but it was strange, whenever she opened her mouth to talk to Wendy about Myra, to explain what it was like to be deposed and pushed out, to have Myra down there, the words remained trapped inside her and what came out were things about the weather and the price of food.

She tried to get on with her sewing but it was neither so easy nor so pleasant up there. Mrs. Collins, who had been her best customer, had varicose veins and refused to climb all those stairs for fittings. There was no way out of the house except through the hall whether Dolly sought the street or the old railway line. She got to know when Myra went to work. Monday and Wednesday and

Friday mornings and all day Thursday, and she tried to pass through the hall only at those times herself. Thursdays she longed for, just to feel herself alone and free in her own home again. The rest of the days she took to spending more and more time in the temple, just sitting in there and being quiet. Or she would sit on the cushions, reading his books, with a single joss stick burning. Unlike her father, Dolly had never been a reader of fiction. Fiction was about beautiful women and handsome lovers and adventure and the great world, about which Dolly knew nothing and which frightened her. It was about people who had friendships with other people.

The books were always back in their right places when Pup came home from work. Like a wife, she had ready for him the food he liked: cold barbecued chicken, pork pies, turkey roll, tomatoes, potato crisps, tinned peaches and evaporated milk, real dairy-cream-filled sponge, chocolate digestives, dry roasted peanuts. She always offered him a glass of her wine but he nearly always refused. He spent all evening in the temple and she was mostly invited to be with him. But like a wise mother she knew better than to obtrude into his life to that extent; she knew when to say no.

"I don't think I will tonight, Pup," she would say and go and sit in the dormer window, her left cheek turned to the street.

On the window sill there and on her bedroom window sill at the back she kept a little mound of stones to throw at Gingie. But he never sat on the post as Fluffy had done or ventured into the Yearmans' back garden. Those evenings she sometimes drank a whole bottle of wine.

"She's practically an alcoholic, that girl," said Myra to her mother. "You should see the bottles. I shall have to get a second dustbin. You should see that house! I'd no idea. To be perfectly honest, it needs thousands spent on it. She never cleaned it and I don't suppose the first wife did. I've got my work cut out there for years to come."

"Marriage isn't all roses," said Mrs. Brewer. "You've got your hubby and now you're paying the price."

"For Christ's sake, Mother, there's no pleasing you."

"Got married to please me, did you? You can tell your little bitch of a stepdaughter if she lays a finger on my Gingie, I'll have the RSPCA on her."

Myra had married principally to have a home of her own. She saw a future in which she gave little dinner parties or even quite large cocktail parties, in which the cavernous drawing room was furnished dashingly with stripped pine and Korean canework, corner units and glass tables with upholstered surrounds. That was the way she imagined the interior of the house in Hampstead Garden Suburb, home of her dentist employer and his wife. It was a little dream of hers one day to invite George and Yvonne Colefax to Manningtree Grove, to a home she need not be ashamed of.

Already she had livened the place up with some of her own pieces from West Hampstead, the Athena Art Van Goghs, the gold chrome spotlights, the reproduction wine table. Her plastic apron had on it a map of the London tube system. If Peter and Doreen didn't want a bathroom of their own, she might as well spend the money having a really super Wrighton kitchen put in here. She called to her husband.

He came into the kitchen, still holding the open copy of *Her Grace of Amalfi* by Grenville West, which was providing him with a little light relief from a life of the Princess Frederick, mother of the Kaiser. Myra put a tube-map dishcloth into his hands. Before his second marriage and during his first he had never dried dishes but had rinsed cups and plates under the tap and left them to drain. Plates had never got sticky because he had lived contentedly off Cornish pasties and Scotch eggs and apples and tomatoes and tubs of ice cream, foodstuffs which scarcely need plates at all.

Dolly, in her window, watched them go off down the road for a drink in The Woman in

White or perhaps to bingo. Harold had never played bingo before, but Myra had and Mrs. Brewer had frequently. Pup was in the temple, performing a Lesser Pentagram ritual as an opening for a piece of practical work. He had told Dolly nothing of what this practical work might be but she guessed it was something to do with the changes he was bringing into being at Hodge and Yearman. Already he had had the sign over the shop altered to "Yearman and Hodge," the Hodge part in very small letters. The name of the company had been changed, he told Dolly, but she didn't follow that, she wasn't interested.

She looked down on Myra, who was dressed as usual in her favorite green, the emerald blouse tonight with all the gold chains, black cotton satin trousers, and black patent sandals. Dolly had very good taste herself, she had a fine color sense, and she knew that people with Myra's coloring should never wear bright greens and blues but rather shades of stone and brown or even pink or the red of their hair. It exasperated her, but her face, to any passer-by looking up, gave no sign of this. Long ago she had learned to control its natural movements so that an observer's attention might not be drawn to it. Like Diane de Poitiers — her father might have told her — she never smiled and never frowned.

She was holding the talisman so tightly in her hand that the rather sharp-sided heptagon made a red imprint on the palm. From the other side of the wall, Pup's low voice could be heard maintaining a low regular chant. He was invoking archangels. Dolly refilled her wine glass, stood up against the wall with her ear to it and listened to Pup.

"Ateh malkuth ve-geburah ve-gedulah le-olam . . ."

He was conjuring strength for himself to make something come to pass. What seemed irrelevant. Was there a limit to what could be accomplished? She put up her hand and touched the surface of the nevus . . .

"Before me, Raphael,
Behind me, Gabriel,
On my right hand, Michael,
On my left hand, Uriel . . ."

The walls were thin in these big houses.

Carrying the glass of wine, she walked back to the window. There were blobs and streaks of orange light on the walls and ceiling now and the sky was parrot-colored, scarlet and gray, with sunset. Up here Dolly felt herself cut off on a limb of loneliness. The room was stuffy and close and Pup's voice droned behind the wall. She would have liked to break things, smash a window and shout out. Down in the street, trotting fast towards

Hornsey Rise, came Miss Finlay, moving as she had done that evening in the winter, as if hastening away, without actually running, from some peril behind. Dolly had heard no more about the velvet skirt, wanted none of Miss Finlay, yet as she saw her scurrying along, going about her business whatever it might be, she felt a pang of resentment, of jealousy almost — though jealousy of *what?* — that Miss Finlay had no more desire to have her as a friend than she had to know Miss Finlay better.

Had she perhaps said something to offend her? Dolly thought back. Their conversation relayed itself to her from the whiff of lemon verbena to the parting at the gate. And then, her father and Myra in the kitchen . . . She had told Miss Finlay about Pup's magic, mentioned it and his powers, and Miss Finlay had said something silly, something about sticking pins in wax images. It had seemed silly at the time. Dolly recalled it in detail. Circumstances alter cases and time alters them.

She had no wax. She would hardly have known how to handle it if she had. There were materials in the room she knew how to handle. She searched through the old fiber trunk, the cardboard crate in which she kept remnants and cut-offs of material. She went into her bedroom and fetched a pair of very light-colored tights that had a run in them. It was going to be a longer job than she had thought at first. For one thing she had never done anything like this before. She would need kapok and that meant going to the shops tomorrow. Taking a sip of her wine, she outlined a shape on the tights with French chalk, and then she began cutting.

When Pup came home on the following evening she showed him the doll. It was about fifteen inches high, a rag doll with knitted nylon skin and rust-colored wool hair and a face embroidered in lipstick red and rouge pink and eyeshadow green. The doll's chest was the fattest and most prominent part of it. It wore a bright green blouse and a navy, green and white check skirt and round its neck and over the bulging chest Dolly had hung gold chains. In the ironmongers in Muswell Hill she had found some plumber's chain, the sophisticated sort that is composed of tiny balls joined by links, the whole being of gilt rather than silver metal.

Pup laughed. "Our wicked stepmother," he said.

"You can see it's her, can't you?"

"It's exactly like." He gave the doll back. "What did you make it for?"

Dolly told him. He looked rather grave.

"I do white magic."

Even implied reproof made Dolly angry, even when it came from him. Especially when it came from him.

64

"You sold your soul to the devil!"

"Come on," said Pup. "I was a kid."

He walked out of the room and went into the temple and closed the door. There, having put on the orange robe, he began to perform one of the rites of the Pentagram, a Lesser Banishing ritual. It was of a kind specially evolved for the banishing of disturbing or obsessing ideas. Pup had been more and more afflicted with these lately and they had nothing to do with Myra or effigies of Myra.

Tears had come into Dolly's eyes. She clenched her fists. After a moment or two she got her pin box and stuck pins all over the doll, into its legs, its body, its bosom, and its embroidered face. It had taken her all day to make, all last evening and all day, about ten hours' work. She picked it up and hurled it against the wall.

6

A postcard came for Diarmit after Conal Moore had been gone for about three months. The picture on it was of the Cliffs of Moher in the west of Ireland. Conal had printed Diarmit's name and the address. He knew who it was from only because one of the other tenants picked up the card and said, "It's from Conal," though whether she had said it to him, Diarmit could not be sure, certainly she did not look at him when she spoke, she might merely have been thinking aloud.

What Conal said on the card, Diarmit never found out. Perhaps something about paying the rent, for next day the landlord spoke to him and said Mr. Moore owed a month's rent. This time Diarmit was in no doubt that he was being addressed, though he did not feel, so vague and fidgety did the landlord seem, that he was being spoken to as a real, solid, flesh-and-blood person but rather as a guessed-at presence or a shape just discerned at the end of a dark room. He paid the back rent and some rent in advance out of his accumulated Social Security. He had plenty of money; there was nothing to spend it on.

Conal's postcard joined the note in his pocket. It puzzled Diramit terribly as to what Conal meant by offering him that butcher's job. It had been a firm offer, surely, but it had all been done by word of mouth, and now Diarmit could not positively remember if the name Budgen's had actually been mentioned by Conal. Perhaps Mary had said Budgen's as people say Hoover when they mean a vacuum cleaner. It might have been some other supermarket — Tesco, Finefare, Sainsbury's, Spar, International, Safeway. Diarmit knew the names so well because he had taken to walking about all over north London looking for the supermarket where the job was waiting for him. It bothered him that they might have been angry because he had never turned up for it. He went into supermarkets in Holloway, Crouch End, Muswell Hill and Wood Green, wondering which it could have been but never actually asking, hoping that somehow, when he came to the right place, he would know.

He was an unobtrusive person, neither tall nor short, with darkish brown, dusty-looking hair, features that might have been roughly molded from putty with careless fingers, gray puzzled eyes. He had brought with him all the clothes he possessed: Hong Kong–made jeans and shirts, a thick gray duffel coat, a quilted nylon jacket. In a second-hand shop in the Archway Road he had bought himself a pair of dark wine-red cord trousers and he wore these most of the time with a dark red shirt which did not show the dirt. He carried the olive-green bag with Harrods printed on it in gold about with him in his other pocket (the pocket which did not contain the card and the note) in case he bought anything.

After he had been, for the third or fourth time, into Sainsbury's at Muswell Hill, looking in vain for a butchery department, as if it might be hidden in some corner of the store he had not yet penetrated, behind the cigarette kiosk, for instance, or in the corner between the vegetables and the turkeys, he crossed the road and went into the big iron-mongers where Pup had bought his magic knife and Dolly her gold chains. There he selected, as nearly as was possible in a domestic hardware store, the implements of a butcher's trade: a steel cleaver for chopping and two long knives. The girl on the check-out was talking to a friend of hers and she did not look at Diarmit or speak to him except to say, "Seventeen pounds, forty-five."

From Woodside Road he walked all the way

back along the old railway line, carrying the knives in the Harrods bag. It was warm and sunny and there were red and black butterflies on the purple spires of buddleia between Highgate and the old Mount Pleasant Green station. Being in possession of the tools of his trade made Diarmit feel a little better. He would be ready now if the job were to present itself. How this might be he hardly knew, though he had vague ideas of someone coming to the door in Mount Pleasant Gardens and asking for him or of Conal coming back.

Back in the house, he used the pay phone for the first time. To do this was a tremendous effort for him, an act of will comparable in anyone else to braving naked an icy river or confronting a savage dog, for by now he had gone a long way along the road towards a split-off from reality. It was as if one of those knives, grasped and held poised, was waiting to strike and cleave a great chasm between himself — whatever "himself" might be, for that was already fast becoming lost — and the natural, normal, real world where others lived their natural, normal, real lives. But he used the phone. He phoned his sister Kathleen in Kilburn, having held her number in his memory for many months. As the bell rang he trembled, he trembled as the pips sounded, for suppose he should put his money in and speak but Kathleen not hear him?

His five-pence piece went into the slot and

he spoke on a drawn breath.

"It's Diarmit, it's your brother, Kathleen. I'm here, not far from you, at Conal Moore's."

A man's voice. He hadn't seen her for years and she had married since he had seen her. "She's got a lot of brothers."

"She has. I'm Diarmit, I'm the youngest. Now I don't recall your name, what would your name be?" Diarmit went on desperately because there was no answer, "Are you there? Will Kathleen be there?"

"She's at work."

"She's lucky, then, lucky to have work." Diarmit experimented with a pleasant laugh. "I could do with work myself. When do you expect her back now? This is her brother, you see. This is her little brother Diarmit. Where is she now? Could I ring her at her work?"

"She'll be home half-five."

The phone went down. At least he had heard his voice, Diarmit thought, he had known who he was. And Kathleen really lived there, she lived in Kilburn, at where that number was, it was all right, it was true and real. Instead of going back into his room, he left the house again with the note and card in his pocket and the Harrods bag in his hand and went down the steps that had been cut out of the embankment to the old station. The rosebay willow herb was in bloom and the white campion. There were pink and white and yellow weeds flowering among the green grass and the rusty cans and the blown feathers. It was warm and hazy, it smelt of cow parsley and diesel fumes. Diarmit walked along the edge of the platform and jumped down and walked on the grassy bed where the track had been.

A woman was coming along with a white Pyrenean mountain dog on a lead. As big and incongruous as a polar bear it looked to Diarmit. He spoke to the woman courteously.

"Good afternoon. A lovely afternoon."

She made no acknowledgment of this. Her eyes were fixed rigidly ahead. He spoke again, "Lovely sunshine . . ." and this time, as if to confirm that she could neither see nor hear him, she bent down and whispered something to the dog, fondling its head. He stood still, watching her go. She tripped along fast, hauling the dog behind her up the steps. Diarmit walked along the old railway line, swinging the Harrods bag, singing as he went like Bottom the Weaver who sang so that others might know he was not afraid. Diarmit would have liked to sing Irish songs but there were none he could remember, so he sang "God Save the Queen," the only verse he knew, over and over, that others might know he was not afraid and for himself too, to know that the sound came from something and that that something was himself.

He got off the line at Stapleton Hall Road and walked to Crouch Hill Station. There was a real railway line there and a real train that would take him to Brondesbury near his sister Kathleen's. It was nearly six when he got there. He walked along the concrete path and up the two concrete steps and rang at the door.

Kathleen had just come in from work and her husband had just gone off to work. Before he went, he had told her that her brother Diarmit had been on the phone, on the scrounge too by the sound of it, no work, on the dole, and hadn't they had enough of her family, for God's sake? Kathleen didn't know what to do. She was tired, she was pregnant, and they hadn't got a spare room anyway. And everyone knew what Diarmit was, going to Mary for a fortnight and stopping three years. He had been funny ever since that bomb.

For all that, she meant to have him in, she meant to talk to him and explain. It was the sight of him and the stink of him that unnerved her. He looked as if he hadn't had a wash for a month and he smelt of old vegetables. Dressed in dirty dark red, his face pale like clay, a carrier bag over one arm and the other hand stretched out towards her waving a paper, he frightened her so much that she stood there staring and quivering for a moment in silence. She smelled his smell and

72

the heartburn she had came up and scalded her throat. She pushed the door and shut it in his face and leaned against it, breathing hard.

Diarmit knew she had not seen him because he did not exist anymore. He had had that feeling before, that he did not exist, after the bomb in Belfast. But since then he had recovered his being more or less consistently, only occasionally had he doubted that he was there. Now he knew for certain he had become invisible and inaudible, no one could see or hear him and it had been going on at that level ever since the morning when he went hunting round Sainsbury's for the butchery department. They had tried to take away his existence so that they wouldn't have to give him a job, and they had succeeded if Kathleen couldn't see him, if his own sister didn't know him.

And now, as once previously, he was aware of how large the things of the world were. He felt very small. Most people, even children, were much bigger than him, buses and cars were enormous, seeking to mow him down, roaring at him, as he crossed Kilburn High Road. It was useless to attempt to go back by train. The man would not hear him ask for a ticket, even supposing he were tall enough to reach the ticket window. He would walk. Though it was a long way, six or seven miles, on this fine sunny evening he would walk. He felt the hard sharp edges of his knives through the green plastic and they comforted him. With them he would defend himself if the big people, not seeing or hearing him, tried to trample him underfoot.

Up in his room, Conal Moore's room, he felt safer. He was like an insect, safe in its cranny in the wall but in peril when it has to run across the floor. An insect can sting feet with the knives in its belly. Diarmit held the Harrods bag close against him as he climbed the stairs.

Two people came running down from the top, laughing, making a noise. He flattened himself against the wall so that they should not bowl him over and sweep him down as they passed. Inside the room it was better. He made a pot of tea, he slept. But after that he began to feel besieged and threatened. He felt that his life was in danger; what ego he still had, which he knew he had but which the others, the Conal Moores and the super-market people, discounted, that was in danger. During the day he was aware that the house emptied, it was a hive only by night. He went down listening outside doors for sounds of life within. It was entirely silent but for music coming from behind one door.

The Dalmatian and the mongrel collie ran about the green, scavenging from litter bins. They looked very large to Diarmit even from this distance. Next to Mount Pleasant Hall they were pulling down a row of old houses and the air was yellow and thick with plaster dust. Next they would pull this one down. Diarmit understood how it would be. There was no one in the house but himself and he was as invisible as an insect, so they would pull the house down around him, not knowing he was there or not caring. They would care no more for him than they would for the woodlice and mites and spiders and silverfish that also lived in the house. He would be crushed in the rubble, overwhelmed by a cloud of yellow dust. He sat in the window and trembled.

By night it was safe. The workmen did nothing after five, he had observed that. He could come back to the house at night and hide there all night but by day he must be gone, taking whatever he valued with him. He might come back and find that the house had disappeared but that was a risk he must take.

Next day, after they had all pounded out of the house, banging doors, laughing, crashing down the stairs, they made enough noise for devils in hell, he crept out with his knives in the Harrods bag. He carried them as a wasp carries its sting or a security guard his gun. There was no doubt in his mind where he was going; he had it all worked out. Down the steps in Mount Pleasant Gardens and on to the old railway line where it spread out wide in a grassy valley, on to where it narrowed at the old Mount Pleasant Green station, and thence to the Mistley tunnel.

The tunnel was as dry as it ever got inside. It had an earthy oily smell and there were feathers everywhere. That mattress must have contained a million little white and gray feathers, for thousands had come out and blown away, had embedded themselves in the clay or adhered to the curved roof or lay in quivering heaps, yet the old torn mattress was still cushiony, still padded with down. Diarmit sat down on it and took his knives out of the bag.

From where he sat, well back under the curve of the roof, he could command a view of both the tunnel's openings. He could assess what kind of a threat presented itself. As for himself, no one could see him, so there was no need to be hidden. But after a while he raised the mattress up on its side edge, making it into a curving wall which he propped in place with a roll of rusty wire netting and an oil drum. It was not for concealment but protection. He squatted behind it, as in a dugout or beind a wind-break, and it did protect him. Three or four people came through the tunnel, one walking towards Highgate, the others to Mount Pleasant, and although they were giant, lumbering, hostile creatures, their bodies nearly filling the tunnel space, none of them even brushed against the mattress and he was safe.

Diarmit understood then that he had found a way to live. Each night he could sleep in the room but by day he must come here, wary and armed, and station himself behind his barricade.

7

*T*he doll, Mrs. Collins said, was exactly what Wendy wanted. No, she didn't think ten pounds too much, ten pounds was very reasonable. Wendy wanted it as a birthday present for the little girl whose godmother she was. The doll was very obviously a little girl itself with a pink smiling face and yellow plaits and scarlet shirt and blue checkered pinafore dress. Dolly had made several, all different, since the Myra doll and had had no difficulty in selling them.

Mrs. Collins gave Dolly a ten-pound note which Dolly, crossing the road from Mrs. Collins's little terraced cottage in Orchard Lane, spent on stocking up with wine at the off-license. Five bottles, wrapped in tissue in two carriers.

It was a dull warm, white-skied summer day. Dolly climbed up the steps and got on to the old railway line by the bridge in North-wood Road. A woman was walking along with a white Pyrenean mountain dog on a lead. Dolly was wearing a pink and yellow and brown plaid cotton dress with a wide brown belt, tights, and low-heeled sandals. The tights were new, on for the first time, and to protect them she decided not to climb up the embankment but to go through the Mistley tunnel to the station and up the steps.

It was absolutely dry underfoot; there had been no rain for a fortnight. Usually it was a bit muddy inside the tunnel but not today. Footprints and cycle tire marks were etched in the hard, pale, feather-strewn clay. Dolly walked through the tunnel, carrying her bags of wine bottles. Someone had stacked the mattress up on its side and propped it up with an oil drum and some wire. Perhaps, rather, the council or the railway people or some-body or other were collecting up the rubbish in here at last before taking it away. Dolly nearly went over to the mattress to see, at closer quarters, if it did look as if some genuine tidying work had been done, but she thought better of it. The bags were heavy, and the smelly dirty old tunnel was no place in which to linger.

She mounted the steps. In Manningtree Grove, outside the house, she paused for a moment. Myra had lost no time in revitalizing the garden. The Michaelmas daisies and

Solomon's seal were all gone and in their place she had planted annuals — lobelias and tagetes and petunias — and these were in flower. Dolly was not one of those people who think all flowers beautiful and here she thought the juxtaposition of cobalt blue, orange, and shocking pink particularly inharmonious. Gingie, for once, was sitting on the post.

"Get off!" said Dolly and clapped her hands. The cat fled.

She let herself into the house but not quietly or cautiously. It was a Monday and Myra worked till lunchtime.

"Doreen!"

Dolly froze. The door to the front room opened and Myra came out, wearing jade green dungarees and a navy-and-white striped T-shirt.

"Caught at last," said Myra but not unpleasantly. "I always seem to see the tail end of you disappearing. Now I've got you, come in here and give me the benefit of your advice."

"Why aren't you at work?"

These were practically the first words Dolly had ever addressed to her but Myra gave no sign that she realized this. "I've started a fortnight's holiday, my dear. I'm going to begin on the painting tomorrow. Now don't look like that!" Dolly hadn't looked like anything. Her face, as usual, was expressionless. "Yes, I mean me with my own two hands," Myra said. "To be perfectly honest with you, I spent so much on converting your kitchen I can't afford to have the men in again."

"They only put a sink in," said Dolly, "and we didn't want that."

Myra gave her tinkling laugh. "Oh, well, that's frank if you like. We won't argue about it. I didn't bring you in here to argue. I want you to tell me what color scheme you think I ought to have."

This was something Dolly had plenty of ideas about. For a moment she forgot her hatred of Myra. "It's a light room. You could have a strong color. You could have a white ceiling and brilliant white paintwork and deep russet walls. That would tone in with the carpet and those chairs."

Myra was astonished. She had spoken to Dolly because she had genuinely thought it would be better to be on speaking terms with her. But in answer to her question she had expected some such rejoinder as "I don't know" or "Whatever you like." "I'm not keeping that filthy old carpet or those chairs," she said scornfully. "I'm having haircord and stripped pine. And I think a natural beige for the walls, there's a shade they call papyrus."

"Suit yourself." Dolly shrugged her shoulders. It was still early in the day but she suddenly felt she needed a glass of wine badly and she made for the door.

Myra had hoped for an offer of help which she now saw she wasn't going to get. She remembered, though, the original purpose of accosting Dolly. "Want a coffee? I was just going to have one."

Coffee was no substitute for a tumblerful of Spanish burgundy. "No, thanks."

"Well, if I can't twist your arm, I can't. Come and inspect the work, though, will you? I hope to have a good bit done by Friday. Come and have a look and tell me what you think. We ought to be friends, Doreen, two girls living in the same house."

Instead of putting up the real objections to Myra as usurper and iconoclast, Dolly chose a less obvious impediment. There was little she had to be proud of but she was proud and jealous of her youth. While she had her youth, miracles could still happen, her blind prince might come or some genius find a cure. "You're older than me," she said.

"A little bit," Myra said, going red.

"I'm twenty-six. How old are you?"

The flush deepened. "When I'm asked that I usually say 'somewhere between thirty and death.' To be perfectly honest with you, I'm thirty-eight."

"I thought so." Dolly picked up her bags and went off upstairs.

She poured herself a big glass of wine and sat down to drink it. Four dolls sat on the

82

mantelpiece, two little girls with yellow plaits, Myra, and an Indian boy doll in a silk turban. Dolly sipped her wine, watched by the dolls.

"Sunbeach" was the name of the color Myra chose for the living room, a compromise between her choice and Dolly's. She thought Dolly might come down and see how she was getting on but Dolly did not. She worked every day and when she had finished the living room she started on the dining room, bought cheap but smart-looking brown haircord to carpet the floors and a three-piece suite in pine with brown-and-white check cotton upholstery. Pup looked in sometimes to give her a kindly word of encouragement, and occasionally Harold, conscious of the huge sacrifice he was making on the altar of marriage, turned his back on the shabby delightful solitude of the breakfast room and sat reading his book in a chair by her stepladder.

After that initial nasty feeling that he was indulging in necrophilia, Harold had only twice made love to his wife and neither time had been particularly satisfactory. For a while he was uneasy about denying her what he thought of as a wife's right. He lay in bed waiting for the touch or the question, and when neither came but instead a cheerful "Good night, Hal," he felt he had been given another night's reprieve. But in fact, though he knew nothing of this, Myra had not married him for love, still less for sex. She had had all the sex, and indeed all the passion and fulfillment, she had wanted with the married man. She was a trumpery, shallow, insincere woman was Myra, but she had her happinesses and her miseries like anyone else and for her, all the happiness of love had gone when the married man went. In a husband, in Harold, she wanted a man to go about with and be seen with, someone of the opposite sex to talk to, and a provider of a big house and the security it brought. She was not dissatisfied with her bargain, and all the better if she could honor her part of it with her skills and her savings rather than a pretense of sexual enthusiasm.

By daylight, Harold was proud of his wife's appearance. When they went out together, it gratified him to be seen arm-in-arm with her. Harold was one of those men who like to say they don't understand women, women are a mystery. His mind ranged sometimes over the incomprehensible women of history — Messalina, Catherine de' Medici, Anne Boleyn, Charlotte Corday — their unaccountable behavior lending weight to his convictions. Women were an enigma and his own wife as great an enigma as any. He derived an almost complacent satisfaction from thinking this way. It absolved him from having to consider why Myra accepted his lack

84

of ardor so equally, why she was wearing herself out painting, and why, instead of having a bit of hush now the dining room was done, she should wish to invite people to eat in it.

Myra couldn't catch Dolly in the hall again, so she went upstairs and tapped on the door. Dolly guessed who it was, snatched up the dolls and put them in the remnants box out of sight.

"We're having a few friends in for dinner on Thursday week," Myra said in her best suburban wife manner. "I hope you and Peter will join us."

"I've got to go to a meeting." The Adonai Spiritists were holding another seance and Dolly had almost decided not to go but she would now. "What friends? Dad hasn't got any friends."

"Quite frankly, Doreen, I think I'm a better judge of that than you are. Of course he's got friends. If you must know, we're having my boss Mr. Colefax and his wife and a very nice couple Hal and I got to know at bingo. If you won't come, I expect my mother will."

The dining room had apple-green walls now, beige Dralon curtains, haircord on the floor, aluminum-framed Constable prints, and on the table Ravenhead glass and stainless steel cutlery and tablemats of British game birds.

Pup didn't refuse the invitation. He

performed an Elemental ritual and went out and bought himself a suit, gray flannel, plain and elegant, and a gray shirt with a small pink and white pattern on it. He thought it unnecessary to mention this to Dolly or that he had cast the I Ching and it had told him that the desires of the superior man are not thus to be pacified.

He came out of the temple, wearing his robe, and kissed Dolly, who was just leaving for her seance. Just as she closed the front door behind her, Miss Finlay came tearing along at her usual pace. There were police everywhere, she said, and did Dolly know what it was about? When she, Miss Finlay, had tried to get on to the old railway line down the steps at Crescent Road, a policeman had turned her back. There was nothing in the evening paper and she hadn't got television. Dolly hadn't got television either, though Myra had just bought a color set. They walked down Manningtree Grove towards Mount Pleasant Green and in that short time two police cars passed them with blue lights flashing.

Myra's guests all had television and they had all had their radios on while getting ready to come out. When they were having their pre-dinner drinks in the pine and cane living room they talked about nothing else, not that it wasn't a horrible thing to talk about, a horrible thing to happen, the man who did it must be a monster, no better than an animal.

"I've yet to hear of animals cutting each other's heads off," said Mrs. Brewer.

Pup said nothing. He was sorry it had happened on the old railway line and inside that very tunnel where, long ago now, he had performed the first ritual of his career. On a fine summer evening like this one it was hideous to think and talk of murder. He was looking at Yvonne Colefax, a very pretty blonde who wore a white dress made of some clinging pleated material. What would make a man want to kill a girl — a *girl,* of all possible victims — and then sever her head from her body with a hatchet?

"Unresolved aggression," said George Colefax as if Pup had spoken aloud. "A hatred of women whose challenge he can't meet." He said it with an emphasis that seemed heartfelt and his wife gave him a glance. "Cutting off the head would silence a mocking tongue and make certain the eyes could no longer see him."

Myra came in to announce dinner. They trooped into the dining room. Harold had never before sat down to a three-course meal at 8:30 in the evening. All this talk of decapitation made him feel queasy, especially as he was halfway through a book mostly concerned with the torture meted out to Madame de Brinvilliers. He had to sit between Mrs. Brewer and Eileen Ridge, the bingo friend.

Myra wore a long green polyester skirt with black daisies on it and a very tight, sleeveless, black polo-necked sweater and all her gold jewelry. Mrs. Brewer, in blue Crimplene, picked at her food and actually sniffed a dish of courgettes in cream sauce. Besides the courgettes, Myra had cooked strange food in elaborate ways, chicken with walnuts, potatoes gummed together with egg and cheese, cabbage that had bits of bacon and caraway seeds in it. George Colefax picked all the caraway seeds out of his very white, even teeth with a gold toothpick. He was a doctor of medicine as well as a dentist and had no compunction (did not even realize such talk might be distasteful) about explaining to the company what a difficult job cutting someone's head off would be and how the perpetrator, whoever he might be, would have needed knives and perhaps a saw as well as a hatchet. Myra brought in raspberry Pavlova cake.

"It was a woman with a dog found her," said Mrs. Collins outside the hall after the seance was over. "She's a woman who lives in Stanhope Road that's got that great big white dog, great big white Pyrenean something. She was on the old line and the dog started sniffing at something and she saw it was this girl without a head. Then she saw the head a little way away. They took her into hospital for the shock."

"What an experience," said Miss Finlay. "It would haunt you to your dying day." Today she smelt, Dolly had noticed, only of Pear's soap.

"You'd never get over it. Who'd do a thing like that? Only an animal, an absolute animal."

Dolly was tired of hearing about it. She stood by the gate, picking leaves from a bush of lemon mint which grew there, crushing them in her fingers and smelling the scent. Her mother had not appeared during the seance, had spoken no word. The leaves had a pungent lemony scent.

"My mother used to use cologne like that," Dolly said, holding her fingers under Mrs. Collins's nose.

"Brings her back, does it? You don't get over losing your mother. I know I never have. You don't want to go off on your own, you two, not after what's happened today. You'd best wait here with me, my daughter's coming for me in the car and she'll drop you both off." It was barely dark yet. Miss Finlay looked fearfully along the street and across the green. "We can expect you both, I hope," said Mrs. Collins, "for Mrs. Fitter's seance on the fifteenth of next month. You've heard of her, haven't you? She's wonderful. The tickets are going like hot cakes. Five pounds a seat but you can take my word for it, it's cheap at the price. Oh, that lemon scent is strong, isn't it, dear?"

When Wendy Collins dropped off Dolly, the party was still in full swing. She went straight upstairs and just avoided encountering Yvonne Colefax, who had gone to the bathroom to dab herself with more Balmain's Ivoire. Back in the living room, Yvonne sat on one half of Myra's new two-seater settee. Pup hesitated, remembering the I Ching and the Pentagrammic Banishing ritual, and then he went and sat next to her. At a loss for what to talk to her about, he offered to tell her fortune. He had overheard Myra regaling his father with details of the Colefaxes' private life, so he was able to give her a very accurate assessment of her past. She thought he was amazing and said so, looking into his eyes.

"How *could* you know I lost my first husband when I was only twenty-one?" said Yvonne, having forgotten she had imparted this fact to Myra during the previous week.

"Your eyes told me," said Pup gracefully.

"Load of wicked rubbish," said Mrs. Brewer.

"Excuse me, but everything he said was the absolute truth."

Mrs. Brewer's face was very red as if she were going to have some sort of attack. Yvonne could hardly take her eyes off Pup, was looking at him as if he were a seer or guru, and Pup felt quite weak and faint. He had to keep telling himself how precious and requisite was the retention of virginity to a young geomancer. Yvonne smelled wonderful and her white silk thigh, the whole smooth slippery length of it, was pressed softly against his own. She had a rather breathy, childlike voice, full of wonder, a wide-eyed voice if that was possible. And although she must have been seven or eight years older than him, she seemed younger.

It was half an hour since he had heard Dolly come in. He ought to go, it would be wise to go. Myra was telling her guests how she and Hal were planning an autumn holiday in Cyprus.

"I don't know about that," said Harold. "It's the first I've heard of it."

"Oh, darling, you and your memory!"

"I must be going now," said Pup. "Goodbye. Thank you for the delicious dinner." Some impulse made him go up to Myra, lift her hand and kiss it.

It was a signal for everyone else to make a move. Myra could have killed him. Mrs. Brewer wanted Harold to accompany her next door, put all the lights on and search the flat in case an intruder had got in in her absence. Like the man who cut off heads, for instance. Pup went upstairs. Dolly was in their living room, drinking rosé. Often on summer evenings, instead of putting the light on, she lit a candle. She was sitting in the half-dark with her single candle burning, looking down from the window at Ronald and Eileen Ridge getting into their car.

"Pup," she said, "did you hear about the girl on the old railway line?"

He nodded. "We don't have to talk about it, do we? How was your meeting?"

"It was all right. Listen, we've got a physical medium coming in three weeks' time, what they call a materialization medium. You will come with me, won't you? You have to say by tomorrow because the tickets are going to sell like hot cakes."

"I never knew anyone actually buy cakes when they were hot, did you?" Her puzzled, slightly offended expression made him smile. "Of course I'll come, dear."

After Harold had left her, Mrs. Brewer began to feel very ill. She thought she had indigestion as a result of eating Myra's strange food. It had begun as heartburn while she was still next door, sitting in one of the uncomfortable pine armchairs. Now this had intensified into a deep pressing pain down her left side, paralyzing her left arm and clamping her as if in an iron cage. It might have occurred to Mrs. Brewer that she was having a heart attack except that she believed women never have heart attacks and no one had told her that this immunity ends with the menopause.

Gingie came and lay on her bed. She passed an uncomfortable night and felt so tired that she stayed in bed all day and the next day, but when Myra came in on Sunday, she was up and about again and she said nothing of her illness.

8

One hundred and four people passed through the tunnel before the fateful one. Diarmit counted them. Three or four a day they came, occasionally more, and he had been stationed behind his barricade for twenty-three days before the attack came on the twenty-fourth.

By then he was becalmed in a false security. Huge though they were, they kept to the center of the tunnel and he was just outside the range of their sweeping strides and great stamping feet. But the girl on the twenty-fourth day left the path and came juggernauting towards the mattress. She was in search of something, he thought in his terror, the roll of wire perhaps or the wooden cask or the old chair with which, through the weeks, he had bolstered his fortifications. Her head reached the roof, and her great flailing

94

arms, swinging above the mattress, made a gale in the air. He jumped up in his fear, though he knew himself too small and too faint in substance to be seen, but he jumped up with a spurt of courage, a knife in each tiny feeble hand to defend himself.

The sound she made was a screaming roar of fury. He almost quailed at that, he almost yielded. It was as much as he could do to keep on his feet, not to shrivel into the ground and scuttle, certain prey for her foot. But he remained there with unflinching bravery, stabbing his sting at her, his double sting, pounding into that vast threatening mass, until the weight of it subsided, sinking on to him, a bloodied hulk.

He had done it, he had won. He struggled free. He stepped back, gasping, looking at the thing at his feet as a knight might have looked at a slain dragon. His hands were red and sticky with blood. In death his attacker had shrunk rapidly. Her body was no bigger than an ordinary girl's now, a small young girl. Diarmit marveled that such things might be, that courage and defiance might reduce a powerful aggressor to this little dead thing.

Perhaps he should reduce it more. After all, he knew all about dismemberment. Wishing he had a saw, he got to work with the cleaver, then the knives. He abandoned the task because he got tired and, as he heard in the distance by the chiming church clock, it was 5:00 now and safe to go home.

The sunshine felt as strong as at noon. A warm curtain of it met him as he came out of the tunnel mouth, carrying the hatchet and the knives in his Harrods bag. The buddleias and willow herb and marguerite daisies were thronged with bees, a white butterfly pursued its waving, fluttering flight, and a ginger cat walked along the edge of the old station platform, but he met no one and passed no one until he had gone up the steps and was in Mount Pleasant Gardens.

Although he was covered with blood, the splashes and great soaked areas did not look like bloodstains on the red shirt and the red cords. In any case, no one looked at him, he remained invisible. On the demolition site beyond the green the workmen had knocked off for the day and the dust had settled. There was very little left of the houses; there were only bricks and rubble and an empty site. Diarmit went upstairs, up and up and up to his top floor. There was one bathroom for all the rooms on the top and in the mornings and the evenings it was always occupied but it was empty now. He took the cleaver and the knives out of the Harrods bag and washed them under cold running water. Then he turned the bag inside out and washed that.

In his room he felt more safe and sound

than he had done for a long time. He made himself a pot of tea and sat drinking it by the open window. The Dalmatian and the collie lay on the grass, sleeping in the sunshine. How good it would be if Conal Moore were to come now! Diarmit felt somehow that his existence, his selfhood, was seeping back; first, the act of defense in the tunnel, then the warm sun, then the tea — all this was bringing him out of limbo, out of nothingness. Conal would see him, know him, he felt sure of that. Kathleen would know him if he went to her door now. The brave stand and the shed blood had made him recognizable, solid, whole.

I kill, therefore I am.

It was not until the next day that the woman with the Pyrenean mountain dog found the girl's body and not until two days after that that Diarmit knew it had been found. He saw a newspaper which someone had left on top of a pile of them on a dustbin in the side entrance. The photograph was of that face which, hugely enlarged and violently colored, had loomed over him in the tunnel and had let out those terrible sounds. He sat on a bench on the green and deciphered the headlines, then the text, working very slowly and moving his forefinger along the lines of print. It was then that he understood they were calling him a murderer. "The Headsman," they called him.

That was like calling a soldier in a war a murderer! If anyone came and asked him why, he had his explanation ready. You see how you would feel, driven out of the only home you've got by a threat of being buried under tons of rubble, only allowed home during the hours of darkness, forced to take shelter out of doors and barricade yourself in lest the stampeding hordes trample you. You try it and see how you'd feel when a huge scavenger threatens to crush you. You'd lash back with all your poor little strength, wouldn't you? If you had the nerve, if you were brave enough.

They had not worked on the site the day before and no workmen had appeared today. Diarmit sat on the bench and watched the site and the house where his room was. The weather was still warm and sunny and the stains on his clothes began to give off a hot fetid reek. The Dalmatian came and sniffed at him. A woman, passing, pushing a bicycle, wrinkled her nose, stared at him and turned away. These evidences of his existence pleased Diarmit, but after a time the dogs annoyed him, the Dalmatian and the collie had been joined by a rough-haired mongrel, and all three sniffed him and followed him. They followed him to the door of the shop where he bought his bread and milk and teabags and they followed him back across the green to his doorstep.

Diarmit took off his clothes for the first time for many weeks and washed them in the bathroom, using Camay soap for he had nothing else. It was Sunday tomorrow and he could stay in. No demolition was ever done on a Sunday. His clothes dry — he had spread them over the window sill and closed the sash on them — he put them on and watched for Conal. A strong presentiment told him Conal would come back today but the hours passed and still no Conal and the sun departed in a long, slow sunset, followed by a long, smoky-violet dusk, and he had not come. When it was dark Diarmit tore up the note and the postcard and flushed the pieces down the lavatory in the bathroom.

Next morning he was dressed and ready to leave when there came a sharp knocking on the room door. That would be the men come to tell him they were about to begin demolishing the house. They could see him now, they could be aware of him, he had a real existence. He opened the door.

Outside on the landing, in plainclothes, were two policemen.

They told him their names. They were a detective sergeant and a constable. Diarmit let them come in and they stood, looking about the room. The longer and larger of the knives lay on the table where he had used it to cut a slice of bread.

The sergeant said, "We're anxious to know the whereabouts of Conal Patrick Moore."

Diarmit smiled at them. He felt how much he liked them, how grateful he was that they had said nothing about the girl in the tunnel. Their eyes had rested with indifference on the knife.

"So am I," he said. "So am I anxious. I don't know where he is at all."

"And who might you be, sir?"

Diarmit told them his name. He told them his story, how he had come to London to Conal and a job but there had been no Conal and no job. To speak and be spoken to was enjoyable, to exist and be recognized. He talked on and on because it was such a novelty. The sergeant had to stop him.

"Don't you want to know what we want him for?"

This had not crossed Diarmit's mind. He didn't much care, no. He savored only the delight of being addressed as "you," of being able to communicate, of being treated as a normal ordinary person.

"There've been a lot of robberies from shops in this area," said the sergeant. "They stopped round about the time you say Mr. Moore went away. Now there's a similar pattern of robberies in a district of Birmingham. Would he go there?"

"He might," said Diarmit. Mary's husband

and his brothers had an old father in Birmingham. He told the sergeant this. He was shocked. The Bawnes and their family connections had always been law-abiding, respectable people. "You'll be letting me know when you find him?"

"And you let *us* know if you hear anything."

They left. Diarmit reflected on what they had told him. Of course, no supermarket would give a job to a friend or relative of a thief, he could understand that. It was a blessing, too, that Conal had been gone before he came. He had no wish to be associated with a criminal. So the room was all his now. He was free. He felt strong and brave and young and free and, stretching up his arms, he capered about the room, doing a little dance of freedom and happiness. What a clearing and cleansing of life had taken place these past few days!

The realization that today being Monday might be the day for starting demolition of the house sobered him. He was pretty sure they would know of his presence and come to warn him but he ought to go out and be on the safe side. Besides, it was a fine morning. He took up the Harrods bag with the knives in it and ran down the stairs. No point in leaving valuable things to be buried under rubble.

Once he was out in the street, a daring idea

came to him. Why shouldn't he try to find himself work? Why not start looking for a job?

9

*F*rom her bed, lying there propped up on pillows, Mrs. Brewer could see the green valley through which the old railway line ran. At previous times when she had been ill, she had liked to watch the people coming and going, using the green track as a short cut — schoolchildren, dog walkers, young people who seemed to spend so much of their lives aimlessly wandering. Since the murder no one used it. Only Gingie could be seen, stalking through the long grass, in quest of real or imaginary prey.

It was August, red-hot, sultry, dry as a bone. Mrs. Brewer was going to get up at about twelve in time to think about lunch. This gastritis or whatever it was knocked you sideways; she didn't know when she had felt so tired. And it wasn't as if she was old yet, only sixty-four and good surely for another twenty years.

She would have to get up in a minute to open the window, the heat in there was getting unbearable and the sweat was beginning to roll off her. Mrs. Brewer had always been proud of not sweating much and had sometimes boasted of this to Myra. Perspiration was so unfeminine. She began to wish Myra would come in. Thursday was her day off and there was nothing to stop her. For God's sake, it was her duty and she only lived next door!

Gingie had appeared outside the window, making soundless mews, or soundless no doubt because he was on the other side of the glass.

"All right, I'm coming," said Mrs. Brewer and she pushed back the bedclothes and put her feet over the side of the bed and got them on to the floor. Another wave of heat washed over her and she broke into sweat.

The phone was in the living room. She would have to phone Myra. But should she try to reach the phone first or open the window to Gingie first? Fresh air might be what she needed. She could walk — just. Very slowly she shuffled towards the window. Gingie was on the sill, screaming silently.

"I'm coming, boy," said Mrs. Brewer.

Suddenly she was filled with passionate tender love for the little cat and it seemed to her that never before, not for long-dead John

Brewer or the infant Myra, had she felt as she now did for this mewing scrap of orange fur. Her love made her pant and gasp. She wanted to feel Gingie against her, to squeeze him in her arms. She struggled with the window, the heavy sash bar, while the cat's face grew enormous, a huge open mouth of misery and frustration. The iron vice and the iron claws which had grasped her on the evening after the party clamped again, resuming their grip. Her love burst inside her like a shower of needles. She hung on to the window but her knees and then her whole body gave way and drooped to the floor in an agony no one could endure for long.

It was not long before Mrs. Brewer ceased to endure it.

Myra had rather disliked her mother but it was a shock to see her lying there, so great a shock as to make her feel faint and have to sit down with her head between her knees. Later that day, when the doctor had been and the undertakers, when the body had been removed to the undertakers' chapel of rest and Gingie had been taken home with Mrs. Buxton, Myra sat down with a glass of sherry and realized that *her mother was dead.*

She had thought her mother would live for twenty years. Her mother had even seemed quite young as mothers went. Now she would never again be told that Mrs. Brewer thought she was never coming or that she had made her bed and must lie in it or have her clothes and her manners and her cooking criticized. Harold was kind, made no complaint about being given a defrosted TV dinner and kept saying, "It's a bad business, a bad business."

Dolly remembered how she had felt when her mother died, and though it went against the grain with her, she made herself go downstairs and say stiffly to Myra: "I'm sorry about your mother."

When Myra woke up in the morning, the first thought that came to her was that her mother was dead and the second, a new one, that the flat next door for which her mother had paid 30,000 pounds two years before might not be hers.

She phoned George Colefax's home in Shelley Drive off the Bishop's Avenue. Yvonne answered.

"I shan't be in till Monday. My mother passed away yesterday. It's been quite a shock."

"Your mother?" Yvonne's little girl voice rose an octave. "But I was only talking to her last week," as if this guaranteed Mrs. Brewer could not have died, must be shamming. "But that's incredible, Myra, that's really awful."

"She had a very peaceful end," said Myra. "Very quick. She didn't suffer. Could you tell George, please, Yvonne?"

Yvonne said she couldn't because George

hadn't spent last night at home, he had been working late so had stayed at the flat over the surgery, but she would phone him, of course she would do that. Myra had her own ideas about George working late and where he stayed but she was too preoccupied to think about that now.

During a quarrel some months before, indeed before Myra's marriage, Mrs. Brewer had said she would get herself a will form and dispose of her property not to Myra, the natural legatee, but to the Cat Survival Trust. She even went so far as to look their address up in the phone book. Myra, enraged, bought the will form herself and gave it to Mrs. Brewer next time she went over.

Had her mother ever filled it in and signed it and had it witnessed? It was unlikely but she must find out. Her mother had cooled down and come round, of course, and been very gratified about the marriage, but suppose she had made the will in the heat of the moment and never unmade it? Myra was in possession of a key to the flat next door. She went off and registered Mrs. Brewer's death. She went to the undertaker and fixed up the cremation, and when she got home again, the police phoned her to say the coroner's officer's decision was that no inquest would be necessary. Pup and Harold came home and still she hadn't been next door. By now she felt sick with anxiety. She served Harold with his beef stroganoff and chocolate mousse, and when he had finished, she said she really thought she ought to pop next door and check everything was locked up and as it should be, et cetera. Her hand shook as she inserted the key in the lock.

Dolly and Pup had a pot noodle snack, Ryvita and Sainsbury's pâté, Waldorf salad, tinned peaches and cream. Pup changed into his best jeans, the pink and gray shirt, and a new black velour sweatshirt. Dolly wore a dress she had just finished making for herself, a long-sleeved shirtwaist, the dark green material with a pattern of tiny strawberries chosen to go with her talisman. It was a very warm evening and there was as yet no autumnal chill in the air. The sky was a deep clear blue and the sun sinking in dazzling gold as they walked down Manningtree Grove towards Mount Pleasant Hall. Dolly had their tickets for Mrs. Roberta Fitter's seance, at five pounds apiece, in her black suede handbag. She wore rather smart, lowish-heeled black court shoes. For most of the way Pup talked about magic, about self-initiation and spiritual exercises, about providing new insights into the psyche.

A corrugated iron fence had been put up round the demolition site. The plaster dust had subsided but it still clung like pale mold to the leaves on the shrubs in the hall garden, the laurel leaves and the rosemary and the lemon mint. The hall doors stood wide open. Dolly handed over their tickets.

The medium was late in arriving. The twenty-three people who had come to see Roberta Fitter do her stuff sat waiting patiently on the twenty-three rush-bottomed chairs Mrs. Collins had assembled for them. Each bore a card with the intended occupant's name printed on it. Dolly and Pup were in the front row.

At the end of the hall in one corner a curtain rail had been fixed diagonally across, a little way down from the ceiling, and from this rail hung a pair of black curtains. Inside it was a chair with a padded seat and back and wooden arms, and behind the chair, another pair of curtains, dark green this time, hung flat against the wall.

Miss Finlay was sitting next to Dolly and next to Pup sat a very old man who wore, in spite of the heat, a raincoat and a cloth cap. He was chewing tobacco, a habit Pup had never actually come across before. Miss Finlay pointed out to Dolly a big frog-faced woman sitting in the row behind them up against the left-hand wall.

"That's the lady who travels with Mrs. Fitter. It's her job to look after her."

"A sort of road manager," said Pup but smiling so sweetly that no one could have taken offense.

"She's called Mrs. Leebridge and Mrs. Fitter's control is called Hassan. He was a sepoy that was killed in the Indian Mutiny defending a British officer from a maddened subahdar."

From a room at the back of the stage, Mrs. Collins appeared with her arms full of black clothing: a loose dress, a pair of knickers, a pair of tights, and black velvet Chinese button-up slippers. These she dropped in Miss Finlay's lap.

"You have to pass them round," Miss Finlay said. "You have to check there's nothing concealed in them in case of fraud."

Very painstakingly she pulled the tights inside out and stuck her fingers into the toes of the slippers before passing them on to Dolly. The frog-faced woman got up and closed all the windows and the room seemed immediately to become stuffy. She pulled down the thick dark green blinds and switched on the central light. The black garments went round from hand to hand, and when they reached the back row, Mrs. Collins came on to the stage with a tall slight woman she introduced as Mrs. Fitter. She said she wanted three ladies to come forward and watch Mrs. Fitter dress herself. Dolly would never have put herself forward so far as to volunteer but Mrs. Collins didn't wait for volunteers; she summoned Dolly and Miss Finlay and a Mrs. Bullen.

In the room behind the stage, Roberta Fitter said not a word as she stripped off her clothes. She was too important and her business too serious for idle chatter. Dolly thought how wonderful it would be if Pup could someday be revered like that. Mrs. Fitter had a thin, brown, wrinkled body with breasts like pigskin purses and gray pubic hair. While they were waiting, Miss Finlay had told Dolly that at a recent seance someone in the audience had shouted at Mrs. Fitter that she was a fraud and as a result the ectoplasm had rushed back into her body so rapidly that it had left a burn mark where it went in by way of her chest. Dolly, holding her hair instinctively across her own face, looked for the burn scar on Mrs. Fitter's chest but she could see nothing except beads of sweat and a sprinkling of hairs.

When Mrs. Fitter had dressed herself in the black clothes, she walked across in front of the audience and sat on the chair behind the open curtains. There was a red light on now from a table lamp on a plant pot stand about a yard to the right of the cabinet. Someone switched off the overhead light so that only the red one remained and this was very dim. It was just light enough to see that Mrs. Fitter had gone into a trance. The curtains operated on cords and these Mrs. Leebridge now drew to conceal Mrs. Fitter from view.

Myra tiptoed in a reverent sort of way across the hall and into the living room. She had an idea she ought not to be in the flat, that she was perhaps breaking the law and that if a policeman or a solicitor were to see her she would be in grave trouble. This made her look uneasily about her, it made her keep on looking over her shoulder. A rolltop desk that had been her father's was her quarry. It wasn't locked. Myra opened it, lifted out a stack of yellow packets of holiday snaps and there underneath them, still blank, still untouched, lay the will form. Myra expelled her breath and momentarily closed her eyes. Then she went through the rest of the papers which Mrs. Brewer had kept in an orderly way, found National Savings to the value of 3,000 pounds and a bank deposit book showing an accumulation of nearly 2,000 pounds.

How long would she have to wait before she came into possession? Some months, she feared, remembering that when her father died intestate, letters of administration had had to be applied for. In that case, she might as well take her mother's fur coat with her, a very good ranch mink it was and only two years old. It would be a pity not to have the benefit of that next spring.

Harold was in the breakfast room. He had been doing a lot of serious reading lately — James Pope Hennessy's *Queen Mary,* no less,

and a book called *The File on the Tsar* — so
for light relief he had turned to an historical
novel about the twin sons its author said Mary
Queen of Scots had secretly borne to the Earl
of Bothwell. He had just reached the point
where one of the twins was about to rescue
his father from the dungeons of Elsinore,
when Myra came in wearing a fur coat.
Harold stuck a finger in his book, half shut
the covers, and looked at her because it had
been a very hot day and the temperature was
still over seventy.

Myra took the coat off and threw it over
the back of a chair.

"Well, Hal, I think you and I can count on
being thirty-five thousand pounds to the good
by next year. How does that grab you?"

"The old dear never made a will, then?"

"Of course she didn't. I knew that. It was
all talk. Why bother when it'd naturally go to
her only daughter? I think we ought to celebrate, we ought to have a bottle of
champagne. It's not every day you come into
money like that, we ought to have a real celebration."

"I don't know about that," said Harold. "I
don't fancy the idea of celebrating your
mother's death."

"We're not celebrating her death, don't be
ridiculous, we're celebrating coming into
money. It's not the same thing, surely you
can see that?"

"Go down The Woman in White, then, shall we?"

"I'm not going there. Let people see me in a pub with Mother not even cremated yet! What a thing to suggest. Celebrate at home is what I meant, like civilized people do."

Harold said nothing. He returned to the windswept ramparts of Elsinore. Myra looked in the cupboard in the dining room and found about a quarter of a bottle of sherry left over from her party and half that quantity of Dubonnet. While she was thinking what to do, she drank up the sherry direct from the bottle. It was a Friday, pay day, but because she had not been to work, her pay was still at the dental surgery. She had about forty-five pence in her purse.

"You could go to the wineshop and get us a bottle of sparkling white," she said to Harold.

Harold laughed in an absent way without looking up. "Good job you didn't take me up on my offer. I'm skint." He pulled out his trouser pocket. "Not a sausage."

By this time Myra wanted a celebration very much indeed. An excited restless feeling had come over her. She was in that euphoric state in which one wants to dance about and sing, and as people do, she wanted a companion whose mood would match hers and who would dance about and sing with her. Harold Yearman was not ideally cast in this role but he was all she had. These days Myra seldom thought of the married man but she thought of him now, of how he had liked to enjoy himself and how wild he could be.

She stood in the hall, which she was halfway through papering and which smelt of wall-paper adhesive, and she wondered if, considering the state of her current account, she dared give a check to the man in the wineshop. Even if she did dare, the shop closed at 8:00 and it was five to now. Myra looked up the stairwell. Doreen wouldn't miss a couple of bottles from that hoard of hers, probably didn't even know what she had there, and in any case Myra could replace them on Monday when she had been paid. Hal, she felt intuitively, wouldn't like the idea, so she wouldn't tell him. She went upstairs.

There were locks on some of the doors but none was locked. Myra opened the door into the living room and went in. The first cupboard she went to, in a shallow alcove beneath some shelves, was full of bottles of wine and she helped herself to two of Asti Spumante. Turning round, she nearly dropped them out of her arms. Four dolls were looking at her from the mantelpiece, two little girls with yellow plaits, an Indian boy, and — herself. Though it was not flattering, though it was very nearly grotesque, she recognized it at once as herself from the hair, the bosom, the colors, the gold chains. Myra felt angry and a little afraid. She was glad she had taken the wine now, she didn't feel a bit guilty or apprehensive, she was glad she had thought of it.

Harold took it for granted that his wife had been the 200 yards or so down the road to buy the wine. He would not have involved himself in an argument over it or consented to the licensee of The Woman in White cashing a check or anything of that sort, but since she had got the wine and there was, after all, something worth celebrating, he put a bookmark into *Twins of Destiny* and followed Myra into the dining room.

The French windows were open. The garden was green and leafy and full of shadows but glanced, too, with dark golden beams of sunshine. It was peaceful and still and very warm and a pigeon was cooing in the pear tree. Myra thought about the doll, pushed the thought fiercely away, and poured the wine.

"To us! We're in business, Hal."

"I don't know about that," said Harold. "There's many a slip between the cup and the lip."

"How can there be when she never made a will? We can go to Cyprus for a fortnight now. First thing we'll do when we get the money is — buy a car!"

"You'll have to drive it then."

"And have the kitchenette all done with pine units. And fitted carpet in our bedroom, a sort of amber color would be nice."

They talked for a while about what they would do with the money. The warmth of the evening and the wine spread through Harold, a delicious, languid calm. He answered Myra amiably while reflecting on the dismal fate of Mary Stuart. Presently Myra got up to close the windows.

"Or we'll have gnats in. There's one bitten me already." She rubbed her thigh.

Harold said facetiously, "Let's have a look."

She had drunk the sherry before they had started and now she staggered a bit, lifting up her skirt to show him. Harold got hold of her and pulled her down on his knee. Her face was brightly flushed, that damask rose skin of hers, and he wondered why he had ever thought she looked like Edith; there was no resemblance. Plumped on Harold's lap, Myra was face to face with herself in the mirror on top of the sideboard. With the married man, she had sometimes looked at her own reflection in a narcissistic way and she did this now, suddenly seeing how beautiful she was, how young and voluptuous with her smooth skin and big round breasts, her mane of chestnut hair and her long legs in black spotted tights. For the first time she thought how lucky Harold was to have her for a wife, a beautiful young wife and he such a meager little gray scrap of a man. Thinking of them like that, of her having so much to give and him unworthy but greedy to receive it, excited her. She put his hands on her breasts. She reached for her wineglass.

"D'you feel like a bit?" said Harold.

Normally she would have reproached him for his vulgarity. But she was sluggish, feeling sexier than she had done for nearly a year. "Of course I do."

"Better go upstairs then," said Harold.

In Mount Pleasant Hall there was for a moment no human sound and it was dark but for the feeble red glow beyond the cabinet. You could make out the shapes of the persons sitting next to you and in front but no more. It was about as dark as it is in a theater when the lights have gone down and the curtain not yet risen.

Mrs. Collins, from her seat at the end of the front row, suggested they should all sing something. Hassan's favorite song was alleged to be "Pale Hands I Loved Beside the Shalimar" but no one knew the words, so they sang "The Volga Boatmen" instead.

At the third repetition of "Heave, my brothers," the curtains parted a little and a figure in a turban appeared between them. You could just make out the shape of the turban and a long white robe.

Miss Finlay whispered to Dolly, "That's Hassan."

"Sssh," said Mrs. Leebridge.

The figure spoke in a voice like that of the man who kept the Tandoori takeaway shop in the Seven Sisters Road. "Good evening, friends."

There were murmurs from the audience and Mrs. Leebridge said, "Good evening, Hassan," in a loud schoolmistressy way. "Are you going to show us any spirit friends tonight?"

Hassan made no reply but disappeared between the curtains. A moment or two later his voice said:

"I have a lady here who passed on with a wound to her head, a car accident or something of that kind."

There was silence. Dolly heard someone whispering behind her. Then a man from the row behind said rather hoarsely:

"Is it for me?"

Hassan said, "That's the voice," and the curtains parted to disclose another draped white figure, bulkier this time and with what looked like a bandage tied round its head. From behind Dolly came a sound as of indrawn breath. The figure spoke in a subdued girlish voice.

"It wasn't my fault, Michael."

The man behind said, "Let me see you close to."

There was a mumbled something that sounded like "too soon" and the figure glided back between the curtains. Dolly heard the man say, "Oh, dear God," in a voice tremulous with emotion.

"His wife was killed last year," said Miss Finlay. "She drove her car out into the road in front of a lorry. They lived next door to Mrs. Bullen. Listen, Hassan's speaking again."

"Is there anyone who has lost a gentleman who was in the forces perhaps? Anyway who wore a uniform?"

A girl from a row behind called out, "Is it you, Dad?"

"That's the voice."

From between the curtains came another white-robed shape. Mrs. Leebridge said, "Look, you can see his peaked cap."

"Sssh," said Miss Finlay.

Pup could see no peaked cap, only someone tall and thin, wrapped up in a sheet. The figure stood to attention and saluted.

"Isn't it wonderful?" said Mrs. Leebridge. "And you can see Mrs. Fitter in the cabinet there lying in a deep trance all the time."

Nothing in the cabinet was visible to Pup. It was too dark. He had looked carefully, though, as one taking a professional interest in something not too distant from his own line of country. The back of the hall, however, was a little less dark owing to one of the blinds having ridden up a fraction and let in a shaft of twilight. This was sufficient to show him the owner of the voice who had been claimed as his daughter by the figure in the peaked cap. It must be her, for everyone else (in Pup's own phrase) was as old as the hills. He saw the profile of a round youthful face, the plump curve of a cheek, an upturned nose, and a mass of dark curly hair, and he was trying to see more when Mrs. Leebridge got up and tugged down the blind.

The curtains closed quickly. Hassan's voice asked if there was anyone who had lost a four-footed companion. There were several replies to this, so it remained uncertain whose pet was the flickering white something that appeared briefly between the curtain hems or even what kind of animal it was. A bird materialized after that, or Mrs. Collins said it was a bird, she said she saw it come out between the curtains and perch on the red table lamp. Dolly didn't see it but she was certain she felt its wings brush her face as it flew down the center of the hall. A woman sitting next to the man called Michael claimed it as her dead parakeet.

No more animals materialized but several more white figures came out, their robes reddened by the lamplight. The body of the hall was now totally dark because it had grown dark outside. There was a stillness and a quiet and then a fidgeting and whispering among the audience so that Dolly began to think the seance must be over. Hassan's voice made her jump.

"Are there a brother and sister sitting together in the front row?"

Dolly could not speak. It was Pup who answered.

"That's the voice!"

Dolly began to tremble and Pup took her hand and held it tight. A strong lemony scent drifted from the stage and pervaded the hall.

10

The figure was tall and thin, faceless, a swaddled pillar of white sheet. The lamp-light laid a red glaze on it, as on a cloth that has been used to wipe away blood. It swayed a little as it walked with mincing tread across the stage towards them.

"Is it you, Mother?" Dolly's voice was unsteady.

Hoarsely, as if its throat were constricted, it spoke. "It makes me happy to see you two together."

Dolly gasped. She reached out a hand yearningly. Then Pup too put out his hand and the apparition, swaying over them, clasped both in hers. Dolly felt thin bony fingers and a palm slippery with a clammy dew. In the darkness she tried to make out a feature, to recognize some defined angle of shoulder or hip, to sense the essence of her mother. The smell of lemons was over-powering. Pup raised himself up to look more closely, but immediately he did so, their hands were relinquished and the shape retreated. It glided away from them into the bloodstaining light, into the red air, and for a moment, before it disappeared between the curtains, its robes looked crimson. The curtains quivered and fell closed. Dolly gave a heavy sigh that made Pup turn and look anxiously at her, but she looked tranquil, she looked happy.

There were no more materializations. Hassan came out and said the medium had used up all her supply of ectoplasm and was in any case exhausted, that was enough for tonight, friends, and thank you very much. Dolly closed her eyes and breathed deeply. She felt as if her mother were still with her, still present in the hall. The central light was switched on and she blinked and sighed.

"Wonderful, isn't she?" said Mrs. Leebridge. "You've never seen anything like that before, I'm sure."

Mrs. Collins said it amounted to genius.

"There's not a doubt about that." Mrs. Leebridge went up to the cabinet and drew back the curtains and gave Mrs. Fitter a ciga-rette.

There was a scraping of chairs as people got up. The blinds were raised and you could see the dark blue night, a sliver of moon made dim by the shine from street lights.

Dolly said in a vague dreamy voice, "Mrs. Collins's daughter is going to give us a lift home in her car."

They filed out along the passage. The double doors were sheltered from the street by a porch with a gable and just inside the porch, beside the notice board, was standing the girl whose father had come out and saluted. In the quite bright electric light, Pup could see that she was a very pretty girl indeed. In fact she was not at all the sort of girl likely to be found in this company of the drab elderly, being about twenty and dressed in a very short navy blue dress with white coin spots, white tights and high-heeled red sandals. When she saw Pup she gave a nervous giggle.

"I know I'm a fool but I'm scared stiff to go out there in the dark."

Mrs. Collins was indignant. "It makes me cross, that sort of thing. As if there was anything to be frightened of in our friends from the Other Side desiring a glimpse of their loved ones."

"I can't help it, I'm scared."

Pup made a decision. She was looking at him, her soft red lips slightly parted. There was no doubt in his mind what was happening. Like Coward's Amanda, his heart had always been jagged with sophistication, inexperienced though he was. The strange thing was that he hardly knew whether he was yielding to temptation or resisting it. All that was clear was that the time had come.

"Let me have the pleasure of seeing you home," he said in his grave courteous way.

"Would you?"

"Of course."

Dolly was too preoccupied to feel much resentment. Besides, she wouldn't be on her own, she would be in Wendy Collins's car, so there was no need to feel nervous about "The Headsman," as the papers called him. Of her mother she could not be afraid, though that gliding presence had in any case slipped away.

The car dropped her outside the house. She unlocked the front door and let herself in. The house was in darkness and there was a draft blowing through from the back. Dolly hesitated and then she went through into the dining room where the draft was coming from and put the light on. The French windows were wide open and the breeze had blown Myra's new curtains so that one of them had wound itself round the standard lamp and the other been caught up on the back of a chair. There were two empty wine bottles on the ceramic top coffee table, which Dolly recognized as from her own stock, an empty glass and one half empty, and on the floor by the window one of Myra's sandals and a pair of black spotted tights.

She closed the windows. She understood

fairly well what had taken place and she shivered. The memory came to her very sharply of her mother in the white shroud and she seemed to feel again the damp coffin-cold hand. Somehow, although she knew her father was not really old, although Myra was quite young and what some would call attractive, she had believed the marriage had been made for convenience and companionship, what the French call a *mariage blanc*. Again she shuddered with disgust. On an impulse to admonish and insult, she stuck the heel of the sandal into the neck of one of the bottles and tied the tights round the other like a scarf round a snowman.

When she had done that, she was breathing like someone sobbing. All the joy and comfort of the evening was gone. She went upstairs, opened a bottle of wine and poured herself a tumblerful. If only Pup were there to talk to, if only he had come home with her! She had never discussed matters of that kind with him, he had seemed to her too young and innocent, but now she would not have been able to keep silent. Pup, though young, was wise; Pup had great ability to console. Thinking of the couple down below, directly below her, lying in a drunken satiated sleep, Dolly took her wine and sat in the window to wait for Pup to come.

Pup was in Hornsey. He was walking along

slowly in the soft breezy late summer night.

"My girl friend got the tickets," the girl was saying, "and then she couldn't go. Well, she chickened out, if you ask me. I thought I'd go though just for a laugh. It was laugh, wasn't it? My dad's alive and well and living in Slough. What's your name?"

"Peter." Pup was digesting the implication of her last remark. "You don't live at home then?"

"Me? You must be joking. I share with two other girls but they're away. They're students and their college isn't back yet."

Pup took her arm to cross the road and did not bother to release it when they got to the other side. She said she was called Suzanne. Her rounded golden-skinned arm was covered with soft down which for some reason had become erect.

"You want to come in for a bit?"

They had arrived outside a house not unlike the Yearmans' but with a dozen bells by the front door. Suzanne's flat was a very large room and a very small bathroom and a tiny kitchen. The overhead light failed to come on when she pressed the switch and she groped for the table lamp. Pup touched her arm, shook his head and put a match to the half-burnt candle that was stuck in a wine bottle by one of the beds.

She giggled. "I'm going to tell you something. I waited for you on purpose. There was

128

an old woman offered me a lift but I said no."

"I was looking at you all the evening," Pup said. "I was thinking how beautiful you are."

"Were you really?"

Pup put his arms round her and kissed her. He felt he did it rather well, considering he had never done it before but only seen it done by couples in the street and on Christopher Theofanou's television. Suzanne responded so enthusiastically that Pup felt quite ill with excitement. What he would have liked and wondered if this was what all men would really like, would have been to tear all her clothes off and rape her in one minute flat. Impossible, of course. He said in a cool conversational tone: "I've got news for you. I'm an innocent virgin."

She stared. "You're kidding."

"No, it's the truth." He smoothed back the dark curly hair, looked into her eyes. He let his hands slide to her shoulders and then enclose her soft full breasts. Pup had read a lot of books, including novels. "But I'm young and strong. You'll have to teach me. Will that be all right?"

"Wow," said Suzanne. "You bet it will."

Dolly waited for him. She refilled her tumbler with wine. It was an hour and a half since Pup had parted from her to see the girl home. Of course the girl might live miles and miles away and perhaps they had had to wait for a bus and perhaps now Pup was waiting for a bus home. She might live in Wood Green or Hackney or almost anywhere in north London.

Pup was so small and slight. In the dark or at a distance he might easily be taken for a girl. The Headsman might take him for a girl. Dolly began to pace up and down but she was unsteady on her feet, the wine had done that for her. Midnight, half-past, ten to one. Suppose he had missed the last bus? Would he attempt to walk? Dolly poured herself more wine. She wanted to scream out her terror that something had happened to Pup. He might be walking home, he might meet The Headsman or that gang that roamed the council estate.

She longed for him. She began to count, one, two, three, when I get to a hundred I shall hear his key in the lock, I shall hear him coming up the stairs. Ninety-nine, a hundred . . . The house was utterly silent, the world was silent, even the perpetual traffic seemed to have ceased. Dolly fell on her knees.

The Yearmans were not a religious family. God had not inhabited Dolly's childhood or done much more than nod in passing through school RI lessons. She found herself praying to the specter that had swayed across the stage in Mount Pleasant Hall.

"Mother, protect Pup and bring him safe home to me . . ."

She would never be able to sleep. What was the use of going to bed? She finished the wine in the bottle, opened a second one. It was two o'clock. Another tumblerful finished her. She crept, she crawled, across the hall and fell on to her bed in a stupor.

At 7:30 on Saturday morning Pup came home. It was a beautiful morning and he felt jaunty and light on his feet and full of joy. As he let himself into the house it occurred to him that it would not behoove him to show these feelings, so, with his story ready, nursing the secret knowledge of his date for six o'clock that evening — a story prepared to cover that, too — he came in a contained and rather diffident way up the stairs. He need not have worried. Dolly was still asleep. Harold was still asleep. Myra was awake and up and in the bathroom, taking aspirins, remembering what had happened. Her former lascivious feeling of exultation in sacrificing her beauty to gray old Harold had changed to revulsion, even shame. She pulled her bright green toweling dressing gown round her and tried to face the day ahead.

The day ahead was faceable for Dolly when she saw that Pup's bedroom door, which had been open when she went to bed, was now closed. Her head was pounding and she felt weak at the knees. Never before had she drunk so much wine at one go. She went down to the bathroom and had two aspirins out of the bottle Myra had left standing on top of the lavatory cistern. Her hair was all over the place. She damped it and combed it out and pulled a curtain of it carefully down to cover half her cheek. Instant coffee would help but she and Pup were out of coffee. She got her purse and key.

Myra was in the hall, her face haggard, her hair scooped up and pinned on the crown of her head. The green she wore looked iridescent to Dolly's morning-tender eyes, it was so bright. She pounced on Dolly.

"Surely it wasn't necessary to do that? I mean, go in there and shut the window, yes, but my sandal stuck there like that and my —" Myra could not bring herself to say the word. Her face was red and working. Nor could she mention the doll. She had meant to, had planned to, but she couldn't.

"It was my wine," Dolly said.

"Well, agreed, of course it was. And if you'd been at home I wouldn't have dreamed of such a thing without asking. I was going to put it back. First thing this morning, I was going to replace that wine and the fact is if you hadn't gone in there to shut that window, which to be perfectly honest was no damn business of yours anyway, you'd never have known a thing about it."

"A person likes privacy."

"You'd better lock your doors then." Myra had forgotten all about wanting to be friends with Dolly. She thought she could see in Dolly's eyes knowledge of what had happened on the previous evening, knowledge and scorn, so she lashed back in the way some people do when their antagonist has a disability.

"You don't imagine doing your hair like that hides that thing on your face, do you? Frankly, Doreen, it draws attention to it."

No one, ever, had referred to Dolly's nevus in any fashion comparable to this. She could hardly believe what she had heard. But she had heard it and she was aware that she would feel the full pain of it later. Blushing deeply, she turned instinctively away; humiliated, she performed the more deeply humiliating act of presenting her "good" cheek to Myra.

"Pancake make-up would be better," Myra pursued. She loved giving cosmetic advice, advice on clothes, on "making the best of oneself," and in doing so she forgot her original malice. "Or even Leichner stage make-up, a greenish powder maybe. You'd need an expert in techniques for covering scars, that sort of thing, but that's not a problem, I mean, these people do exist." She put out a hand and lifted the long lock of hair. Flushed with blood, the nevus burned a rich purple.

Dolly jerked backwards, pulled her hair out of Myra's grasp and ran out of the front door. It was cooler this morning, quite cool and fresh, and the breezy emptiness of the street was like her own loneliness. She hated Myra, that went without saying, she loved Pup. Yet last night, simply by staying out, simply by not being there as he always was, he had taken a step away from her. Dolly felt colder than the temperature warranted. She longed for a friend to talk to. Why couldn't a friend have come into the house instead of an enemy like Myra? When she reached the corner shop she realized she was holding her hair across her cheek, holding it with both hands, her shoulders hunched.

Myra never said a word about the doll. Perhaps she hadn't seen it when she went in to take the wine, Dolly thought, or perhaps if she had noticed it she hadn't recognized it, vain as she was, as representing herself. One afternoon when she had nothing else to do, Dolly made it an emerald green jacket from a scrap of material left over from a client's dress. Emerald had been a fashionable color that summer.

The doll soon lost its companions. Miss Finlay bought one of the little girls with yellow plaits, Wendy Collins's best friend had the Indian boy, and Mrs. Leebridge wanted the other little girl.

Dolly took it to Mrs. Leebridge's flat herself. This was in Camden Town, in a block not far from the tube station. Mrs. Leebridge, large, flabby-fat, frog-faced, was perhaps the only person Dolly had ever known who could be in her company without reacting in some way or other to her nevus — without staring at it in fascination and then quickly looking away or ostentatiously not looking at her face at all ever or darting swift covert glances. Mrs. Leebridge behaved with Dolly just as she did with everyone else, noticing her only as a sponge to suck up the stream of self-love and boastfulness which poured from her thick flapping lips and the almost equally effusive adulation of everything pertaining to Roberta Fitter.

The doll was paid for, glanced at, then set aside and ignored. Mrs. Leebridge talked about how she herself had been privileged to see ectoplasm coming out of Mrs. Fitter's chest and forehead in white streams. She showed Dolly photographs of spirit faces surrounded by ectoplasm and floating in the air and one of Mrs. Fitter in a trance with a long white tube coming out of her chest and a man's face in a kind of balloon at the end of it.

"I hope you'll come to another of our seances, dear."

Dolly said she would think about it.

"I hope you'll do more than think, dear. Only five pounds, that's nothing these days, that's less than you'd pay to go to a show in the West End."

Dolly didn't much like underground trains.

You had to sit facing people and people in trains had nothing else to do but look at other people. But Mrs. Leebridge lived so near the station that it seemed stupid to hang about waiting for a bus.

It was just after 5:30. She was a hundred yards or so from the station entrance when she saw Myra ahead of her with her red bushy hair down on her shoulders and wearing the very sandals one of which Dolly had stuck by its heel into the neck of the Asti bottle. George Colefax's practice was in Camden High Street and Myra must be on her way home from work.

Vaguely Dolly knew that Myra traveled by tube from Camden Town to Archway and caught a bus or more usually walked the half-mile or so home to Manningtree Grove. She disliked the idea of traveling home with Myra and she hung back a little until Myra had passed into the station and was lost to view.

Dolly wondered what Myra would say if she warned her off wearing that awful emerald green. No doubt it was all right for Myra to give people unwanted advice but not for them to give it to her. By the time Dolly came into the station Myra had disappeared and Dolly did not see her again until she came on to the platform.

There were a lot of people on the Barnet Line platform, though it was not densely packed. As usual, people had gathered themselves into groups, each separated from the next by a few feet, at the very edge of the platform. How they would know exactly where the doors would be when the train came in (for this was the reason for the mode of waiting), Dolly had never been able to understand. Myra was in the center of one of these groups in her emerald green cardigan. At some point between Dolly's first sight of her and now, she had scooped up her hair in the way she often did, no doubt because of the heat — it was very hot down here in the tunnel — and had fastened it on to the back of her head with a large tortoiseshell slide Dolly had not seen before. It was interesting to someone fond of clothes and color to notice how a fashionable shade such as that green would occur regularly in every crowd, when you half-closed your eyes you could see dozens of bright spots of it against a uniformly drab background. It had been the same, she remembered, a year or so back when purple grape was "in" and during the months she called the "yellow summer." Dolly herself was wearing a sand-colored coat and skirt, with a sand-and-blue-and-red check shirt and Pup's amulet tucked away inside it because it did not quite "go."

She made her way through the press of people until she was behind Myra and within four or five feet of her. On the left of her stood a tall businessman in a chalk-stripe suit and on her right a plump elderly woman. Their bodies slightly overlapped Myra's; she was a little nearer the edge of the platform than them. A bright segment of green cardigan, a scrap of green, white and navy check skirt, showed between their more sober gray and fawn, and this, as Dolly watched, was in turn covered by the slim shape of a young girl in the same fashionable green spotted with black. Dolly moved forward. The notice which announced incoming trains had lit up to indicate that the next one would be for Mill Hill East.

It seemed to Dolly that everyone was staring directly ahead, reading for perhaps the hundredth time the advertisement posters on the concave wall of the tunnel opposite or, as in the case of the man in chalk-striped gray, a folded newspaper held three or four inches from the eyes. Dolly hooked her handbag over her shoulder and looked down at her hands. She turned her hands over, palms uppermost, and looked at them. Images filled her mind: her mother shrouded and gliding across the dark stage, the rooms she and Pup now lived in, a pair of spotted tights lying by an open window, an amorphous greenness on which lay fiery hair. Suddenly she fancied she could smell lemons.

The girl in the green with the black spots on it stepped a little to one side. Dolly had not exactly pushed her but had thrust herself behind the man in gray and rather to the right of him so that the girl was obliged either to move or argue. She gave Dolly a huffy look and turned her head away. Dolly was aware of two more people, perhaps more than two, coming to stand immediately behind her and the girl. They pressed against her, not pushing, but standing very close. She could feel their warm breath on the back of her neck. It was very warm indeed in the tunnel and sweat prickled Dolly's upper lip.

No one but the girl could have seen what she did with her hands and the girl had turned her face away in offense. Dolly held her now shaking hands at waist height. She could not see the train lines, the rails on which the wheels ran or the electrified rail between them but she knew they were down there, in the deep gulf between the platform and the concave wall. Last week, Pup had told her, the line between Mornington Crescent and Euston had been closed for two hours because someone had thrown himself on the line. Not in front of a train but just on to the electrified rail, and it had killed him. Of course, for good measure, if you wanted to commit suicide it would be a surer way to throw yourself over just when the train was coming in.

The light up the track at the far end was green now, awaiting the coming Mill Hill East train. Dolly could hear it in the distance and feel the wind that blew ahead of it. She held herself perfectly still, her eyes on that bright, virulent, poisonous green, which was all she could now see, which had expanded itself into a great green field crowding all her vision. Her throat was constricted and dry. She unclasped her hands and raised them, the palms a spare centimeter from the green jacket, the woolly pile of it brushing her hands. The train burst out of the tunnel mouth into the station and Dolly braced herself to push.

The elderly woman in brown turned round sharply. The twitch or start Dolly had made must somehow have alerted her. She took in the position of Dolly's hands a second before Dolly snatched them away and her face, bun-like, motherly, one of those determinedly cheerful faces, was overspread with horrified disbelief.

The train stopped and the doors opened. There was a surge forward. Dolly turned and fought her way back through the crowd eager to get into the train. She pushed with her hands, with her arms and shoulders, coming, as she retreated in a panic, face to face with Myra.

11

She needed air. She sat on a wall, breathing deeply, feeling the damp breeze on her face. It was horrible to think of what she had nearly done, sent some stranger to her death by electrocution and under the wheels of a train. Myra had not even been at the front of the waiting crowd but well in the rear. Perhaps there had been some difficulty over her ticket or she had been delayed, talking to someone she knew. Whatever it was, the woman in the green coat that Dolly's hands had almost pushed over that subterranean precipice had not been Myra, though she had been almost more Myra-like than her apparent double, for Myra, when Dolly came face to face with her, stared at her, passed her speechless, had been wearing a tan-colored skirt and her red fuzzy hair still hung about her shoulders.

And now Dolly thought of the pleasant bun face, briefly become horrified. Suppose that woman should pursue her, tell the police of her? Attempted murder, she thought, and she put up her hand to the nevus by which anyone who had seen her could identify her. She got up. She was afraid to go back into the station and began to walk rapidly up the Kentish Town Road.

A taxi came and she got into it. It was perhaps only the second taxi she had been in in her life, but she felt she couldn't face any form of public transport. She was overwhelmed with dread of the police coming and the bun-faced woman with them, of knowing herself identified and hearing her action described. As soon as she was home she poured herself a big glass of red wine and it comforted her, it gave her courage. The second glassful she took with her into the temple. She thought she would hide there if they came and tried to find her. Before settling herself on the cushions, she moved to the altar to look at the elemental weapons as she always did on coming in here. Amid her fear it brought her a separate feeling of unease to see a film of dust lying on the dagger's blade that Pup had used to keep so bright.

The doorbell ringing fetched her out on to the landing. Her father went to answer it and she expected the deep sound of men's voices and the tramp of feet. But it was only Myra, who had forgotten her key. Dolly refilled her glass.

"I couldn't get in the first train that came," Myra said crossly. "It made me hours late. You'll just have to have an omelette or something."

Harold would rather have had tinned ravioli or a pork pie but there were no such things in the house or not down here. He was obliged to accept what Myra called a "soufflé" omelette, this being the kind in which the whites of the eggs are separately beaten into stiff peaks. Harold thought it was like eating peppered and salted cotton wool but he didn't let it bother him. He ate it with a fork held in his right hand, using his left to turn the pages of a reconstruction of the life of Henry II's paramour Rosamund Clifford, which he had propped up against the cruet. Myra, breathing hard, took away his plate and handed him a crème caramel she had made the night before.

"I thang you!" said Harold, continuing to read. He had the lady encaged by the king in the middle of Woodstock maze.

Myra snatched the book and threw it on the coffee table.

"Steady on," said Harold. "You've lost my place."

"Well, for God's sake, always reading at mealtimes."

Harold licked his spoon. "I've finished now," he said mildly. "Want to go up The Woman in White?"

Myra shrugged. They went. Ronald and Eileen Ridge were in the pub but they had little to say and Harold never said much. Myra, who had rather more to drink than usual, was almost silent.

"What's up with you?" said Harold on the way back. "You got your visitor, is that it?"

Myra shook her head. She couldn't be bothered to answer him, not even to tell him off for using vulgar euphemisms. She only wished she had got her "visitor." Thirty-nine was young to have the menopause but not out of the question, she supposed. Not long ago she had read in a magazine at the hairdresser's that it was normal to have the menopause any time between thirty-eight and fifty-five. But she was such a young thirty-nine! She was so pretty and with a young girl's bloom on her, she couldn't be having the change, could she? She couldn't already be sliding into the gray sexless trough of middle age. Hair growing on the face, she thought, her waist thickening, hot flashes and all the rest of it. The other possible reason for a woman of thirty-nine missing a period she wasn't even going to consider.

It was pointless worrying about it. She was eagerly awaiting the arrival of the letters of administration so that she could get at her mother's bank account. Harold said it wasn't right for her to keep going next door taking what she wanted out of the flat; she ought to wait till she got the okay to go ahead. Myra didn't care. She seldom attended to Harold's wishes these days. In the meantime she finished doing up the hall and when the paint was dry and the carpet down she fetched in two rugs from Mrs. Brewer's living room, a console table and a framed reproduction of *The Laughing Cavalier*.

Yellow leaves fell gently on to the yellowed grass of the old railway line. A sinking sun put forth mild gleams through the smoky autumnal haze. Pup and Suzanne walked along hand-in-hand. They had been to the cinema in Muswell Hill because on Saturdays the students spent all afternoon beautifying themselves and did not go out before evening. From time to time, they stopped and kissed or stood embraced or simply stood still, hugging each other and gazing into each other's eyes. They behaved as all young lovers do who are suffering from temporary frustration, causing embarrassment to the few people who passed them and who had forgotten what it feels like to be nineteen or so and forced by circumstances to go to the cinema instead of to bed. By six, the student who was going to see her mother would have gone and seven would see the departure of the student who was going out with her boy friend. Pup kissed Suzanne on the bridge at Stanhope Road and hurried her down the steps. They did not see Myra but she saw them. She had been down to Crouch End Broadway for an evening paper and a packet of Rennie's for her indigestion and she saw them as she was walking back to Manningtree Grove. Dolly was coming down the stairs as she let herself into the house and would have walked past Myra with averted eyes.

Myra said loudly, "It's ridiculous you taking this attitude, Doreen. What have I done, I should like to know? Tried to help you, that's all."

Dolly opened the front door in silence.

"Let me tell you," said Myra, getting closer to the bone than she guessed, "you're going to need friends one of these fine days. When you're all on your own you're going to need friends. You won't always have your brother."

Still Dolly did not speak but she hesitated.

"You won't always have your brother dancing attendance on you. He'll want to lead his own life, he'll want to get married, won't he? As a matter of fact I've just seen him walking along with a girl — hand-in-hand, to be perfectly honest with you. Rather a tarty-looking girl, I must say, but we'll let that pass. You didn't know? You actually didn't know, did you? Well, I'm sorry if it's been a shock but it's always better to know, isn't it? I can't honestly say it didn't look like they'd got a serious thing going because, frankly, it did."

Dolly, as on the previous occasion, went quietly out into the street and closed the door behind her. A feeling of sickness which had nothing to do with what had just passed, which had in fact come over her in just the same way on the previous evenings, now overwhelmed Myra. She retched, clapped her hand over her mouth, and rushed for the kitchen sink. Harold, sitting in the breakfast room in one of the few remaining old armchairs, looked up from Robert K. Massie's *Nicholas and Alexandra* at the sounds of vomiting. This was his last remaining sanctum but even here the wallpaper had been stripped from one of the walls and Myra's paintpots already stood on newspapers on the gateleg table. He got up, put his head round the door, and called out that it must be the paint getting at her, maybe she had a paint allergy.

"You're just trying to stop me making the place look nice," Myra shouted back.

It can't be true, it can't be true, a voice cried to Dolly. The voice was in her head but it was like her mother's voice. She had been going out for wine. Not to the shop in Northwood Road — since The Headsman she went there no more — but to the nearest place, the wine supermarket in the Broadway. She had one bottle left, she could get more tomorrow. She walked round the block, came back to the house and ran upstairs. On the top landing she thought she smelt lemons, just for a moment and then the whiff of it was gone.

Her mother's voice said quite clearly, out loud, "It's true!"

Could she ask Pup? Would she dare? How could she ask him anyway, when she never saw him, when he was never there? It *was* true and she would lose him. She had never thought of the possibility of this before, that Pup might leave her for another woman. Somehow, without formulating it in words, she had believed he and she would be together, celibate and holding themselves apart, all their lives. She imagined him and this girl, hand-in-hand, walking home through the October twilight to her home. The mother opening the door to them, tea with the family, Pup the recognized accepted suitor. Oh, the pain of it, the unspeakable agony of it!

She opened that last bottle of wine and poured a tumblerful and drank it down like a thirsty person drinks water. If only he would come! If he came now, she thought she would have the courage to ask him. But he wouldn't come, he wouldn't come till the deep middle of the night. She tried to think of other things. Often she felt it should have weighed on her more, what she had done on the station platform at Camden Town, or what she had meant to do and would have done but for the bun-faced woman. Her mind reverted to it and sweat broke over her as she thought of what might have happened.

But it was not a powerful enough diversion to distract her from Pup for long. The tears were running down her face. She took a duster into the temple and dusted the things on the altar, and as she worked she cried. Pup's golden robe hung neglected on the back of the door, a half-burned candle lay on its side in a heap of joss-stick ash. Dolly blew off the dust that had settled on the books, the four volumes of *The Golden Dawn,* the heavy tome that was *The Chaldean Oracles of Zoroaster,* the slimmer *Book of the Dead, The Key of Solomon.* She cleaned it all up and tidied it and then she sat on the floor and wept. Just before 8:00, she went out to buy more wine and, passing the bathroom door, heard Myra being sick inside.

In the hairdressers' on Monday afternoon Myra read in a magazine an article called "Those Different Pregnancies" which said that some pregnant women were sick in the evenings, not the mornings, they might even be sick or feel queasy all day long. Myra, under the dryer, felt hot already. Now the sweat broke from her and ran down her sides. She couldn't be pregnant, could she? It was seven weeks since she had had a period and five weeks and a bit since that stupid business when they had drunk the wine to celebrate her mother's money. But even so, she couldn't be pregnant by old Harold, it just wasn't possible.

With the married man she had been on the pill but it wasn't wise to stay on that indefinitely so, when she had come off it, sometimes she had taken care of that side of things and sometimes he had. Often she hadn't been very careful. A psychiatrist would say, Myra knew from her magazines, that this was because she had unconsciously wanted a child. And maybe she had, maybe she had thought that would have fetched him permanently to her, in spite of his wife. Yet for all that passion, for all that lovemaking, two or three times in an afternoon sometimes, Myra had never even had a false alarm. And she had been young then, she thought sadly, and he young and strong, a big virile man who had fathered two children on his wife. It wasn't possible that she had never conceived in all those years, yet now be pregnant by puny old Harold.

Walking home from the station over the Archway bridge and down Hornsey Lane, she met Harold and Pup coming home from the shop via the library. Pup was carrying his father's books under his arm. That was something that maddened Myra — the idea of being married to someone who had to have things carried for him by a younger and stronger man. It was half-past five and she was starting to feel sick again.

"Not going out with your friend tonight then?" Dolly said as Pup walked in.

Pup shook his head. Suzanne had a week's holiday and, long before she had met him, had fixed up to go to Corfu with a girl friend — the same one who had chickened out of the seance — and she couldn't cancel it, she'd paid 100 pounds in advance. Pup was wondering how he would get on without her. He sat down to his corned beef and Marks & Spencers ratatouille, a carton of tropical fruit juice, and a rum baba.

All day Dolly had been screwing herself up to this, rehearsing what to say. And there was always the fear he wouldn't come home anyway. When at last she did speak, it was with apparent insouciance.

"This friend of yours, it's a girl, isn't it?"

Pup hesitated. He put down his knife and fork. He knew very well, almost precisely in fact, how Dolly felt about him. She was even more possessive of him than Dilip Raj's mother was of her son. And Dilip Raj's mother didn't have a birthmark slapped on the side of her face like a great crimson pancake. Pup understood it all. "Yes, it is," he said gently, and then, "How did you know?"

Dolly didn't answer. "Pup, is it serious? You aren't thinking of getting married, are you?"

"Of course not," said Pup with perfect truth.

Dolly had gone white but now her color came back, though she was still breathless.

" 'Of course not' to what? It isn't serious or you aren't getting married?"

"Both," said Pup. "Neither. Anyway, she's not here any more, she's gone away. Now you can tell me how you knew."

She used his name for Myra. She was happy and she made a sound that was nearly a giggle. "Our wicked stepmother."

He shrugged at that. Dolly watched him eat the rum baba and drink up his fruit juice. She was drinking Mosel herself, just starting on the second bottle, and working on a new doll, a ballet girl with black hair and a tutu.

When he had finished, Pup went into the temple. It suddenly seemed very small. Virginity is an asset to a geomancer. Maiden virtue holds some special qualities that are dissipated by sexual experience. Pup had known this long before he yielded to temptation (or resisted the temptation to keep himself pure and aloof) because the price he was paying in avoiding sex was very high and his diffuse, urgent desires had to be constantly assaulted by invocation and banishing rituals.

But the effect of terminating chastity was

dramatic. He could no longer do magic. It was true, just as the books said, the gift was lost, the power vanished.

He stood in the temple and looked about him and saw a poky attic bedroom with streaky black walls and bits of rubbish lying on an old bamboo table. The idea of making holy water or burning incense seemed grotesque. He could not imagine chanting all that Hebrew mumbo-jumbo, at least not *seriously*. He had abandoned his chastity and the power had gone.

Or could it be that something more easily explainable had happened? Here Pup's strong vein of common sense asserted itself. Could it be instead that now he had discovered sex, the things which he had done before now seemed mere childish substitutes for it? Very likely. Most probably it was both these explanations which contributed to his feeling of boredom about the temple and what had gone on in it.

He looked regretfully as his collection of books. He thought of all the knowledge he had accumulated. It was a pity to waste it. Perhaps he need not waste it. Considering the enormous store Dolly had learned — had been taught, he thought, by him — to set on magic and the rituals and all the jiggery-pokery of it, it would be unkind and unwise altogether to abandon it. He loved Dolly. But, oh, how he loved this new glory that had entered his life! The two loves seemed incompatible unless he could achieve some compromise and achieve it through his lost magical skills.

Pup stood at the window in the temple, thinking of all this, holding the silly knife with its crudely painted handle, watching the blackened leaves drop from the fruit trees and float slowly down on to the wet grass. A plan, daring yet simple, was beginning to take shape in his mind.

12

Dismay was what most women felt in the presence of Yvonne Colefax. If a woman knew she was going to see Yvonne, she would dress carefully and pay particular attention to her face and hair only to find that she was still inadequate, she was still not in competition. Yvonne inspired dismay and a resigned sinking of the heart. One remembered her as beautiful but generally as less beautiful than she was, so that each time one saw her afresh, it was with shock that she was so much lovelier than one had expected.

Two things about her consoled Myra. One was that Yvonne was nice, she was what people call "always the same" and that sameness was to be simple, childlike, and friendly, and the other was that the one person on earth Yvonne wanted to be noticed and admired by did not seem to see his wife as

155

anything out of the ordinary. More than that, he seemed to prefer almost anyone's company to hers, and if there was ever a case of a man treating his wife like a servant and his home like an hotel, this was it. Myra wouldn't have put up with it for a moment, let alone five years or however long it had been that George and Yvonne had been married. Yvonne might have a Porsche to drive about in and a wonderful house just off the Bishop's Avenue but that, Myra reflected sententiously, was no substitute for respect and consideration. And here was Yvonne, being George's doormat again or at least his errand girl, running down to Camden Town with something else George had forgotten when she must surely have better things to do with her time.

Yvonne came up to the desk where Myra sat in the front hall. Myra had forgotten just how pale and fair and soft her hair was, like dandelion fluff. And how slim she was, slender enough to bring a pang to almost any woman's heart, and how aquamarine blue her eyes. She was never overdressed, never unsuitably dressed, but for all that she didn't dress like other people but rather like someone in a film or television play whose garments have been carefully chosen by experts and whose accessories are all exactly the same shade. The expert was, of course, Yvonne herself and this morning she looked like the young Faye Dunaway dressed for the part of a woman from the East Seventies going shopping in Saks Fifth Avenue. Camel-colored suit with a thin brown belt and tall, narrow, shining brown boots as bright as chestnuts and a rakish little white felt hat with a brown ribbon. The scent of Ivoire overcame that of the pine air-freshener with which they sprayed out the waiting room each morning.

"You look absolutely amazing," said Myra generously. "You off somewhere exciting?"

"Just out shopping," said Yvonne as Myra had known she would. "George rang and said would I get him a Higginson's and bring it in, so I have. Here it is."

"A what?" said Myra but by that time she had unwrapped and exposed the long cardboard box labeled "Higginson's Syringe." "What does he want that for?"

"He's got this patient swears it's her teeth and George says it's not, it's her ears, so he's going to syringe her ears out."

"I could have popped out and got that," said Myra. "Want a coffee now you're here?"

"I'd love some coffee. You are kind, Myra. I'm afraid I'm just an awful nuisance, aren't I?" Yvonne said this with the air of one who is accustomed to being told she is tiresome and her jewel-like greeny-blue eyes sparkled as if tears always hung suspended in them. "You look a bit pale. Are you all right?"

Myra thought how nice Yvonne was. Why

couldn't Doreen be like that, friendly and down-to-earth and meeting you halfway? After all, if there was anyone with a reason for putting on airs, it was Yvonne, and yet here she was as natural as a child. For a moment she thought of confiding in Yvonne but she dismissed the idea. It was more than possible that Yvonne actually wanted a child and would have scant sympathy for a woman with an undesired pregnancy. So she only smiled and said she was a bit tired and they chatted about clothes for a while over their coffee and Yvonne told Myra how she had been all the way to Florence specially to buy her boots and handbag and belt and Myra didn't think she was too awful, did she?

Half an hour after she stopped work for the day Myra had an appointment with her GP. She had brought a specimen of urine with her but she knew it was too late to bother about that. She knew she was pregnant, eight or nine weeks pregnant, and it was not confirmation she needed. She needed advice, consent or maybe, hopefully, only the making of arrangements.

Walking up the windy hill to Camden Town station, Myra thought about the married man. She had been thinking about him a lot lately. It was in autumn that he and she had met and in autumn that they had parted. Myra thought of how she had stood in the bay window of her furnished room, watching for his car to come and for him to step out of it and slam the door and walk towards the house, walking with that supple grace of his, his head held high. He had stayed slim, never put on an ounce of weight, and the frosting of gray in his hair only made him look more distinguished. Every Wednesday and every Friday and most Monday evenings for year after year he had come and then one day he had told her there was no way he could desert his wife and she had rejoined that she had had a better offer anyway. Did he know where she was now? Did he ever think of her?

In spite of the appointment, she had to wait nearly half an hour to see her doctor. He examined her and confirmed the pregnancy. He began scolding her for not having come before, at her age early attention was vital, an amniocentesis would have to be carried out. Myra interrupted him. She didn't want a baby, she wanted an abortion. The doctor looked rather severe and Myra, made defiant, angry, and unhappy too because fearful doubt is not at all the same thing as certainty, said aggressively that she thought any woman in England had the right to an abortion just by asking for it.

"Before we take any steps," the doctor said, "I should like to talk to you and your husband together."

From that, in spite of her pleas of it being her baby, her body and her business, Myra could not move him. He would do nothing for her until he had spoken to Harold as well. Myra had never discussed with Harold the possibility of having children. It had no more occurred to her than it would to discuss men with Dolly or clothes with the perpetually sweatered and trousered Eileen Ridge. But now that she thought about it, she was not at all sure that Harold would be as dismayed at the prospect of a child as she was. Lazy, slow, apathetic people often liked children. Harold, in a half-hearted way, seemed to like the children he already had. Suppose, when she told him, he were to react with thrilled excitement? Suppose he were to be, in one of his own phrases, tickled to death? Suddenly Myra knew beyond a doubt that this was how it would be — Harold thrilled, Harold flattered at this proof of his virility, Harold adamant when it came to discussing with any doctor the termination of the pregnancy.

Myra walked home up Crouch Hill. She reflected dismally that, no matter how frightened and fed up a woman might be, she still had to think about what to have for supper. She went into the shop that was part butcher, part delicatessen, and the Irishman with the peculiar eyes and the rubbery face served her with two pork chops. He never smiled, he never said much, he always seemed to be listening. Next door was a news-agent. Myra bought an evening paper. She was in search

160

of an advertisement she had seen before, directed at women requiring abortions, and there it was, a box among the small ads.

She rang the number when she got home. The woman she spoke to was friendly and forthcoming and she said she must warn Myra that, on admission to the nursing home, before anything was done, a fee of 500 pounds would be required from her. It was only fair to tell her this from the start. Myra put the phone down. There was 20 pounds in her current account and this amounted to all her resources. The letters of administration had not yet come, might not come for weeks, and until they did, though she might drop in next door picking up unconsidered trifles, there was no way she could get her hands on her mother's money. These things always took ages. It was over two months already. Myra could remember precisely when her mother had died, for the date of that death was the day before the conception of this hated, unwanted child.

Pup had plans for the expansion of Yearman and Hodge. As soon as he had passed his driving test, they were going to buy a van. He had started going out servicing typewriters but it would be better when they had the van. These new electronic machines were the thing, Pup said to his father, big and efficient but light as a feather with all the works a mere microchip. They could still do well and make a profit if they took twenty-five percent off for cash.

"You've got drive," said Harold in the sort of tone one might use to inform someone he had a nasty cold.

"We'll have to think about photocopiers for the future," said Pup. "Photocopiers are the coming thing."

He walked up to Queen's Avenue in Muswell Hill, though it wasn't a very nice day but wet and windy. When he got home, he resolved, he would do some magic for Dolly. To make her happy. Like in the old days, he would perform one of the great rituals with incense and wine and roses. He owed that to Dolly.

The girl who opened the door to him said she typed theses for people. She was in the middle of doing this philosophy thesis for someone seeking a Ph.D. and the typewriter was sticking on the g. Well, the carriage return was sticking too. She had had it three years and it had never had a real service.

Pup set to work on it. It was an Adler and he knew all about Adlers. The girl watched him. She was rather a plain girl with a long face and a big nose but she had waist-length blonde hair and a very good figure. The figure was shown off to the best advantage in Lycra stretch jeans and a red T-shirt. Both looked brand new and Pup wondered if she had put them on because he was coming. They had met once before in the shop.

After a while she produced a bottle of Asti Cinzano. "But perhaps you don't drink on duty?"

"I'm not a policeman," said Pup.

"It's a well-known female fantasy," the girl said, "sort of daydreaming what it would be like with the man who comes to mend the TV."

"Or the Adler Gabrielle Five Thousand."

"Well, if you say so." She poured generous fizzy pink drinks. "What's your name? I mean I know it's Yearman but what's your first name?"

"Peter. What's yours?"

"Philippa. How much longer is that going to take you?"

"About five minutes, Philippa."

"Do you know, I suddenly got scared your father might come instead. I mean, I couldn't have fantasies about him, could I? Can I refill your glass?"

"Not if you don't want me to spoil this very nice expensive typewriter for good and all." While he still had his chastity, Pup thought, he had been able to handle this sort of thing. It had sometimes happened and he had pretended not to understand. Ah, those were the days! Or were they? "There you are, I don't think you'll have any more trouble with that *g*. Are you registered for the Value

Added Tax?"

"What, me?"

"One mustn't take anything for granted," said Pup, very close to her now. He lifted some soft locks of fair hair that clung to the front of the T-shirt. In spite of Suzanne he felt less than fully confident, so he used the ploy that had succeeded so well with her. "For instance, you're probably acting in the belief that I'm an experienced man while the fact is I'm still a virgin."

"That's unbelievable!"

"There are more things in heaven and earth, Philippa, than are dreamt of in all the philosophy you type on that machine."

"Well," said Philippa, "you don't want to go on being one, do you? I mean you'd like to sort of put an end to it?"

"I should love to," said Pup with fervor.

He felt a bit tired at the end of the day. Walking slowly homewards, he turned over in his mind the plans he had made to keep Dolly happy and give him a measure of freedom. Tomorrow night he had a date with Philippa and he meant to spend all day Saturday with Suzanne. Dolly, alerted by Myra, would never be made to believe he was spending all that time, half the day and half the night, with Chris Theofanou. He was generally free from vindictive feelings, but these days he felt quite savagely towards his father's wife. Pup had a special dislike of wanton malice.

An evening class or a club, or better still, a combination of both were what was needed. And a club-cum-class that would seem to benefit him in the one pursuit of his that interested Dolly. Pup had no qualms about telling quite ferocious lies in a good cause. He was pleased with his plan, it seemed to him foolproof.

Dolly began grumbling as soon as he got in. "I hate being forced to live up here. I hate this poky room and having to go down all those stairs every time I want to use the bathroom. It's so unfair! People won't climb up here and it's not worth my while making their clothes if I've got to spend pounds on bus fares."

"I've got something to tell you," Pup said.

She had been putting food on the table in front of him, cold sausages, potato salad, a bowl of tomatoes, but she stopped, holding the bowl, the gesture arrested in mid-air.

"It's not about that girl, is it?"

"Of course it isn't. Have you ever heard of the magical Order of the Golden Dawn?"

She nodded, relieved. "I read about it in one of your books."

"Well, I've joined it. The Highgate branch. I thought I should. There'll be a lot to do, meetings and seminars and special courses, quite a few evenings every week, I expect, and sometimes weekends. But if I want to

165

succeed as a geomancer I don't really have an alternative.''

In the relevant book, Pup recalled, it also said that the Order of the Golden Dawn, founded by Eliphas Levi, Crowley, Yeats and other like-minded dabblers in the occult in 1888, had under its later title of the Stella Matutina collapsed in the 1930s. He thought it unlikely that Dolly would wade through the innumerable dull pages in the book before this fact was reached. If she did, he could always say the Stella Matutina had been revived a few years ago.

Dolly's face was ardent. ''I think it's wonderful, I'm so glad. Did they ask you to join them?''

''Well . . .'' said Pup, not exactly committing himself.

''They must have done. It'll be a help to you in your career, won't it? It'll put you on the road to success.''

As far as Pup thought about having a career, it was as one of the directors of an expanding business machines company. He started to eat his sausages. Like a woman conditioned by a patriarchal society — in fact, very much like Dilip Raj's mother — she never ate with him but waited on him and watched.

''I'm going to be formally admitted as a member,'' said Pup, beginning as he meant to go on, ''tomorrow night.''

After supper, remembering his resolution, he went into the temple and beckoned to her to follow him. She came joyfully, lit the candles and then sat on the cushion under the fire *tattwa,* gazing at him. Pup stood by the altar looking at his elemental weapons and felt like groaning, the whole thing was such a bore. Why had he ever begun on it? Why hadn't he gone in for football or Tai Chi or stamp collecting?

"Well, then, what shall I do?"

"You're asking *me?*"

"I mean is there anything special you're embarking on? Any piece of work? Or anything particular that's bothering you? D'you want something invoked? I haven't got any holy water but I could make some."

She hesitated. "One day," she said, "you'll be a master, won't you? You'll be able to do anything, miracles?"

Her hand had not gone up to her cheek but he knew her meaning and he was aghast. A kind of panic rose in him, impatience with her and the whole business, self-disgust. Better to have told her it was finished, better to have destroyed the temple and thrown away the robe. But only let him think of something before she put that monstrous question directly to him . . .

"I know," he said. "We'll clobber the wicked stepmother!"

She was immediately diverted. She was

surprised, presumably because he had shown such distaste before. As if it mattered, he thought, white magic, black magic, all quackery, all rubbish. Pup pulled the robe over his head and thrust his arms into the wide sleeves. The night was dark and moonless and the wind which had been blowing all day had sprung into a gale, whipping tree branches and driving clouds in black flocks across a sky lit red by the lights of London. It was nearly 9:00 and he was weary but Dolly was not. She went into the other room and came back with the Myra doll in one hand and a tumbler of red wine in the other. Pup very nearly laughed. He thought how shocked he would once have been at the idea of profaning temple and rituals with any alcohol except that used strictly in the ceremonies.

He drew the curtain. The temple was now lit to a suitable cabalistic flickering dimness by the flames of four candles. The whole thing was going to be a bore and to satisfy Dolly he would have to go on for at least an hour. His father and Myra had already gone to bed, or at least his father had. He had heard the click of a light switch below him and the bathroom window had shed a rectangle of yellow light on the dark wet grass. Pup drew a circle in chalk on the floor and inside it he drew a pentagram. Something that would make this business less tedious was that he was no longer trammeled by rules and instructions.

He could do what he liked, say what he liked, jumble it all up.

Dolly was sitting with the doll on her lap. With her legs crossed, her hair hanging forward over her bent head, the crude metal talisman dangling from her neck, she looked like a little girl. Pup felt a fierce yet exasperated pity for her, he felt she was like an albatross or a millstone around his neck. He put out his hand for the doll and dropped it so that it flopped on its back in the middle of the pentagram.

"Give her a pain," Dolly said viciously. "She's had a lot of trouble with her stomach lately. Give her — give her appendicitis!"

"That's a bit strong," Pup said.

He turned to the east and made the Cabalistic Cross and then he began on the Inscription of the Pentagram. This was a Lesser Banishing ritual but he had forgotten the proper order of words and soon he was muddling it up with bits of consecration formulae and Hexagrammic rituals and invocations and all sorts.

For a short while at school he had done Latin. He recited the few declensions and conjugations he remembered. Then he abandoned that, prepared holy water, and scattered it about, walking round and round the circle until he was giddy. His sleeve, falling back as he raised the wand in his hands, showed him the time by his watch.

Ten-fifteen. He could stop soon.

When he had recited all the Hebrew names he knew and all the Egyptian ones and all the names of Greek gods and goddesses that he could remember, when he had said prayers frontwards and repeated them backwards, he seized the dagger from the altar. He held the dagger high above his head, a tall, commanding figure whose golden robe shivered and shimmered in the light from the candles.

Dolly gave a little gasp. Pup plunged forward in a swoop that was almost that of a *samurai* in its grace, and thrust the dagger's point through the belly of the doll with a sure stroke. For a moment or two the doll remained impaled on Pup's dagger and he had to draw it off with his other hand. Some of the stuffing came out and a fat worm of cotton wool like an entrail. Dolly looked as if she were going to clap but as if clapping would somehow be out of place. She got up, leaving the wounded doll where it lay. Pup pulled off his robe and blew out the candles.

Back in their living room, Dolly poured the last of the wine into her glass. The wind sang round the house and rattled the old window sashes in their frames. As she had come into the room after the ceremonies, her mother had spoken to her quite clearly and in her normal speaking voice:

"It's going to be a wild night."

Edith had always been one to comment on the weather. "Cold enough for you?" she would say or "This rain will get rid of the fog," or something like that. Now, as Dolly stood by the mantelpiece on which the ballet girl doll now sat alone, as she stood sipping her wine, Edith came very close to her in a breeze of lemon scent and whispered: "I never did like a wind, I'd rather anything but wind."

Pup came in and Dolly hoped their mother would speak again so that he could hear her, but Edith was silent.

"Can you smell anything?"

"Candles?" said Pup.

Dolly shook her head. "Come on, I'll make us both a cup of cocoa."

They were out on the landing, in the dark, and this time it was he who asked the question: "Did you hear anything?"

"The wind," said Dolly. She put out her hand for the light switch but could not find it.

"It sounded more like a cry," Pup said. He put the light on and they went into the kitchen.

In there, the window was too small for curtains. The panes rattled with a monotonous regular thudding. Dolly began heating milk in a saucepan and got out the tin of drinking chocolate. The window rattled, the wind made a keening sound as it rushed through the old railway line, and downstairs from immediately below them came a slither and a heavy thud.

Dolly clutched Pup's arm. "Whatever is it? D'you think someone's got in down there?"

"It was in the bathroom. The bathroom light's been on for ages. You can see in on the grass out there." He went back to the landing and looked down the stairwell. "I wonder if Dad's all right."

"We'd better go down."

The milk rose up in the saucepan and streamed down over the gas ring. Pup turned the gas off. They went down and tried the bathroom door. It was locked. The door to Harold and Myra's bedroom stood ajar. It was dark inside but Pup could make out a humped shape, a down quilt tucked round it, on the far side of the bed. He went softly over to the bed, expecting to see Myra, and saw his father lying there, fast asleep.

Dolly was rattling at the bathroom door. Harold didn't stir. Pup went back upstairs, got a piece of wire and poked it through the keyhole on the bathroom door until the key tumbled out. He could see the key under the door and, inserting his wire, hooked it through.

Still the door would not open more than an inch or two. Something was pushing against it. Pup pushed too and the door opened enough to admit him and then Dolly and he saw that it was Myra, whose head and shoulders had prevented the door yielding.

She was lying on the floor, wearing only the top half of a pair of green nylon pajamas. Near her, on the marbled tiles, lay a small pool of cloudy water and a big tube thing with a nozzle on one end and a bulb on the other. Her face was white and stiff as wax and when Dolly, trembling, shaking, and gasping, remembering some ancient recommendation of Mrs. Collins's, unhooked the wall mirror and held it to her lips, there was no mist of breath on the glass.

"She's dead," Dolly whispered.

"She can't be dead! There's no blood, there's nothing."

Her eyes met his and hers were full of wonder, of a deep, almost incredulous admiration. "Of course she's dead," Dolly said. "Of course she is." She drew in her breath in a sobbing way. "I'd better go and wake Dad."

"I'll do that," said Pup.

Dolly picked up the tube thing and dropped it in the basin. In lifting Myra's pajama trousers she uncovered what lay beneath them, a cardboard box labeled: Higginson's Syringe. Something prompted her to cover Myra's body with a bath towel. She mopped up the pool of water and then she stood, silent and trembling, looking down at the dead, mummy-swathed thing on the floor at her feet.

13

The doctor at the inquest said Myra had been ten weeks pregnant. She had tried to syringe out the uterus with a solution of water and shampoo and had continued pumping after the liquid was used up and there was only air left in the syringe. This had caused a bubble in her bloodstream, an air embolus, which, when it reached her brain, had killed her. She would have felt nothing, known nothing, simply collapsed and died.

Pup, sitting with Harold, thought that it was not true she had felt nothing. He remembered that cry. It seemed strange to him that a woman could damage her brain and kill herself merely by introducing water and air into her womb, although the doctor said this was not uncommon among women trying to procure abortion. To Pup, it still seemed nearly incomprehensible that in big, vigorous, energetic Myra, life had hung so precariously. It was as if she had been struck down, not by a little bubble of air in her blood, but by some external force that took no account of strength and vitality and love of live.

Dolly did not attend the inquest or the cremation. She had always avoided as much as she could public places and gatherings of people. The funeral was at Golders Green Crematorium, where Edith's had been. George and Yvonne Colefax came and a cousin of Myra's who had been a witness at her marriage to Harold. Apart from Pup and Harold himself, there was no one else in the crematorium chapel but a tall, good-looking man with graying black hair who walked with an easy grace. He slipped in and sat at the back while they were struggling through the Crimmon Version of the Twenty-third Psalm. George Colefax knew who he was and nodded to him. It was George Colefax who had rung him up and told him Myra was dead. By the time they were standing outside looking at the flowers, the man had disappeared.

Harold went home in the black funeral car he and Pup had come in but Pup accepted a lift from the Colefaxes. George's car was a large silvery-white Mercedes-Benz. He was going to drop Yvonne off at a friend's house in Muswell Hill, and since Pup also had a friend to visit in Muswell Hill, that would suit him too. George drove in grim silence.

Yvonne sat beside him, crying quietly for Myra. She was dressed in a suit of very fine black wool and a ruffled blouse of black and white crêpe de Chine and on her thistledown hair she wore a tiny black hat with a veil. Pup, sitting in the back, wished he could still see her legs. Yvonne's legs and slender feet were miracles of sculpting in black gossamer stockings and black patent court shoes. She cried softly, sometimes saying what a fool she was to cry but she had been so fond of Myra, it wasn't as if she had all that many friends. George kept silent, his shoulders hunching just a bit more. The tears did nothing to Yvonne's Arthur Rackham fairy face but trembled on it like drops of dew. Pup hoped he and she might be allowed to leave the car together but Queen's Avenue was reached before Cranmore Way and he was obliged to get out, thanking them politely for the lift.

Without Myra the house was quiet and strange. It was an altered house, new and clean, and the cheap new furniture had a pathetic look. Once she had it to herself again and Harold and Pup were back at work, Dolly began moving things downstairs. She brought down her sewing machine and put it back in the living room that had been Myra's pride. She brought down the chest of remnants and the box of patterns and the ballet girl doll. The other doll, the Myra one, its body ravaged by Pup's dagger, she had removed from the temple some time in the small hours of that dreadful night. When she looked at it next day, her feelings had been strange ones — awe, wonder, guilt, remorse, triumph.

That same day she had destroyed the doll. No fireplace in the Yearman home had been used since Harold's mother died but the fireplaces were still there. Dolly lit a fire in the one in the room that had been hers and Pup's living room. Smoke billowed out and filled the top floor, unable to escape properly up the clogged chimney, but at last, set among Dolly's firelighters and screws of newspaper and bits of wood, the Myra doll was consumed. She opened all the windows to cleanse the place of smoke.

It was with a feeling of relief, almost of triumph, that she moved back into her old bedroom and moved Pup's things back into his. That evening they all ate together in the kitchen once more: tinned spaghetti, corned beef, granary rolls, St. Ives cheese spread, defrosted chocolate éclairs. If Harold noticed this reversion to the old ways, if he was aware of an end having come to the reign of stuffed peppers and moussaka and eggs Florentine, he gave no sign of it. He read with his book propped up against the cruet, and when he had finished, he shuffled off to the breakfast room. Dolly had asked him if he would like her to clear it up a bit, do something about all those pots of paint, but Harold said no, to keep it just as Myra had left it.

Ron and Eileen Ridge, who had been on holiday in Spain at the time of Myra's death and funeral, paid a visit of condolence.

"I did it," said Harold. "I killed her."

Ron was embarrassed. "Don't say that."

Harold spoke with lugubrious pride. "I do say it. But for me she'd be alive today. We men have a lot to answer for in this world."

"True enough," said Ron.

Harold showed them the breakfast room, the gateleg table still covered with a dust sheet, the paintpots still standing on newspapers, Myra's brushes in a glass jar.

"How touching! It makes me want to cry."

"It's the least I can do, Eileen," said Harold, "seeing it was me killed her."

"He's no right to say that," Dolly said to Pup, and then she said what he had been dreading to hear from her: "It was you killed her." Pup held the living-room door open for Dolly and let her pass in ahead of him and then closed it firmly. He thought his face must have gone white, it felt very stiff and cold. Dolly had flushed. The nevus was a dark, sore-looking purple.

"You must not say that."

"Why not? You made holy water, you said the words, you stabbed the doll with your dagger and she died. Half an hour later she was dead. You stabbed the doll in the stomach and it was that part of

179

her killed her."

"Dolly," he said, "it was a coincidence. Myra killed herself. She caused her own death by doing a mad thing to herself with that syringe. I told you what the doctor said."

"Yes, and you told me you couldn't believe a bubble of air like that could kill anyone. You know it couldn't. It was your magic killed her, you killed her. And why not? You've studied, you've got the power, I think you could do anything. You're as good as that Mrs. Fitter. You're equal to her, you're in the same class as her and she's famous. You can be famous now. Isn't that what you want?"

There were a good many statements among what Dolly had just said whose accuracy Pup doubted. As for Mrs. Fitter — he was on the point of telling her the truth about Suzanne's father but he thought better of it. Dolly had been strange since Myra's death, perhaps since before Myra's death, intense, preoccupied, sometimes seeming to listen or stare as a cat may do, erecting its fur at nothing. If Pup had pinned himself down to it, had really wanted to think of it, he would have said there was something disturbed about her and he might have gone even further. But he did not want to think about it. He did not want to think about Myra's death, about Dolly's loss of balance or about anything that was in any way connected with magic, the occult, the supernatural, ectoplasm, rituals, good and bad spirits, incense, archangels, Crowley, or any of it.

What he wanted was to go upstairs and dismantle the temple. Put the dagger, the wand, the cup and the pentacle in the plastic bag for Haringey Council to take away, give the golden robe to Oxfam, sell the books down the Archway Road and paint over the black walls with some of Myra's "Sunbeach." Walking home from work, he decided to do this or some of this, once he had had his supper. But as soon as he saw Dolly, as soon as she had come up to him and put up her face for his kiss, he knew that, of course, he couldn't do it. Get rid of the temple, deny his powers, his commitment, and then what would become of the alibi he had used so successfully last night in order to see Philippa? He had probably gone too far already in refusing to accept responsibility for Myra's death. Unless he could invent something else. Chess? Car maintenance classes? Cinema club? She knew he was interested in none of those things. She knew what interested him, what *had* interested him. Pup nearly groaned aloud.

Dolly was so close to him she could read along the line of his thoughts. Not read them, thank God, but read along the periphery of them.

"You've got a meeting of the Golden Dawn

tomorrow night, haven't you?"

Pup nodded. He was going round to Suzanne's.

"Will you tell them?"

He looked at her. The question that came into his mind was, would a normal person ask that? "Tell them what?" he stalled.

"How you did magic and made Myra die."

His own steady sanity recoiled. Every word was an affront. He suddenly saw clearly what he wanted from life and meant to have: pleasure, joy, peace, material things, money, worldly success, women. And, looking hopelessly at her, he saw something else, too. It had all come about because of him. If he had never sold his soul to the devil, Dolly would never have heard of the occult, if he had done no magic, not made the temple, Dolly would have thought magic something conjurors did for kids at parties. He had begun it and for her sake as well as his own he couldn't let her down now. He smiled at her.

"We — you — can tell people I can harness certain powers. I can make things happen, if you like, but we mustn't tell them about Myra. Can't you see that, dear? You're not allowed to kill people, you know that, it's against the law."

She nodded. When she spoke after a moment or two, he thought with relief that she had changed the subject.

"You've got your driving test tomorrow?"

"Yes, at ten."

She laid her hand on his arm. "Let's go into the temple and perform a Pentagram ritual for success."

"I'm going to pass anyway."

"Isn't that what you learn magic for? Isn't that what you sold your soul for? For success and getting what you want?"

How well she had learned the lessons he had taught her! He had run out of joss sticks but that was no excuse as she had bought some herself to keep in stock for him. She sat on the cushion with her glass of wine, watching him make the Cabalistic Cross and utter the prescribed words for success in a coming venture.

The next day he passed his driving test as he had known he would.

"Now you'll be wanting us to get that van, I daresay," said Harold.

"I'm taking delivery this afternoon."

Harold, who had been in the middle of an account of the sorrows of Prince Leopold after the death in childbirth of the Princess Charlotte, a subject fairly appropriate to his own situation, stuck his finger in the book to keep his place. "You haven't wasted much time."

"What were you thinking of doing with the money you get from Mrs. Brewer's flat?" said Pup.

"Now you wait a minute, you hold your

horses, that'll be months and months."

"Maybe. We should be able to get a good big bank loan on the strength of it, though. I want you to put it all in the business. We could take over one of those shops in Crouch Hill when the leases fall in in the summer and go into word processors. I've got it all worked out."

"I don't know about that," said Harold, turning pale. "There's a recession on or hadn't you heard?"

"That's the time to expand. There won't always be a recession. I've got my eye on that new tower block going up at the Archway."

"We're not moving into any tower block."

"Of course not. It's something else I've got in mind."

Harold gave him a hopeless look and returned to his reading. "All this drive," he said. "I don't know where you get it from."

"I don't know where we're going to go," said Suzanne, sitting on her bed and handing Pup his cup of herb tea. "They say they'll go in the bathroom for half an hour but I draw the line at that."

"I've got a car," said Pup. "Well, a van. No windows in the back and I've bought one of those duvets."

"You're kidding."

"Come and see. I thought we might go up on the Heath."

"You know, you're pretty amazing," said

Suzanne, twining herself round him.

They were putting up a block of old people's flats on the site at Mount Pleasant Green. It was so cold that the frost lay white on the builders' tarpaulins and stacks of bricks. The air was still but with a cutting edge to it and the sky sparkled with stars rarely seen in the London suburbs. There was a starry-eyed look about the lighted houses that surrounded the green as if surprised by the bitter cold that had suddenly clamped down on them.

"I always feel better once the winter solstice is behind us," said Miss Finlay, scurrying along so fast that Dolly had to trot to keep up with her. "You know the days are getting longer even if you don't feel it."

A handwritten and hand-drawn poster advertised Roberta Fitter's seance. Dolly had paid her five pounds, she was coming willingly, but she rather resented that poster. "They ought to have my brother here."

"He's not a medium, though, is he, dear?"

"He could be. He's got amazing powers. I had this cold last week and he cured it. My colds usually go on for weeks but my brother did this special invocation and next day it was practically gone."

Talking about him recalled to her mind how he had refused to come with her. Well, not refused exactly. He had a meeting to go to.

But she felt the lack of his company. It had been so nice last time. He was always out now and she was always alone. That was why she had come here tonight, to see Edith again, if possible to bring Edith more positively back with her, to have more of her than an occasionally heard voice. And as she entered the hall she sniffed the air, hoping for an early foretaste of lemon scent, but the place smelt faintly of some kind of cleaning fluid and tonight Miss Finlay had used lavender water.

It was cold, in spite of the two wall heaters with their thin, glowing elements. The curtains to the cabinet were open and you could see a green and black tartan blanket thrown over the chair Mrs. Fitter would sit in. This time Dolly was not asked to assist the medium with her dressing. Graciously, as to a favored novice, Mrs. Leebridge gave her the black clothes to hand round among the audience. Again Miss Finlay pulled the black tights inside out, her face drawn into a frown of concentration. Roberta Fitter was rather a long time getting ready, and a murmur of relief went up from the twenty or so people there when at last she appeared in the shapeless dress and the black Chinese slippers, crossed the stage with bowed head and hunched shoulders, and sat in the chair, drawing the blanket around her knees.

"It's no trouble to her, going into a trance, is it?" Miss Finlay whispered. "It's a knack I could do with. I find it more and more difficult getting off to sleep these days."

"Sssh," said Mrs. Leebridge.

When the lights were turned off, it was much darker in the hall than it had been in August. It was so dark, pitchy black, that at first Dolly thought they would be able to see nothing. Then Mrs. Collins put on the red lamp by the cabinet. It was a relief. The brief blackness, the icy cold blackness, had for a moment been alarming, bringing her a choking feeling of panic. Her hands, though in fur-lined mittens, still felt as cold as when she was walking along the street. She moved them about, rubbing the fingertips together. The red lamp gleamed but not warmly, not with the suggestion of a glowing brazier, but rather as a red warning light may shine in the darkness on a lonely road.

The curtains were drawn and the medium lost to view. Mrs. Collins came on to the front of the stage and suggested they sing the "Indian Love Call." Miss Finlay put up her hand like a child in school and said she didn't think it was the right sort of Indian. So they sang "The Volga Boatmen" once again, out-of-tune elderly voices mostly, cracked voices but for Dolly's clear soprano, and after a chorus or two the curtains opened and the thin, turbaned figure of Hassan appeared between them.

"Good evening, friends."

One or two people said good evening. The curtains seemed to move and he was gone, though it was too dark to see him go. The fidgeting among the audience ceased and there was silence, stillness, the dark and the cold. Someone had switched off the wall heaters. Their light would have been a distraction but the air seemed to be growing steadily and rapidly icier. Miss Finlay, her hands in woollen gloves, was pulling the front of her coat down to cover her calves. Dolly glanced to her right and she could just see, now her eyes had become used to the dark, that the woman who sat next to her was holding hands with the man on her other side. They were not young or good-looking or well-dressed, they were just an ordinary, middle-aged, working-class, married couple, but they had each other and each had the other's hand to hold. Dolly hunched her shoulders, tense with increasing, incomprehensible alarm. If nothing happened in the next few minutes she wouldn't be able to stand it, she would have to leave. Someone coughed slightly, a nervous clearing of the throat.

Then, when it felt as if you could have cut the cold, tense air with a knife, Hassan spoke from the cabinet:

"Is there someone here who has lost a gentleman who liked growing things? A market gardener perhaps? A gentleman with green fingers?"

The audience was silent.

"He's waiting to come through," Hassan's voice said. "A florist, could it be?"

A woman behind Dolly piped nervously, "My husband had his own greengrocery business."

"That's the voice!"

The curtains quivered. A figure appeared in something whitish that caught the red gleam from the lamp. It suddenly struck Dolly, for the first time it truly came to her, how terrible and wonderful it was, how it changed your whole life and way of looking at things, to have spirits brought to you thus from the abode of the dead. She trembled and stared.

"Is it you, Stan?" the woman said. Dolly heard the chair behind her creak and scrape as the greengrocer's widow got to her feet. Her voice was yearning. "I've missed you so, Stan. Put out your hand to me, won't you put out your hand?"

The specter extended a long thin hand that quivered. The arm, from which draperies fell back, passed in its own miasma of coldness close to Dolly's face and she gazed at it, that skinny, sinewy arm, very thin for a man's. The woman leaned forward between Dolly and her neighbor and reached out her own hand as if to try and touch the outstretched fingers but the spirit retreated with a slow twirling movement, glided away without even a whisper of sound from its trailing wrappings, and slipped between the curtains.

The widow was still standing up, still half-leaning across the people in front of her. "He didn't speak to me, he didn't speak a word. I wonder if he's angry. They say they know everything on the Other Side. I wonder if he knows I couldn't keep the business going. I did try but it was too much for me. Oh, Stan, why didn't you speak to me . . . ?"

"Silence, please, friends," said Mrs. Collins. "We must have quiet."

The woman's voice dropped to a whisper and then was hushed. People seemed stilled by the cold, paralyzed by it. Dolly was so cold now she was hugging herself for warmth. But there seemed no warmth left anywhere to find and the cold as deep now as in the place where those shrouded figures came from and returned to.

Hassan's voice came hollowly from the cabinet.

"I have a lady waiting to come through. She's a lady who died before her time. An operation perhaps or a wound in the lower parts."

Dolly kept absolutely still. Her mother had had two abdominal operations before she died. She waited for the lemon scent to come and, when there was no lemon scent, for someone else to claim the woman. Somehow she knew her mother would not come without that heralding breath of perfume. It was not Edith who waited there on the edge of the living world for Hassan to lead her over the threshold.

And now she was becoming afraid. Someone surely would claim the woman. Please, please claim her, Dolly mouthed silently.

"A young lady," Hassan's voice persisted. "There's somebody here who must have lost a young lady that passed over in November."

Then Dolly knew no one would claim her, for she knew who it was and knew it was for her. Perhaps she had really known for a long time now and that was why she was shivering with cold. Her teeth would have chattered if she had not held them clenched.

She gathered her strength. Her teeth chattered as soon as she parted them but she spoke. "Is it for me?"

"That's the voice!"

"Myra," Dolly said, "is it you?"

The curtains parted and Myra came out of them. She wore a long white robe like all the specters did but the red light gleamed on her red hair, and when Dolly saw the dabble of blood on her skirts, the flickering spotting of red, she jumped up and screamed aloud. She couldn't help herself. The scream came involuntarily from her throat and she went on screaming until Mrs. Collins seized her and clamped a hand over her mouth.

Myra had retreated swiftly. The cabinet was open and Roberta Fitter sat there, staring wildly about her like a madwoman. Someone in the audience called out:

"Put the lights on!"

"No, you don't," said Mrs. Leebridge. "You'll kill her. Look at her! Look what that girl's done." She went almost fearfully to the cabinet and took one of Mrs. Fitter's hands in hers. "The ectoplasm rushing back like that, it's a wonder she's not all burned up."

Dolly broke away from Mrs. Collins's grasp and ran out of the hall. She knew there was no escaping Myra now and Myra was waiting for her in the porch, not visible, not tangible — unless that tremor against her face was her cold touch — but a voice that spoke in Myra's accents.

"I may as well walk home with you, Doreen."

Dolly pushed open the door and went out. It had begun to snow lightly, a fine icy powder. She began to walk home through the snow with Myra by her side.

14

*T*he cleaver and the knives, Diarmit Bawne's elemental weapons, lay gathering dust. They were still in the Harrods bag on the floor in a corner of the room and he never looked at them. They did not belong to him but to Conal Moore who had been a thief and a murderer and who, when the police were after him, had run away home to Ireland. Conal Moore had a sister and brother-in-law in Kilburn who refused to speak to him and did not want to know him because of his criminal behavior. For this reason, too, no one would have anything to do with him, would not recognize his existence, except the police. The worst of his crimes had been to hide in a tunnel on the old railway line and kill a girl who came through and cut her head off. After that, there was no help for it but to run away back to County Clare. But before

193

he left he had had the sense to leave his room and some of his belongings in the care of a responsible citizen called Diarmit Bawne.

Only Diarmit knew he was in Ireland and knew he had killed the girl. Only Diarmit knew where the weapons he had used were. He intended to make a statement about all this to the police, lay all the facts about Conal Moore before them and hand over to them the Harrods bag of knives, but at the moment he was too busy to get around to it. Unlike Conal Moore, he was a reasponsible hardworking person with a job and he didn't have the time to devote to all these outside things.

Conal had been a mass of nerves, afraid of all kinds of things. One of the things he had been afraid of was that they would demolish the house while he was in it and he would be buried in the rubble. Diarmit couldn't help laughing to himself when he thought of anyone believing a thing like that. For one thing, the men would have seen him if he had put his head out of the window and shouted. He had been a small insignificant creature, Diarmit remembered, but not that small, not so small you couldn't see him. He, Diarmit, could wear his clothes, after all, did wear them every day. It wasn't that he much cared for the idea of wearing a murderer's clothes, especially the dark red trousers and shirts Conal had worn so that they should not show bloodstains, but it was a terrible waste not to wear them. Waste not, want not, as his mother used to say. Diarmit Bawne had no family now, he was alone in the world, standing on his own feet, but Conal Moore had a dozen or so brothers and sisters living all over Ireland and in London and Liverpool and Birmingham. He was their responsibility now, they must do the best they could for him, for Diarmit had done enough, looking after his home and his clothes and his possessions, not many would do as much.

It was only two or three weeks after Conal had run away that Diarmit had got himself the job in the Greek's shop that was part butcher's, part delicatessen. It was only a short walk from Mount Pleasant Green. The Greek could understand very little of what Diarmit said and Diarmit could understand about as much of what the Greek said, but this suited them both. Formerly the Greek had always employed other Greeks who talked all day to him in his own tongue. He wanted someone who would leave him to the quiet and solitude he liked. Diarmit never tried to talk to him much; they had nothing in common and he was busy with his own thoughts. He had begun thinking a lot about Conal Moore.

With his lazy ways, his nerves, the crazy way he had of thinking people were going to knock him over and trample on him, Conal would have made a bad impression on

Georgiou, he would never have got the job. Probably he hadn't got a job at home in Ireland. People like that were always out of work, living on the dole or, worse, on the charity of their families. Conal had thought he was going to do that with his relations in Kilburn but his brother-in-law had been too tough a nut to crack. None of his family wanted him any more, they had had enough to last them a lifetime. It seemed likely to Diarmit that Conal would never be seen again. He would either disappear quietly among the wilds of County Clare and his crimes disappear with him or else he would be caught and spend the rest of his life in prison. Either way they would all be rid of him. Sometimes Diarmit thought that perhaps he wouldn't go to the police after all. What had the police ever done for him? They hadn't even had the common courtesy to come back and tell him how their case against Conal was progressing. Besides, he would have to tell them everything he knew about Conal and that would take hours, take all day, for he knew him as he knew himself, and quite frankly he was getting a bit sick of him, he often thought he'd like to banish him from his mind altogether.

Georgiou had once employed two assistants and a girl part-time but he did so no longer; times were hard and wages high.

There were just himself and Diarmit in the shop. The lease came up for renewal in the summer and Georgiou knew his rent was going up, though he did not yet know by how much. "Sky-high" was what the tenants of the other shops in the row said. Georgiou would not fight it, he said to his wife, he would make the landlords a reasonable offer and if they wouldn't have it, too bad. People talked about the rents going up double, he couldn't pay double, if that happened he'd retire. He was past sixty anyway. No one said any of this to Diarmit. What business was it of his? He was only an employee and if Georgiou retiring meant he had no job, too bad.

Diarmit sat in his window in the evenings and looked across the green at the block of sheltered flats going up next to the hall. Progress had been slow but they were nearly done now. The roof was on. His own mother was dead, God rest her, but Conal's was alive and wouldn't one of those flats be just the thing for her? But Conal would never think of a thing like that, too feckless, too lacking in responsibility.

Sometimes Diarmit gave the room a good clean. The first time he did this he was appalled at the mess Conal had left behind him. Bits of stale food dropped behind things and now coated in mold, a heap of dried-up, mildewed teabags on a newspaper under the bed, dirty clothes in piles, a drawer that had

once had biscuits in it now full of mouse drop-
pings.

Once he had cleaned up Conal's mess, he
felt really clean in himself and he felt free.
Keeping the room and himself that way had
become very important to him. Now he would
have liked to clean his mind of Conal too, but
that was much harder than cleaning a room.
Try as he did, he found himself dwelling on
Conal when he lay down to sleep, on the way
to work, at work and on the way back, when
he sat at the window, watching the green and
the new flats and the hall where all those
cranky people came. He would think of
Conal's past and his present, imagining him
in the green west and weaving about him long
strange fantasies.

And by night he often had a Conal dream
in which the other man sometimes appeared
bound and gagged and led by a halter, and
sometimes, more often, toiling up a hillside,
bearing a heavy sack on his shoulders.

15

*H*arold sat in the breakfast room, surrounded by mementoes of Myra, writing his novel. It had come to him some months before, round about the time of Pup's twentieth birthday, that with his surely unrivaled knowledge, it would be a good idea for him to attempt a work of historical fiction. He wrote in longhand on pads of pale blue Basildon Bond. His subject was the unsavory life of that least exemplary of the sons of George III, Ernest Duke of Cumberland, who was said to have committed incest with his sister and murdered his valet. Harold was treating these allegations as fact. He was in the middle of Chapter Five in which the young prince and the Princess Amelia began their guilty liaison.

He read nothing now but works on and novels about the children of George III. He read them at home and he read them in the shop when the new assistant was attending to customers and Pup wasn't about. Pup was often absent these days, up at the new branch he had opened in Crouch Hill. In an armchair very like the one at home, Harold sat in the storeroom, which was now stuffed full of Pup's word processors, and read about the English court in the late eighteenth century. His writing, what he should write next and how the plot should develop, filled his waking thoughts so that he became quieter than ever and apparently morose. This withdrawal into himself was attributed to the loss of Myra and some said that poor Harold was beginning to break up.

He had told no one what he was doing. In the days before he was a writer and had merely been a reader, he had never talked about what he read. He didn't expect others to be interested in what he did; he wasn't interested in them. His children, in these past months, had become rather shadowy to him. He was aware that Dolly was in the house, that meals appeared and housework was done, but he seldom said much to her. She had her own friends, he thought when he thought about it at all.

Ron and Eileen Ridge came round to ask him if he felt like starting bingo again. They would call for him, they would like to. Dolly admitted them to the house and called out to her father, rather than showing them straightaway into the breakfast room. This gave Harold the chance to hide the Basildon Bond away out of sight and be discovered brooding in his sanctuary.

"You've got to come out of yourself sooner or later, Harold," said Eileen in a mildly scolding tone. "You owe it to Myra's memory."

Harold nodded vaguely.

"I know you'll say you've got your daughter and that's perfect true."

"She has her own friends," said Harold.

Mrs. Collins, Wendy Collins, Miss Finlay, Mrs. Leebridge. Dolly had never much liked the last two, which was just as well, since she never saw them any more. The Adonai Spiritists had closed their doors to her.

"I couldn't take the responsibility, could I?" said Mrs. Collins while Dolly was measuring Wendy for a trouser suit. "You might have another of your fits and then where should I be?"

"I didn't have a fit."

"Whatever it was, dear. You can kill a medium like that. Mrs. Fitter was under the weather for days. And all because you were privileged to catch a glimpse of young Mrs. Yearman."

Dolly said nothing about its having been more than a glimpse. It was only Pup she had told about hearing the tap of Myra's high heels following her up the path that night and up the steps to the door. Only he knew how she heard Myra's whisper as well as Edith's now. Once or twice, with gooseflesh on her arms, she had felt Myra's hand lift up the curtain of hair and a finger run across the nevus.

Wendy bought the Chinese girl doll with the black pigtail and the dark blue quilted jacket. She wanted it for a present for a friend's child whose birthday wasn't until November. She might as well buy it now, she said, since she didn't expect she would be seeing much of Dolly once the trouser suit was finished. Dolly was left alone with the ballet girl and the Chinese boy, who sat together on the mantelpiece staring across the room at Myra's now dead rubber plant and Myra's calendar for the previous year.

Pup did the Rosy Cross ritual to banish Myra. Long ago he had told Dolly that, if you became involved in the serious practice of geomancy, it was likely that the invisible world would begin to intrude on your everyday life. He had told her and then she read it in one of his books. It might take the form of a series of coincidences or of poltergeist activity or simply of strange sights and sounds. The ritual of the Rosy Cross extended a protection against such things; it placed a barrier or veil between you and them.

As soon as Dolly told him about the voices and the invisible hands, Pup wanted to do the ritual. He said she must have faith in the ritual and then she would be all right. They had gone into the temple together, Pup had made crosses and circles in the air with an incense stick and had chanted:

"Virgo, Isis, Mighty Mother,
Scorpio, Apophis, Destroyer,
Sol, Osiris, Slain and Risen,
Isis, Apophis, Osiris,
Ee-ay-oo, el-ewe-ex, lux, light,
The Light of the Cross,
Let the Light descend!"

As Pup and the book had promised, Myra went away after that. But she came back and Edith came back with her. Dolly knew she could have asked Pup to do the ritual again or even attempted it herself and one evening she tried it, chanting the words from the book and making the signs with a sandalwood joss stick. But she had barely finished when she sensed the two women had come into the temple. The lemon scent was so strong it overcame that of the sandalwood. She heard Myra's light brittle laugh.

Edith said: "That's Pup's job, dear. Better leave that sort of thing to Pup."

He was away that night and the next and

the next on a weekend course in Hertford-
shire, learning how to operate the Infra-
Hyposonic XH450 word processor. The
manufacturers liked retailers as well as
prospective customers to be conversant with
the intricacies of their equipment. The course
was in a country house called West Lawn near
Puckeridge. Pup was not the only man there
but he was the only one under forty. Most of
the girls were young and pretty. It was more
like a model school seminar than instruction
in working a glorified typewriter.

Apart from the obvious one, Pup recognized an immediate affinity between himself
and the prettiest girl. She lived in Islington,
a mile or so from his own home. After the
Saturday lesson and the lecture on advanced
techniques, he drove her down into the village
for drinks and chicken and chips at The Green
Man.

"Have you got a girl friend, Peter?"

"She just got engaged to someone else,"
said Pup with perfect truth. Suzanne, having
found out about Philippa and an occasional
pal of Pup's called Terri, had declared on the
rebound her intention of marrying the brother
of one of the students. "Rather sad but I
suppose that's life. I'll survive."

In the van she sat close up to him. She had
a bottle of wine in her room, she said, and if
he didn't mind its not being iced . . .

"The sadness isn't so bad," said Caroline.

"It's the frustration I mind, it's so — well, kind of degrading."

"Here, let me," said Pup, taking the corkscrew from her. He gave her his other-worldly look. "I wouldn't know about that, never yet have succumbed. That may have been part of the trouble with Suzanne. But I mustn't bore you with my problems. Cheers."

"Cheers. Do you mean what I think you mean?"

Pup nodded. "I had this idea of saving myself for the perfect girl, Caroline." He took her hand. "A kind of crazy idealism, I suppose you'll say."

"It's the most romantic thing I ever heard!"

He got home to hear that the estate agents had found a buyer for Mrs. Brewer's flat. Harold seemed to have lost interest, so Pup had quietly taken the matter over himself. Thirty-one thousand pounds to be paid over a month after exchange of contracts which would be the following week. Caroline had told him that her friend's sister was secretary to a man who was managing director of a company taking a lease for two floors of the new tower block. It was a new company, starting from scratch, and Caroline not only got hold of its name for him but also the private phone number of this guy her friend's sister was secretary to.

What with that and opening the new branch Pup was kept busy. The shop had been a butcher's and delicatessen, so the whole interior had to be remodeled and refitted. Pup felt rather proud of getting it because he could afford a higher rent than Georgiou, who had had the place before.

It was time he spent an evening with his sister. It would have been nice to have gone out somewhere, the cinema or for a meal, but one couldn't associate Dolly with those activities. Dolly wasn't normal. He faced that now and accepted it, though he worried. The amount of wine she drank worried him, and the voices and the isolation she lived in. But what could he do about it? He couldn't stay at home every night or lock up her wine or get introductions for her through a marriage bureau. She would never marry. She would never have a job or lead a normal life and he saw that he would have the burden of her for the rest of their lives. He could never leave her, never even contemplate living apart from her.

These thoughts depressed him, and when he reached home, it was as if they had lifted a veil from his eyes so that for the first time in years he looked at Dolly with no comforting glaze between them. He saw the lines that were beginning to mark her face, particularly the deep lines that ran from nostrils to chin, the curious absent look in her eyes and the way her eyes wandered, no longer coordinated but with the beginning of a strabismus. The great blotch of the nevus was a dark, uncompromising crimson. He noticed how carefully dressed she was, just for an evening alone with him, in a new black-and-red striped dress and with the talisman worn ostentatiously on a bright red ribbon. With a sinking of the heart he thought how an evening alone with him was a high spot of her life.

It was useless to talk of going out. He ate his supper and tried not to let her see him looking at her as she finished one bottle of wine and started on the second. Inevitably, they would end up in the temple. He had a constricted feeling in his throat, a sensation of a kind of distasteful embarrassment, when he asked her if she would like him to do another Rosy Cross banishing ritual. Several times he had noticed her seeming to listen or holding herself still and staring the way he had sometimes seen Gingie do, alone on the fence or walking on the garden path.

She shook her head. The voices, at any rate, were company.

"You ought to do something for Dad," she said. "You ought to do a ritual for happiness and peace for him." Even as she spoke she could hear Myra whispering. "He's only had two books out of the library this week," she said.

Pup was relieved. Still she hadn't asked the question, made the request he dreaded to hear. Perhaps she never would now, perhaps she was losing her faith in him, and gradually the temple and its contents might be allowed to fall into disuse. There was no sign of that happening, though, in Dolly's manner as they went into the temple and she, with more knowledge than he now retained, outlined to him the kind of Hexagram ritual he should perform.

It was high summer and from the open window the old railway line could be seen like a bit of countryside lying in sunshine, like a piece out of a Constable painting inexplicably surrounded by buildings. The buddleias made drifts of purple on the green, the poplar leaves trembled in the breeze and showed their silver undersides. Pup closed the window and unhooked his robe from the back of the door. But in doing so he caught it on the hook and tore a rent in the neck opening.

"It's all right," Dolly said, "it's only the facing. I'll mend it for you tomorrow."

"Thanks, dear."

The long tedious ritual was gone through. Pup did his best to make Dolly believe he had generated a solar hexagram. He forgot the names of the Supernal Triad of the Sephiroth, he forgot most of the names of the angels and planetary spirits. Most of what he intoned he made up as he went along. Dolly was enthralled. She had forgotten to bring the rest of her wine with her and it occurred wryly to Pup as he raised the cup and waved the wand that doing this every evening would be a way of curing her addiction.

She gazed raptly at him. He went on for an hour or more, remembering just before he finished to ask whoever or whatever it was he had invoked to call down blessings and riches on Harold, their father.

Pup replaced his weapons on the altar. It had been several weeks since he had handled them, as long since he had worn the robe, and now as he looked down at the hem of it he fancied that it had shrunk. Of course there was another possibility . . . When he was over twenty?

While Dolly, carrying the robe for mending, went downstairs to make their hot chocolate, he slipped into the bedroom that had formerly been his and after Myra's death had become his again. Very faint but still discernible on the wall were the measuring marks he had made when he was fifteen. He stood close up against them and made a new mark with a pencil. Yes, it was as he had thought, he had grown another inch. At twenty he had grown another inch and attained five feet eight. Pup laughed for joy but softly. He ran downstairs. Dolly was in the kitchen, standing over the stove, listening to a voice that spoke to her from invisible lips, her hand behind her ear the better to hear it.

The next day, when the doorbell rang,

Dolly thought it was Wendy Collins come for a fitting, though she had said she couldn't come before Friday. But while she had been sitting with her back to the window, sorting through her cotton reels for one of golden thread to mend Pup's robe, she had heard a car draw up. One glance told her it wasn't Wendy's; even if Wendy had changed her car, she would not have done so for a long, green, expensive-looking sports model.

The bell rang again. Dolly did what she always did when she wasn't expecting a caller and there was someone at the door. She pulled down the curtain of her hair so that the edge of it came a little way further than halfway along her eyebrow and about an inch out from her nostril. This was her only preparation, the rest of her she knew was all right.

The girl on the doorstep was of the kind she most disliked and resented — on sight. They filled her with a resentful misery for which there was no compensation. She did not particularly take against the Myras or Wendy Collinses of this world, the buck-toothed Eileen Ridges or the dried-up Miss Finlays. But those, like this one, who looked as if they belonged to a different, or to a new and glorious, species made her want to turn her back and close her eyes and shut herself up somewhere in the dark.

The voice was not a girl's or a woman's but a shy child's, a piping voice yet not shrill. "I do hope I'm not disturbing you. I don't think we've ever met. I'm Yvonne Colefax." She looked and sounded embarrassed.

Dolly didn't help her much. "Yes? Was it something to do with Myra?" She had noticed her visitor was holding a largish flat brown paper parcel under one arm.

"Well, no, I . . . I mean, I know about you through poor Myra. It was really — well, I'm looking for a dressmaker!"

Dolly had lost a lot of customers through her alienation from the Spiritists and she felt she could not afford to turn business away, however much she might want to shut her eyes and hide. "You'd better come in," she said.

Yvonne had been aghast at the sight of Dolly. Things like that always upset her, any deformity or scar or that kind of thing. She had got it from her father, who had been married to two beautiful women and who taught his daughter that to be beautiful was all she need be and that anything ugly to look at was somehow bad and wrong as well. Not that she felt like that about Dolly; that was a feeling that had long been pushed deep down in Yvonne's unconscious mind. What she felt was revulsion, pity and a wish she had not come. How terrible it must be to go through life with a disability like that! For a moment it made Yvonne's own predicament seem light and trivial. But only for a moment. She put the parcel down on the arm of a pine-framed brown-and-white check settee and looked about this room into which she had been once before.

Dolly was very conscious of what other women wore. She could price their clothes, gauge pretty well where they came from. It was seldom that in her own milieu she saw anyone better dressed than herself. Today she was wearing a dress she had made herself out of a blue linen and polyester mixture with drawn thread work on the collar and pockets, blue sandals and around her neck a small blue, pink and green scarf, casually knotted. But this girl made her look dowdy. It was nothing to do with the nevus, nothing to do with that mark of apartness. She would have made most women look dowdy and clumsy and coarse. Everything about her had a delicate ethereal daintiness; she was a puff-of-wind creature with Chinese porcelain skin, thistledown hair, and her bronze silk dress floated here and clung there like a beech leaf — Dolly found herself remembering childhood book illustrations — on a nymph or pixie.

They eyed each other warily in the bright sunshine which streamed through the living-room windows. Yvonne was the first to look aside. In a rush, she began explaining how Myra had said Harold's daughter was a dressmaker, how she had this piece of silk a friend had brought her from Hong Kong, how she just happened to be passing the house. Dolly's eye was caught by the large diamond cluster engagement ring on Yvonne's left hand. She had no illusions about her work. She was a good, average, little-woman-down-the-road dressmaker. But was she good enough for a woman who wore Cacharel dresses and bought her sandals at Kurt Geiger? Yvonne unwrapped the parcel and let unroll a length of rather stiff silk. It was of a brilliant uncompromising pea green, the sort of color ninety-nine women out of a hundred would have looked terrible in.

"You can wear that color," Dolly said grudgingly. Her dislike was evaporating. The fact was that Yvonne seemed altogether too far removed from her, too remote and different, to feel for her such an ordinary human emotion as dislike.

"Well, perhaps." Yvonne spoke in a serious, concentrated way. She began to talk about colors and textures, about greens and whether you should wear gold or silver with them. Dolly said always gold with that particular color. And garnets, if you happened to have them. A simple shift dress, didn't Dolly think? Dolly had already thought this. She was very nearly enjoying herself. None of her previous customers had had any real interest in clothes; they simply wanted something to cover them or keep them warm, not to be "showy," nothing flattering or distinctive or elegant. She hadn't talked clothes like this with anyone since Edith died.

"You'll have to have a pattern. I should have a Vogue pattern, they're the best."

But Yvonne had never heard of dress patterns. She had never had anything made before. Dolly opened the pattern box, though she had little hope of finding anything in Yvonne's size which was probably a ten or even an eight.

"Couldn't you sort of make it up yourself? What's that?"

Dolly turned round to see Yvonne holding the golden robe which had been hanging over a chair.

"That's my brother's. He's a —" Dolly hesitated. She knew it might sound strange to the uninitiated. Had Aleister Crowley or Israel Regardie had sisters? "— a magician, a geomancer."

Yvonne didn't look amused or suspicious or even very surprised. "I've met your brother. Here and at poor Myra's funeral. He told me my — my past. And he got it right, all of it in detail. Wasn't that amazing?"

"He's a genius," Dolly said simply.

A silence fell. Dolly didn't know why it should have done, for they had seemed to be getting on so well. She said awkwardly, "I expect I could make the pattern up myself if you just want a straight up-and-down shift. Sleeveless, I expect, and with a turtleneck? I

don't know why they call them turtlenecks
but straight across at back and front?"

"Because a turtle's neck comes out of his
shell like that." She sounded like a child of
seven. And it didn't seem to be affectation,
it was real. Myra had said she had had two
husbands; she must be twenty-seven or
twenty-eight. "I used to have a tortoise in my
garden in Shelley Drive but he ran away and
got run over. Well, he walked away, they
don't ever run."

Dolly found herself saying, "Oh, dear,
never mind," as she might have done once to
Pup over some childhood sorrow. "I'd better
measure you, hadn't I? Then I can get it cut
out and tacked."

She drew the curtains against the sunlight
and curious eyes. Yvonne stepped out of her
Cacharel to reveal art nouveau limbs and
Janet Reger underwear. Thirty-two, twenty-
two, thirty-three — Dolly had not yet
ventured into the metric system.

Yvonne put on her dress. She touched the
cheeks of the dolls and smiled at them as if
they were real children. She touched the robe
again. "Like a wizard," she said. "The
wonderful Wizard of Oz."

"Yes."

"When shall I come for a fitting?"

They were out in the hall again. "It's
Thursday today. How about next Monday
afternoon?" Dolly hesitated. She had an

impulse to do something she knew was daring and perhaps reckless, something she had never done before but which now seemed essential. If she let Yvonne go without doing it she knew she would be full of regret. "Have you got a minute?" she said. "I'd like to show you something."

"What sort of something?"

"It's got to do with my brother."

She led the way upstairs. "Poor Myra," Yvonne sighed at the top of the first flight. Dolly heard Myra's heel-taps behind the closed bedroom door but she did not think Yvonne would hear them; Myra appeared to no one but herself. She opened the door to the temple and had the satisfaction of hearing Yvonne gasp.

"What is it?"

"It's the place where he does his magic." Dolly showed her the elemental weapons. "He can do anything."

Yvonne had picked up the pentacle and was holding it rather gingerly between finger and thumb. "What sort of anything?" She lisped a little when she was excited.

It was on the tip of Dolly's tongue to tell her how he had killed Myra but something stayed her. After all, as Pup himself had said, it was illegal to kill people and it might, for all she knew, be a punishable crime to stick a knife into a rag doll. "He can make things happen," she said. "It's a science, you know, it's not like witchcraft or witch doctors or anything. It's just as much a science as — as being a doctor or working in a lab." In her enthusiasm she had forgotten to keep her hair over her face and the nevus was exposed to the strong afternoon light. Dolly's voice rose. "He can do wonderful things, he can do miracles."

Yvonne's eyes glanced into her face and as quickly darted away again. Dolly blushed. She knew what had passed through the other girl's mind.

"You have to ask him to do it," she said. "He's not God."

Yvonne nodded. "When he told me about my past, he got it all right, every bit."

"Last night he did a very special ritual to make our father's life take a turn for the better."

"Oh, yes, poor man. Poor Myra!"

"You'll see, things will come right for him very soon."

They went downstairs and Dolly opened the front door. It was plain to her, inexplicably, that Yvonne did not want to go. She wanted to prolong the visit because there was something she wanted to say or ask. But she didn't know how to and Dolly, who was unaccustomed to long periods of social contact with new people, or indeed with any people except perhaps the Collinses, was beginning to feel the strain of it. Yvonne lingered on the doorstep.

"You did say Monday?"

"About two in the afternoon would be best. Goodbye."

As soon as the door was closed she regretted driving Yvonne away. Not that she was alone. Myra's footsteps came across the hall, the heels clacking as if there were no haircord there but still the old uncarpeted quarry tiles. Dolly pushed past her and went into the breakfast room where Harold kept an *A–Z London Guide* along with the few books of his own he possessed.

"Silly old fool," said Myra's voice. "You'd think he'd have the sense to put those paint tins out for the bin men. To be perfectly honest, you ought to do it, Doreen."

Dolly took no notice. She was looking Shelley Drive up in the index.

"They've got a great big house," said Myra. "George's father was a very well-known specialist. He left everything to George. They've got a sauna in their house and a swimming pool in the garden."

Myra followed her back to the living room. Edith was already there, waiting. The Ivoire that Yvonne had been wearing was drowned in the pungency of lemons.

"You want to pin that silk on to a piece of flannel before you start cutting," said Edith.

Myra gave one of her laughs. "Quite candidly, I think it's peculiar her coming here to Doreen. With the money they've got she could go to anyone."

Dolly sat in the window, stitching the neckline of the golden robe. They did not speak to her again but for a long time she heard them laughing softly and their footsteps as they walked about the room.

16

*T*o celebrate the sale of Mrs. Brewer's flat, on completion day Pup took Philippa out to lunch at the San Carlo, in Highgate High Street. After that they both took the afternoon off, a rare enough lapse for Pup. The people who moved into the flat were a woman and her two teenage daughters. Dolly sat in the window and watched the removal van come. It was raining and the men had to cover the furniture with sheets before making the journey from the van to the front door. The new neighbor was a woman of forty who still dressed in the fashion of her youth — long droopy skirt, scuffed boots, peasant blouse, and shawl — for like many of that Beatles generation she had never noticed that the trend had changed. She stood in the rain, getting wet, looking helpless, and presently Mrs. Buxton came waddling along under an umbrella with a cup of tea and a plate of biscuits for her on a tin tray.

The Porsche, drawing into the pavement, sent a spray of muddy water from the gutter up on to her fat legs. Mrs. Buxton said something to the driver. Dolly couldn't hear what it was but it looked rude, and when Yvonne got out her expression was nervous, even distressed, though by then Mrs. Buxton, with Gingie under one arm, had gone off into her own home.

Yvonne made no reference to the incident. She was wearing a raincoat today, though one that was as elegant as and indeed very like a cocktail dress, being of black proofed silk, and with it a wide black patent belt and high narrow black patent boots. A shimmering of raindrops clung to her fine silver-gilt hair. She almost ran into the house.

"What a horrid day! I hate summer days like this, don't you? Oh, look, it's half done! I'm going to love it!"

Dolly didn't want her making water spots on the silk. "Let me take your coat and hang it up."

Yvonne's manner seemed unnaturally bright today, almost hysterical. She tore off the coat like someone stripping off after waiting the whole of a long hot day to get to the water's edge. And the pink-and-black striped dress she wore was going the same way. Dolly drew the curtains just in time to stop the removal men getting an eyeful of Yvonne in orchid bra and bikini briefs.

The bright green was right on her. Her white neck rose from it like a madonna lily from its sepals. She looked at herself in Edith's pier glass.

"We can have the curtains back now," Dolly said.

"No . . ."

"Well, the lights on, if you like."

"I can see, I can see well enough." She stood there, gazing at her own reflection. Something in Dolly — or perhaps one of the voices — warned her of impending trouble. Yvonne was so still, gazing at herself, but gazing as if she saw nothing, as trance-like as Mrs. Fitter. "I don't want light," she said, her voice growing more childlike. "It's easier when it's a bit dark." She turned round slowly. "Can I take this off?"

"Let me. Mind the pins. You're happy with it, are you?"

"Happy?" Yvonne gave a little light laugh. "Oh, yes, it's fine, it's fine." She stepped into her own dress. "About not pulling back the curtains — I meant it's less embarrassing like this. Do you mind?"

Again Dolly sensed trouble coming. Her apprehensiveness sharpened into fear. She shrugged and laid the green slip down.

In a breathless rapid way Yvonne said, "I've been thinking about what you said about your brother. All over the weekend I've been thinking about it, about how you said he could do anything. You said it was a science, a scientific thing, not like — well, clairvoyants and faith healers and that sort of thing."

Enormous relief flooded Dolly. What had she been afraid of? Something to do with the nevus perhaps. That Yvonne, like Myra, had been going to give her advice about the nevus. But it was Pup she wanted to talk about. Dolly loved talking about Pup, she couldn't have enough of that.

"You see, I've tried everyone. I even went to this fortune teller. I had my horoscope cast. I've been to my doctor and to a psychiatrist, I've talked to my solicitor and they don't do a thing to help me, not a thing. They don't *understand*. One night I phoned up the Samaritans, I felt so bad. Can I call you, Doreen?"

Dolly shook her head. She found herself saying, rather to her own astonishment, "I'd rather you said Dolly."

"Dolly, all right. You don't mind me talking to you like this, do you, Dolly? You see, you're my last chance. Well, your brother's my last chance. I think your brother's absolutely amazing, I really do. All my life I shall remember the way he told me about my past life, he was marvelous. So you don't mind me talking, do you?"

No one had confided in Dolly before. It

was a new experience. You couldn't count Pup describing what happened at meetings of the Golden Dawn. Her friendless existence had contained no sessions of girlish outpourings. No torch-carrying man had opened his heart to her, no elderly person complained of the neglect of children and the exigencies of living on a pension, no girl confessed sexual adventures. Her brother, she suddenly realized with a pang, was self-sufficient and perhaps always had been. Because of her lack of experience she had no idea of the prompting words required, the "Do you want to tell me about it?" and the reiterated "Go on." She simply shook her head, unaware that a look of wonder had spread itself across her usually expressionless face.

"Well," said Yvonne, and she looked away from Dolly. She looked at the ballet girl and the Chinese boy on the mantelpiece and then at the big old black and gilt Singer sewing machine. "Well, it's George, my husband. He's in love with someone and I don't know what to do."

This was mystifying. That anyone who had someone as beautiful as Yvonne could conceivably want anyone else was, for a moment, beyond Dolly's imaginings. But intuitively now, she understood that she had to make some sort of reply.

"She must be," she began awkwardly, "I mean she must be — well, amazing if she's prettier than you . . ."

Her voice faltered and the blood tore into her face. The words had been terrible to say, they had been wrenched out of her, but now, for some reason, she was tiredly glad she had said them. Impulsively, Yvonne put out her hand and laid it briefly over Dolly's. "You are nice, you're a dear." She paused, then gave Dolly a sideways look. "It's not a she."

"But you said . . ."

"He says he's in love with a — a beautiful boy!" said Yvonne and with a little preliminary shriek she burst into tears.

Dolly gave a nervous giggle. Yvonne, drying her eyes, had repeated what she said and Dolly found herself without words. It was quite dark in the room now, the rain pounding on the windows, and inside the atmosphere had become very awkward and strained. It was the kind of atmosphere Edith had used to say you could cut with a knife. Edith and Myra were not there now, they had fled. Yvonne turned her face, impervious to tear stains, unmarked by the redness or puffiness of tears, towards Dolly and dabbed at her eyes with a lacy Y-initialed handkerchief.

"I don't know what you want me to say," Dolly said clumsily.

The delicate, thin shoulders shrugged. "What can anyone say?"

The only source of Dolly's experience in

such matters was the advice columns and answers to readers' letters in the magazines she read, her only mentor the woman journalist who had advised her to go out and meet people and forget about her birthmark. But she did not draw directly from them.

"It's not as if he wanted a divorce to marry this — this person," she said.

"He would if he could! He says gay people ought to be able to marry each other, he says you can find actual ministers who'll marry them, and if he can find one who'll do it, he'll marry Ashley Clare."

"A form of marriage," said Dolly vaguely. She had read this expression somewhere. Yvonne was looking at her eagerly, nodding her head. Evidently, Yvonne expected much from her and suddenly Dolly felt excited, she felt she was enjoying herself. The constraint had gone. The whole experience was so novel, so different. She felt she must enhance it. But how? "Would you like something to drink?" she said, uncertain of the proper form of words to use.

"Tea, do you mean?"

Dolly shook her head. Until the advent (and the demise) of her father's second wife, Dolly had never had anywhere to chill her wine. She now opened Myra's big Electrolux and got out a bottle of Blue Nun.

"How lovely! What a lovely thought! You are kind." Yvonne actually clapped her hands at the sight of the tray with the bottle on it and two of Myra's best wineglasses. "It's just what I need!"

Dolly nodded happily. It was what she needed too. They did not raise their glasses to a toast. Yvonne could think of nothing to toast and Dolly was too used to drinking alone for such a thing to cross her mind.

"Did you know he was —" never before had she pronounced the word in this context "— gay when you got married?"

"I ought to have known. He was thirty-five and he'd never been married and that's a bad sign." The utterance of this sophisticated lore sounded strange in Yvonne's baby voice. "Besides, he was so — well, old-fashioned and gentlemanly to me. Real men aren't like that, are they?"

Dolly had very little idea what real men were or were not like. She refilled their glasses.

"I'd just lost my first husband. He died of leukemia, he was only twenty-two. I've had a sad life really, haven't I?" Dolly nodded sympathetically, though to her it seemed a wonderfully eventful one. Once more the tears gathered in Yvonne's eyes. "I was twenty-one. We were babies when we got married. I felt terrible when he died and I met George and he was so kind to me and said he'd look after me. And you know, Dolly, I hadn't got any money and George had this huge private practice apart from what his dad left him. He said he'd buy me a house anywhere I liked and he'd give me a car for a wedding present." When Dolly's eyes went involuntarily to the curtained, rain-lashed window, she said quickly, "Oh, not that one, I've had two since then."

"He married you to try and cure himself," said Dolly, sagely quoting her columnist.

"I suppose so. Of course, Dolly, it never worked." Yvonne drew a squiggle pattern in the condensation on her wineglass. "I always knew there was something wrong. You see, I'd had a very passionate relationship with my first husband."

Dolly didn't want to hear about that. "What about this Ashley person?"

"I've never seen him, I don't know anything about him except that George says he's a beautiful boy and he met him in a gay club in Earl's Court called The Ganymede." Yvonne's voice gathered speed and the words rattled out, rather like a toy train charging downhill. "And he's madly in love with him and he wants to leave me and go and live with him all the time. He wants to sell our house and buy me a flat with some of the money and go and live with Ashley Clare." On the long vowel of the surname her voice rose on a melancholy wail.

"Don't cry," said Dolly awkwardly. She put out her hand as she might have done to Pup.

Yvonne clutched it. She would have liked to throw herself into Dolly's arms but the nevus repelled her. The nevus usually had exactly the effect on people that Dolly expected it to have. But Yvonne held on to her hand. "So — you see — your brother — he's so clever — I thought —"

"That he could do something for you?"

"That he could make it stop!"

"But do you want a — a husband like that?" Dolly asked.

"I want my house! I want to be Mrs. George Colefax. I don't want to be divorced and dropped and just thrown away for a — a beautiful boy! I just want your brother to make it stop. I can pay for it. He's so clever, he can name his price, I know that, Dolly. I shouldn't mind what I paid, I'm so miserable.

Dolly said almost scornfully, "He wouldn't want paying." She poured the last of the wine. The rain had stopped. She drew the curtains apart a few inches and a shaft of watery sunshine came through the crack between. "Tell me what he looks like, this Ashley. Could you get a photo?"

Yvonne said she would try. She would borrow or steal a photograph from George and get it to Dolly. Relaxed by the wine, she talked about where Ashley Clare lived, what he did for a living and, as far as she knew, what he looked like. Once or twice she called Dolly darling. It had been an eventful and exciting, even exhausting, afternoon, and Dolly, watching the Porsche depart up Manningtree Grove, felt so strung up by it that she had to open a fresh bottle of wine a full hour before Pup was due home.

For that evening he intended to spend at home. He had a date with Caroline's friend's sister's boss at his house in Finchley at 6:00 and he was nervous. But he showed none of this nervousness to Philippa, and in spite of it, he did not leave her flat in Muswell Hill until five to.

Half an hour later he came away jubilant. He drove through Hampstead Garden Suburb in the Hodge and Yearman van, forcing himself to drive slowly and carefully, for his instinct was to be reckless. The sun was shining now and it was as if the rain had never been except that but for the rain the lawns would not have been so green or the flowers so fresh or the leaves so sparkling in the bright soft light. The large beautiful houses seemed to look graciously upon him.

Dolly was a little drunk by the time he came in. She was steady on her feet still but her speech was becoming slurred. Pup looked at her flushed face and at the empty Blue Nun bottle and the nearly empty bottle of Yugoslav Riesling but he made no comment. He didn't want to antagonize her, he wanted to tell her what he had achieved that day. He had to tell someone. Harold would only caution him to hold his horses. Philippa was less interested even than Dolly and Caroline was a gold digger. He could have told his friend Dilip Raj but Dilip had gone to his grandmother in Calcutta for a holiday.

"I've had the most wonderful thing happen," he said, coming across the room to kiss her, almost bounding across. "I've just been to see a man who's going to give us a contract to supply his new offices with everything they need in the way of equipment — word processors, electronic typewriters, the lot — it'll be an enormous contract. And he's given it to me, Dolly." This time, though she noticed nothing, he said "me" and not "us." "I'm on top of the world, Dolly, and I tell you what, I'll have a glass of your wine."

She poured it for him and brought it to where he was sitting on the brown check settee. Pup, for the occasion, had been wearing his gray suit with the pink-and-gray patterned shirt and a slate-blue silk tie. He took off the tie and his jacket and sat there in his shirtsleeves.

"To us!" he said, raising his glass. "To the continued success of Yearman and Hodge!"

She looked at him. It was the look of a mother whose son is a wealthy rag and bone dealer but who would have preferred him to be a poor professor. "I should have thought," she said, "you'd leave all that kind of thing to Dad."

It was rare for him but he was suddenly furiously angry. He controlled himself. "He's not a businessman. I think I am. I think I'm lucky enough to have a flair for it."

She said quietly and dolefully, "I thought you had a flair for — you know what I thought."

The only thing to do with that was ignore it. "Come on," he said, "we'll celebrate. I'll take you out to dinner."

She shook her head. "I'm tired. You know I don't like going out to eat in those places." He saw what she meant and he was powerless. "Besides, I've got your meal here."

Salami, rolled turkey breast sliced thin as paper, cole slaw, potato crisps, chocolate Swiss roll, tinned peaches and tinned custard. He felt disloyal but he was growing out of that kind of food, the child's dream of a feast. Harold was already seated at the kitchen table, *The Daughters of George III* propped up in front of him between his plate and the milk jug.

"Hello, Dad," said Pup, who hadn't seen him since the morning. "Had a good day?"

"I don't know about good. I know I'm worn out."

And this time he was. That afternoon at 5:00, sitting in the room behind the Crouch End Broadway shop, operating one of the new Olympia ES100s, he had finished typing his novel. He was reading *The Daughters of*

George III less from need than habit.

Dolly poured out two cups of tea. She sensed it would be unwise that evening to tell Pup about Yvonne Colefax and her trouble. Wait a day or two, wait until next time he was home in the evening. She had had too much wine to feel like eating but she took a piece of bread and buttered it and made herself a sandwich with the sliced turkey. It was rare for Pup to be home two evenings in succession. She almost trembled when she thought of what that might mean, that he was growing tired of the Golden Dawn.

The ins and outs of why Georgiou came to lose the shop Diarmit never fully comprehended. Not that Georgiou, hitherto taciturn, had not talked of it all day long, grumbling in his thick harsh accent about landlords and rent acts and the iniquity to be found everywhere in the United Kingdom. Not that he had not attempted to explain, his voice snapping and crackling as he stumbled over difficult words.

"That place that sells the typing machines, they are after my shop." Georgiou threw back his head and lifted up his hands. "Oh, nobody is saying but I have ways of knowing. Expansion is the word, expand, expand, that is all — everything — nowaday. Typing machines, photomachines, this is what people like today. Good food they don't like, they don't care."

Diarmit smiled uneasily at him, mystified.

"So if that's what people like," said Georgiou, "let these typers and photoers pay the rent. Me, I don't care, I retire. I leave this rat race for good."

Once more Diarmit was on the dole. He had all the time in the world on his hands and no purpose to put it to. He was ashamed of being without work and even more ashamed to be seen to be without it by the other tenants of the house. They would think him no better than Conal, they would think that birds of a feather flocked together.

Of necessity he now spent hours in his room. If he went out it was never for more than an hour or so. He spent all night and most of the day in that room. The fact that Conal's things were in it, were still taking up space in it, began to anger him. He put Conal's clothes and the knives in the Harrods bag in the middle of the room in a pile. Whenever he moved about, he had to step over them or walk round them but he felt that at any rate he had made a gesture, he had made it plain to whomever might call or look in the window or somehow observe the interior of the room that those things were not his and had nothing to do with him. He stopped wearing Conal's red clothes and went back to the denim jeans he had had on when first he came to take over the room.

Then it occurred to him that Conal's sister

Kathleen was a more suitable person to give her brother's things house room than he was. He made them all into a parcel which he wrapped in newspaper and bound with adhesive tape. It took him nearly all of one day to pack and wrap that parcel, and on the next, a hot day in August, he took it over to Kilburn on the train from Crouch Hill.

A man opened the door to him. He said he was Kathleen's husband and Kathleen was out at her work.

"She's lucky then, lucky to have work," Diarmit said politely. "I could do with work myself." He had heard the man's voice before, he remembered now, when he had made that phone call on Conal's behalf. Cowardly Conal had got him to phone them because he was scared to. "These are her brother Conal's things now that I've brought all the way over on the train. I've no use for them, you see, so you'd best take care of them till he comes."

The man stared. "She hasn't got a brother called Conal."

So that was the way the wind blew. They meant to disown him entirely. Diarmit could not blame them but he persisted. "Moore's the name, same as her maiden name. Conal Moore."

"My wife's maiden name was Bawne."

Diarmit laughed. He couldn't help it. The effrontery of it, the sheer nerve of skiving off

235

out of your responsibilities by pretending to be a member of *his* own family! Bawne, indeed. He laughed humorlessly, tossing back his head, and he tried to thrust the parcel into the man's arms, but before he could do so, the door was shut in his face.

Why had the man refused even to admit Conal was his brother-in-law? That he and his wife might want nothing to do with Conal, Diarmit could readily understand. But why deny the relationship and refuse to take in a parcel of Conal's property? It must be because they had had word that Conal was coming back and they were scared of any involvement with him.

He was coming back . . . . It was a year now since he had murdered that girl and cut her head off, since they had called him The Headsman and written about him in the papers. He was coming back because it had all blown over and he was safe. Diarmit climbed the stairs to his room. He unpacked the parcel and laid the red clothes out carefully on the end of the bed and over the backs of chairs. The knives and the cleaver were clean but he washed them at the sink and dried them and replaced them in the bag. Conal was coming back any day . . .

The letter was in a brown envelope addressed to Ms. Doreen Yearman and it was such as Dolly had hardly ever received in her

236

life before, for it began "Dear Dolly" and ended "Love from Yvonne." With it was a photograph of two men in a living room sitting at either end of a velvet sofa. It had been taken with a flash and both were blank-faced and stary-eyed. George Colefax was smoking a cigar but the other man sat with his hands rather girlishly folded in his lap. A beautiful boy, perhaps, though that surely had been rather a long time ago. His black hair, swept back Byronically, had silver wings at the temples and although the flash had obliterated lines on the forehead and under the eyes, you felt that they were there.

Dolly put the photograph and the letter in her handbag. Something impelled her to keep taking the letter out and rereading that "Dear Dolly" and "Love from Yvonne." She was going shopping in the Holloway Road, walking part of the way there along the old railway line. It was a warm hazy day with the promise of great heat by noon and the grass was flushed pink where the rosebay willow herb was in bloom. You could hear the hum of insects in the flowers above the hum of traffic.

As she stepped inside the comparative coolness and darkness of the Mistley tunnel, it occurred to Dolly that it must be a year since The Headsman's murder. It had been a Wednesday, she recalled, the day before Myra's dinner party at which Pup had accurately told Yvonne the events of her past life. She, Dolly, had been out, making her first visit to a seance of the Adonai Spiritists. Because of that she could remember the dates, Wednesday, 12 August, Thursday, 13 August. And today was Wednesday, 11 August. A year had passed, exactly a year, today was the anniversary.

Dolly quickened her step through the tunnel and felt a certain relief at coming out at the other end into the soft warm light. A black and red butterfly flew across, an inch or so from her eyes, and settled on a spray of buddleia. She walked along the old station platform. Approaching her, in the distance, was the woman with the white Pyrenean mountain dog, the animal ambling indifferently as if a year ago it had never nosed out a corpse and then a human head.

17

*T*he man in the photograph appeared to have an olive skin, so Dolly made the doll's body from the kind of coarse unbleached linen that is called crash. There was a piece left over from Edith's tapestry work. Dolly embroidered Ashley Clare's face, the curved black eyebrows, the almond eyes, the red sensuous mouth. She sewed a headful of black hair on him but she used silk, not wool, and at the temples she stitched in fine threads of silver. Almost by chance she seemed to have caught the man's expression. The face, she felt, would be instantly recognizable.

In the photograph he was wearing velvet cord jeans, a shirt open at the neck and a zipper jacket but Dolly wanted to see him more formally dressed as he must surely be for his daily work, whatever that might be. She made him a suit from gray polyester that had been left over from a skirt of Wendy Collins's, a shirt from one of Edith's lawn handkerchiefs, and a red silk tie from the lining of her own velvet coat. She painted his cardboard shoes with Woolworth's Chinese lacquer. Complete, he was the perfect man doll, the best doll she had ever made.

Even Myra admired him. Myra and Edith had been there with her, watching her work.

"I must say, Doreen, it's a perfect likeness. I saw him once when he came into the surgery. You've got him to a t."

"You've made a very nice job of that, dear, but isn't he a bit cross-eyed?"

It was rare for them to speak to each other but sometimes they did. "To be honest with you, Edith," Myra said, "he *is* a bit cross-eyed."

Dolly put him on the mantelpiece between the Chinese boy and the ballet girl. Making the doll had taken up all her time and she had done nothing more to the green silk dress. While she was stitching in the facings at neck and armholes there was a ring at the door and she was sure it must be Yvonne calling unexpectedly. But it was only one of the girls from next door with a pair of denims over her arm to say that Mrs. Buxton had told her mother that Dolly did dressmaking, so could she find time to turn her jeans up four inches? She saw the doll, said it looked like Robert de Niro and giggled. Dolly took the jeans and said she would have to charge four pounds and would that be all right? She could see the girl trying not to look at her right cheek.

Since the letter, read and reread, especially the opening and concluding words, there had been no sign at all from Yvonne. Dolly had never before known what it is to sit by a telephone waiting for it to ring, longing for it to ring. She tacked the green silk hem and began sewing it with fine slip stitches.

"Once you've finished that dress," Myra said, "she'll be off like lightning. You know that, don't you, Doreen? She won't bother with you. I mean, frankly, give me one good reason why she should."

"It's a difficult shade to match the Sylko to," said Edith. "That jade is a difficult shade to match and a difficult shade to wear."

"Her father was a professional man and her husband's a profession man. It's a question of class really. Well, isn't it always?"

Pup was coming home for a meal. He was wondering — it occupied his mind a great deal these days — how he could get his father to retire. For a long while Harold had been useless in the shop but now he was becoming worse than useless, impeding Pup like an iron on his leg. He mooned about, replying to customers with the vague near-incomprehension of someone who has been addressed in a forgotten foreign language. He was always to be seen stooped over the Xerox or lugging brown paper parcels of the kind that contain a ream of paper.

Pup, however, had a horror of hurting people's feelings, of causing pain. It would be unthinkable to make Harold feel unwanted, he must instead be made to wish to go of his own accord. Perform a Pentagram ritual, Dolly would no doubt advise, but he had lost all belief in the efficacy of that. In the days when he had bargained and cajoled for height, he had had faith — or perhaps the simple answer was that all along five feet eight had been written in his genes.

The first thing he saw when he walked in was the doll. He gave an exclamation which sounded like pure astonishment but was really dismay. Any of these items of evidence that his sister was unlike other women, was growing more and more strange, filled him with foreboding. But he said nothing. Dolly had already begun on her bottle of wine and he started his supper. At the last meal he had eaten at home he had mentioned over the tinned tongue and defrosted sausage rolls that he liked seafood, though knowing as he spoke of it that this would lead to his being served prefabricated prawn cocktail twice a week for years. The first of the series was before him, all the ingredients fresh from a freezer pack and topped with a dollop of bottled sauce.

Dolly was glad to have given him something different, something he would really enjoy. It distracted her from her preoccupation with Yvonne, though only for a while. They were back in the living room and she three-quarters through her Chianti Classico when she made up her mind. She picked up the receiver and dialed, resolving to put it down again if George Colefax answered.

Yvonne's little girl voice said like a receptionist:

"Dr. Colefax's residence."

"It's Dolly. Your dress is finished."

"Dolly, did you get my letter? I was expecting you to phone before."

So it was she, not Yvonne, who had been at fault, she who had committed the breach of conduct. She gave a sigh of relief which made Pup look up from his evening paper.

"Would you — would you like to come over? Would you come over tomorrow?"

But Yvonne said why shouldn't Dolly come to her? She would like to return Dolly's hospitality. Say Monday or Tuesday? It wouldn't occur to her of course, Dolly thought with a flicker of resentment, it never did occur to people with cars, what a difficult and time-consuming journey it would be, getting from Manningtree Grove to the Bishop's Avenue by public transport. But she was too gratified by Yvonne's invitation to demur.

"I'll pick you up on my way home if you like," Pup said. She had a friend, a young, suitable, normal friend at last. The relief was

243

great. He remembered Yvonne Colefax, he remembered the scent of her and the feel of that slim thigh against his leg. And at Myra's funeral . . . He took his eyes from the olive-skinned, red-lipped doll on the mantelpiece. "Ask her what time."

As happy now as she had been tense and fearful before, Dolly sat on the settee beside him and told him of the love affair between Ashley Clare and George Colefax.

"And he's married to that lovely Yvonne?"

"We'll have to do something about it."

"What can I do?" said Pup absently and he returned to his paper.

When he had first come to London, he had put himself into Conal's hands and Conal had had to look after him. Not that he had made a very good job of it. True, he had provided him with a roof over his head but the job had never come to anything and there was no doubt Conal had simply made use of him as someone on whom to unload all his dreads and terrors. Thanks to Conal, he might even have been suspected of the murder and decapitation of that girl, for Conal had had no qualms about returning here with the knives and his bloodstained clothes. But this time, once Conal had returned and they were together again, Diarmit knew it would be him who must look after the other man. It filled him with anxiety.

The knives of the Harrods bag and the heap of clothes still lay in the middle of the floor. Diarmit cursed them, for every time he crossed from his bed to the sink or from the cupboard to the window he had to step over them and once or twice he stumbled and fell headlong. Dressed in blue jeans, a gray shirt and a gray sweater, he went to the Job Center but still they had nothing for him. He dreaded having to confess to the feckless criminal Conal Moore that he was out of work, that he was on the dole.

The two dogs scavenged from the litter bins on Mount Pleasant Green, the Dalmatian and the mongrel collie, dissecting the wrappings of takeaway food, running on the grass like a pair of jackals. The old people had moved into the sheltered housing and a woman of seventy or so could be seen in the window of the communal room, arranging flowers in a vase. A lawn had been started in the garden and little evergreen trees planted. The workmen had long been gone. That would worry Conal, Diarmit thought, he would wonder where they were and expect them to come demolishing this house. He would be afraid to stay in in the daytime, it would all begin again.

Sitting at the window, looking across the green in the direction of Crouch Hill station which was the way Conal would come, Diarmit told himself that to avoid Conal he had only to run away. He had only to leave and go back to Liverpool. But it was not realistic thinking, for he knew he would never so shirk his responsibilities, and besides he had no family in Liverpool, they were all dead and only Conal's relations lived there. He could go down on the old railway line and hide out in the Mistley tunnel, taking provisions with him and sleeping on the feather mattress. But that would be no good when the fine weather broke and the autumn came. Diarmit shivered, resigning himself to his doom, waiting for his doom to come across the green from Crouch Hill station.

As it happened, though, when Conal came Diarmit did not see him come. He must have slipped into the room during the night. For when Diarmit awoke he was there, wearing dark red clothes and taking his knives out of the Harrods bag, examining them closely, to check no doubt that Diarmit had taken care of them in his absence. Conal the murderer, Conal the criminal, Conal the outcast. Jobless, friendless, hated, mad Conal.

Because he knew what would happen if he left the house, because he dared not go out yet must have exercise, he began pacing the room. Up and down, he paced the small cluttered room with a heavy dogged tread that after a while grew weary, but he paced on.

He did not speak. There was no one to speak to, for Diarmit had gone.

It was the girl's first day in the Unisex salon in Tottenham Lane and Pup's first visit. They closed at lunchtime on Mondays and he was her last client. His was also the nicest hair she had handled that morning, fair and wavy, more like a girl's than a man's.

"You could do anything with your hair," she said.

"Like what? Knit it? Grow it up a beanstalk?"

She giggled. "I mean have it in any style. You know what I mean."

"Okay, stop that cutting and I'll have dreadlocks. They said your name but I didn't catch it. Anthea?"

"Andrea. I'm going to start the blow-drying now."

"Wait a minute. The racket it makes kills me. Look, Andrea, I don't know how I'll get through the day if you won't say you'll come out with me tonight."

"I don't even know your name," said Andrea.

"You've only got to ask. It's Peter. And you like my hair, don't you? That's a start. We can go to the new disco in the Broadway . . ."

Pup had to pick up Dolly first. He got to Shelley Drive at two minutes past six. Because he was going dancing, he was wearing his tightest jeans but, changing

247

quickly on his return home from work, an idea had come to him that for Dolly's sake he should impress Yvonne Colefax with some sort of weird or magicianly air. Dolly had told him how she and Yvonne had been up to the temple together and how Yvonne remembered him as a clairvoyant. So he put on a plain black velvet sweatshirt and hung round his neck on a long thong the solar talisman — gold letters on black painted metal — he had made for himself when he was sixteen. It was a costume equally appropriate for the disco. Perhaps this thought rather summed up the attitude Pup had come to take towards the practice of magic arts.

The Colefax home was a white-walled, green-roofed hacienda whose architecture also owed something to art deco and Moroccan influence and had in its pillared porch a hint of Palladio. It was not the largest house but among the larger houses in quiet, luxurious, bosky Shelley Drive and its grounds ranged extensively. Those in the front were an intricate lay-out of little rockeries, cypress trees, gravel walks and geometric flowerbeds, while on the far side at the back a red lacquer Chinese bridge, such as one associates with the Summer Palace of Peking, could be glimpsed. The lawns, as smoothly green as the jade silk dress Pup had seen Dolly making for Yvonne, obviously required the at least twice-weekly attentions of the old-age pensioner who was at present steering round the turf with an electric lawn mower. Yvonne came down the steps when she heard the van's tyres crunch on the gravel. She was in a candy-pink lawn dress and she looked very young and fragile.

"It's lovely to see you again. Come in and have a drink. Do you know, I always think of you as some sort of supernatural being, a kind of guru perhaps."

Pup smiled. They walked across expanses of oak parquet on which pink and yellow Kashmiri rugs were artlessly spread, to where Dolly sat on a terrace in a white cane chair. There was an empty wine bottle on the white wrought-iron table and another bottle which Dolly was rapidly emptying. Pup said he would have a glass of sherry. From the terrace you could see no other houses, only lawns and shrubberies and, surrounding it all, an apparent woodland whose foliage doubtless concealed other scattered palaces. The Chinese bridge spanned a little lake in which swam fish as vermilion as its lacquer. Dolly said the swimming pool was behind that hedge over there.

Yvonne came back with sherry and dry roasted peanuts in a glass dish. She sat in the swing seat and her wispy pink skirt rode up a little to show off her legs that the sun had tanned to a very light biscuit color.

"I was reading something in a magazine the

other day. About ESP and harnessing energy and making use of powers we don't know we have. It said that, in the future, we'd take it for granted these powers existed, we'd accept telepathy as a fact like — like electricity. It said there was about ninety percent of our brains never got used but still there was this enormous — well, potential in them. That's the kind of thing you do, isn't it?''

She spoke as if she had learned it all off by heart for him, like a little girl reciting a poem she barely understands for a teacher she admires. He was curiously touched. He nodded.

"The power of your mind could alter the way another person's mind thinks and feels?"

"That would be the theory."

She turned away. "I shall be all alone after you've gone. I haven't seen George since Saturday morning. I don't suppose he'll bother to come home tonight."

Dolly said, "I could stay for the evening. My brother won't mind coming back for me, will you, Pup?"

"Pup?" said Yvonne.

"A pet name," Pup said imperturbably. "And I'm afraid I would mind. I've an appointment, I'm going out."

Dolly looked disappointed but proud. "He goes to this society," she explained to Yvonne. "It's a kind of sacred order, like — well, Templars or Freemasons, but they learn to be adepts in the occult."

She was quoting directly from some book, Pup thought, but he didn't deny that the meeting place of the Golden Dawn was his destination that evening. He finished his sherry and got up.

Not much more than an hour later he was gyrating with Andrea under the orange, veridian and purple rippling lights of the Damaria Disco and Wine Bar.

She said nothing to him of the small adventure which had befallen her during the afternoon. She did not yet know him well enough for that. She had gone home to the room she rented in a house at Mount Pleasant Green, expecting the house to be empty at that hour, expecting to have a quiet afternoon setting the room to her liking and arranging her things. On the way there she had bought three small houseplants from a florist: a Christmas cactus, a croton, and a fern.

It was like the continuous low rumble of thunder overhead. But a noise which is, so to speak, an act of God is much easier to put up with than that made, and deliberately or thoughtlessly made, by man. The sound was immediately above her, coming from the room over hers, at the back and on the top floor. There were only two rooms on the top because of the way the roof sloped. Andrea went down to the front door and went outside and read under the topmost bell the name "Diarmit Bawne," printed in a hand that seemed unused to handling a pen.

She had suffered from the noise for more than two hours. Suppose it went on at night too? She would have to move out and she had only just moved in. It took nerve to go up there but she screwed herself up to it and went. She knocked timidly on the door and then had to knock again.

It was a young man who opened the door. He was in his middle twenties but she would have described him as a boy, neither tall nor short, with dusty-looking brown hair — that his hair was dirty she particularly noticed — and features that looked as if roughly shaped out of putty, gray eyes that stared. She spoke in a rush.

"Excuse me, but would you mind not pacing all the time? You've been pacing up and down for nearly three hours, I timed you. I've got the room below you and the noise is really awful. I don't like complaining but I just don't think I can stand any more of it."

She wondered why he was looking at her so strangely. Not with antagonism or resentment, it wasn't that, but almost as if he were surprised she existed and could speak at all.

"I mean," she said in her nervousness, "if it's the exercise you need, couldn't you go out for a walk? Or is it —" she had read in a novel about someone pacing up and down like a caged lion "— that you're worried about something?"

"I can't go out." He spoke hoarsely, in a thick salivary Irish brogue. "I'm allergic, you see."

Allergic to what? Air? Light? She did not feel she could ask. The window was closed and the room had a fetid, sweetish, sweaty smell. The dark red clothes he wore looked as if they had never been washed or cleaned.

"Well, if you could just try not to walk up and down so much." She said it awkwardly, confronted by those curious opaque eyes. "Can't they do anything for your allergy?"

He shook his head. "Nobody can do a thing."

She felt a rush of pity for him. She thought she should speak his name before she went but she didn't know how to pronounce his Christian name. It was a strange way to address someone only a year or so her senior but, "It is Mr. Bawne, isn't it?"

"It is not." He sounded angry and Andrea took a step back. "Conal's the name," he said, "Conal Moore."

18

*T*he flat was a block at the top of East Heath Road. It was one of those Hampstead blocks that from the outside look more like a Georgian country house. Ashley Clare lived at No. 24. Yvonne had told Dolly that he worked in the West End, he was a designer, something to do with stage design, so Dolly knew that if she wanted to see him she would need to be outside Arrowsmith Court quite early in the morning.

She was torn between her desire to see Ashley Clare and her sense of duty that she must be at home to give Pup his breakfast. She got up very early. Pup's bedroom door was ajar and she could see his bed had not been slept in. Dolly no longer worried herself half to death that Pup might have been mugged or run over but these fears had been replaced by another.

Myra's heels clattered across the landing and Myra's voice said: "You know very well he had that girl friend, Doreen. I mean, she went away somewhere but that doesn't mean he's never going to have another, does it?"

Edith whispered in Dolly's ear. "I shouldn't object if he found himself a nice ladylike girl. He'll be wanting to get married one of these days."

"To be perfectly honest with you, Doreen, a nice-looking boy like that who's earning good money isn't going to live like a monk, is he?"

Dolly, tormented, made a striking motion at them over her shoulder. She swatted them away like flies. Harold's snores could be heard, rising and falling, though it was broad daylight. Dolly dressed herself in her blue plaid dress with the plain blue collar, and she put on navy blue tights and her cream sandals. Yvonne was making her more clothes conscious. There must come a point, surely, when you dressed so well, you looked so smart and elegant, that no one noticed your face. Or would they notice it *more?* Hair that was flat on top and frizzed out at the sides had got very fashionable. Suppose she were to have that done, the frizz part covering up her cheeks? Dolly shook her head at her own image. She had never in her life been to a hairdresser. Her mother had cut her hair, and after her mother died, she had done it herself with the dressmaking scissors and a razor comb. She knew she would never dare go to a place like the Unisex salon Pup went to and put her blemished head into a stylist's hands.

She walked to the bus stop and got the No. 210 bus. Hampstead Heath lay mysteriously veiled in the first mist of autumn. Dolly was not entirely sure why she was there or what she intended to do. Principally, of course, to have a sight of Ashley Clare. She began imagining a future in which George returned to Yvonne and she and Pup became their best friends. They would visit each other's homes in the evening and drink wine. Perhaps they would even go away on holiday together. Dolly had not been on a holiday since she was a child when sometimes the whole family went to the Isle of Wight and sometimes to Newquay. She thought she might enjoy a holiday if she had Pup and Yvonne there to cushion her from the world, and George, that unknown quantity, who was a doctor as well as a dentist and who might . . .

By then Pup would have learned all there was to learn about the science of magic. He would be a master. He might still go to the Golden Dawn sometimes — once a month, say — but for the rest of the time he would stay at home, working in the temple. It would be more a laboratory than a temple really, a place where he could make dreams come true for the four of them. Dolly touched her face where the wind had blown her hair aside.

She was outside Arrowsmith Court now. The glass entrance doors were open and two or three people came out, bound for work. A man got into one of the parked cars and drove off down East Heath Road. Dolly worried in case, early though it was, not yet 8:30, she had already missed Ashley Clare. But as she was beginning to feel awkward hanging about there, to feel that soon one of those departing commuters would come over and ask her what she wanted, the glass doors swung open and the man in the photograph came out.

He looked older. That was only to be expected. Photography done with a flash rejuvenates in a way that early morning light does not. He looked thinner, this face was a little worn, and he was formally dressed in a dark gray suit. But he was unmistakably the man George Colefax had called a beautiful boy. Dolly walked along behind him. She followed him down Heath Street. He was carrying a briefcase and, over his left arm, a folded, cream-colored raincoat.

Dolly was sure he must be heading for Hampstead tube station, and as she walked, she got her ten-pence pieces ready for the ticket machine. Ashley Clare went through into the lift with his season ticket. She followed him in just before the doors closed. From the raincoat pocket he took a copy of

The Times — it had presumably been delivered to his door — and folding it as small as it would go, began doing the crossword puzzle.

Sex had played very little part in Dolly's life. She tried never to think of it in relation to herself. And she seemed to have known few people to whom sex was important, though the memory of what she had discovered of Myra and her father sometimes still brought her a small shudder. That Pup was uninterested in sex she was certain — hadn't he told her in innocent confession that he was a virgin? This statement may be perfectly true one day and false the next but that never crossed Dolly's mind. She had never, as far as she was aware, known a homosexual. She was no reader and her social life was sparse. But nevertheless, though near the perimeter of it and in the shadows, she lived in her world and its culture. She had an image of a homosexual, a queer, as a mincing creature with scented after-shave and blusher on his face, one who would give you sidelong looks and call you "my dear." Ashley Clare, though undeniably very handsome, looked like any normal man, smelled of nothing at all and when he encountered an acquaintance on the platform, lifted his head from the crossword and said a laconic " 'Morning."

The train came in and Dolly followed him into a nonsmoker. Ashley Clare sat next to the window in one of the double seats facing the front of the train and Dolly managed to seat herself at right angles to it and immediately behind him. At Belsize Park, the next stop, the train filled up. People were crammed in and standing all down the aisle. That made it hard for anyone to look at anyone else. Dolly knew, anyway, that no one would do more than glance at her and look away. The nevus embarrassed people and made them feel guilty, so no one ever looked at her for long.

Ashley Clare's head and about six inches of his shoulders and back projected above the back of the seat. He was printing in the solutions to his puzzle. Dolly began picking black and silver hairs, mostly black ones, off the collar of his suit jacket. If anyone did happen to see her doing this, they would suppose him to be her husband. They would think them husband and wife who had been unable to get seats side by side and now she was performing a belated grooming on him before they separated to go to their jobs.

He felt nothing. He didn't even twitch his shoulders. She got eight hairs and slipped them into her purse between two pound notes. It was a Bank train, heading for the City, and at Camden Town he left it, presumably to change for Tottenham Court Road or Leicester Square. Dolly also got out and went through the passages to where she could get a northbound train for the Archway. There she stood on the platform, waiting for the train to come and remembering how, on this very spot or close by, she had come within a centimeter and a second of pushing the woman in green over, believing her to be Myra.

But there was no need for such calculated violence when Pup could kindle or destroy with words and water.

Harold sat at the kitchen table, unable to eat. The food was the kind he liked, processed, packaged junk food that Edith and more recently Dolly had always given him, but he pushed it about his plate, staring disconsolately around him.

It was twenty years since he had eaten a meal without reading a book at the same time. When the children were little and Edith busy with them, he had begun to take a book to the table with him and no one had minded or even noticed. It had become a habit. Now he could no longer read, writing had inhibited or exorcised reading for him, and therefore he could not eat. It seemed to him that during the months he had spent writing *Her Highness My Sister*, the library had got in a more than usually rich collection of royal, archducal and aristocratic biographies. They waited temptingly for him when his task was done and the typescript out of his hands, and once he had posted the parcel, off he had gone to the Haringey central library and taken out a wonderful 600-page-long life of Queen Louise of Prussia. He could not read it. The print danced, the sense of the words registered hardly at all, the impetus was gone. The substance of his own novel, which he knew practically by heart, interposed itself between his eyes and Queen Louise and he was forced to lay the book aside in mounting panic.

It made him feel ill. He had hunger pains like a stitch in his side that for a while he thought was the onset of a heart attack and that he might be going to fall down dead like Myra's mother or poor Ronald Ridge. Of course he did not give up at once. He tried a biography of Stanislas II, the collected letters of the Albanian royal family and fictionalized memoirs of Madame de Montespan, all, however, to no avail. Just as working in a sweet factory is said to put one off chocolate, so the manufacture of history had made the finished product revolting to him. It had been a kind of aversion therapy.

"You're not eating, Dad," Dolly said. "If you don't want your pie, have a piece of Battenburg cake. Go on. You must eat."

He shook his head. He was losing weight and he had never had much flesh on him to start with. The next day was Ronald Ridge's funeral, same time, same place, and by the look of the sky it would be raining again.

"Have you got your black tie?"

Harold nodded. He shambled off to the breakfast room and sat in the armchair where, surrounded by mementoes of Myra, he had passed so many happy hours lost in the bypaths of the romantic past. He stared at the rectangle of window, the gray sky beyond, the first drops of rain splashing against the glass.

That day Pup, with mock solicitude (Harold thought), had inquired more persistently than usual after his health, suggesting, though not putting it into actual words, that he might think of early retirement. He had been incensed. He was only fifty-five.

"I'm not getting out for a little whipper-snapper like you."

"I beg your pardon," Pup said in his courteous way. "I'm sorry. You'll do as you like of course. Only you don't seem to be getting much fun out of it."

"Work's not supposed to be fun," said Harold but his mind harked back to when he had been writing his novel. That had been fun, the best fun he had ever known. A gust of anger shook him. "All these big ideas you've got, you'll ruin the business I built up and you not yet twenty-one."

Pup said no more. He watched Harold shamble off the premises, no library book under his arm or in a carrier these days. It would all work out one day, he supposed.

Tonight was not one of those times he was obliged to be in. He locked up, got into the van and drove round to Andrea's at Mount Pleasant Green. She had to work Saturdays but Thursday was her day off, the salon closed on Thursdays. She was the most domesticated of his girls, the only one who was houseproud, who could cook. When she came down to let him in, she was wearing an apron.

Halfway up the stairs she paused and listened. All seemed quiet.

"It worries me when he paces up and down like that," said Andrea. "Like a caged lion."

The room was neat and warm, flowers in a vase, hyacinth bulbs poking through the loam in a pot, a Christmas cactus showing buds. Andrea did her level best to make the bed look as little like a bed as possible with cushions in a stripy cover. This evening there was even a tray on it. She had not yet allowed him into it, the stripy cover was never more than rumpled. On top of the little Belling stove were vegetables steaming in a wok and inside it something emitting delicious smells.

"I've made two chicken pies, one for us and one for the boy upstairs."

"What a kind girl you are!"

"Do you really think so? I like to do what I can. He's really rather pathetic."

"I'd better go up the road and get us some wine."

"No need, I've got it. It's in the sink

cooling." She beamed on him, the perfect manager, the future helpmeet, the prize candidate in the fiancée stakes. She came and sat next to him on the bed. "Peter?"

"Mmm?"

"The boy upstairs, when I asked him his name he said Conal Moore but that isn't his name, his name's Di-ar-mit Bawne, I asked some people downstairs. Someone called Conal Moore used to live there but he went away ages ago, last year, and this boy came. Don't you think it's peculiar?"

"This is a peculiar place," said Pup. "It's a rough area. Not the best place for a girl on her own. Can't you find someplace better?"

"It's only temporary." She looked into his eyes. "Do you think I ought to ask this Di-ar-mit why he says he's someone who went away a year ago?"

"I don't think you ought to have anything to do with him. I think you should keep out of it, Andrea. It's nothing to do with you anyway."

"I read somewhere," said Andrea sententiously, "that no man is an island."

"I am," said Pup. "I'm one of those privately owned islands in the Aegean and I'm very fussy about who comes ashore."

"I'm not sure I know what that means."

"It means to keep clear of unemployed Irish riffraff," said Pup.

264

Dolly was making Yvonne a tweed skirt. She knew it was only to be an ordinary everyday skirt to be worn for shopping in the Market Place or a little light gardening. For anything requiring a higher sartorial standard, Yvonne would have gone to Brown's or at any rate Jaeger. The Ashley Clare doll, its legs straddled on the mantelpiece, watched her as she plied the Singer. After she had put the zip in and tacked the waistband in place there was nothing more she could do until Yvonne had had another fitting. She opened the lid of the remnants box and looked at the figure which, wrapped in a sheet of white tissue paper, lay on top of the pieces of material.

The wax from four white candles had gone to shape it. Dolly took off the paper. Her skill was with cloth and a needle, not in molding wax, and the figure appeared wretched compared to the doll, a sausage-shaped mannikin covered in dirty fingerprints with a tuft of stolen hairs on its golf-ball head. There was something intensely unpleasant about it, something obscene. Dolly, holding it up, could recognize that without knowing why. After all, it was only wax and dust that had somehow got on her hands and hairs from a man's coat collar. She wouldn't have had to make it if Pup had not been so difficult about the doll. He had been home last night and she had carefully prepared the way for asking him. She had watched his face grow wary as she worked up to her question, then harden as the harsh refusal came.

"I'm not making a fool of myself with that, Dolly."

"You didn't make a fool of yourself when you killed Myra."

"For the thousandth time, I did not kill Myra!"

"Well, of course he did, Doreen," Myra said into Dolly's ear. "On the Other Side we know everything and I can tell you for a categorical fact that healthy girls don't drop dead from giving themselves an ordinary douche."

Dolly swatted her away. "You're not going to tell me you're giving up magic?"

He shrugged. Then he looked at her. "No. No, of course not, not white magic. But I won't play at killing people. Right?"

For the wax doll she cut out and sewed up a piece of the tweed for trousers, a scrap of lawn for a shirt. It took her less than an hour. A long loneliness stretched before her, encompassing half the evening and the whole night and all the next day until Pup was home again. Now she half wished that this evening she had done what she had been doing every evening lately when Pup was out, going to Hampstead to watch Ashley Clare.

She hardly knew why. Simply for something to do? Something to break the loneliness? Or because she thought genuine advantage might be derived from it? Since the morning she had secured the hairs, she had twice seen him come out of Arrowsmith Court and make his way down Heath Street to the station. Once in the evening she had witnessed his return home, at twenty to six, and once he and George Colefax had come home together, Colefax dressed very much as he had been in the photograph, so she had had no trouble recognizing him.

After that, she had stood for a long while outside the flats and had been rewarded by the sight of a light coming on and George Colefax appearing for a moment at the window. He did not draw the curtains. With a lubriciousness or voyeurism unusual in her, Dolly stood there waiting, hoping to see the two of them embracing behind the window, in the yellow light. She did not herself want to be seen even by the porter of the flats, but Hampstead is full of trees and creeper-hung walls and leafy shrubs and one of these hung low over the little wall where she sat, where after a while Myra and Edith came to join her, one sitting on either side.

"You'd think a woman'd have more sense than marry a man who's that way inclined," said Myra. "It's not as if she hadn't been married before."

Edith whispered confidingly, "When I was young, things like that weren't talked about in public. The expression 'homo' meant nothing to me. I still don't know what they do and I don't want to."

"To be perfectly frank, it's the mothers make them that way. I read that in an article. They're not born like it."

"Put the blame on the poor parents," said Edith, "that's always the way these days."

George Colefax and Ashley Clare did not embrace, or not where they could be seen from the window, and they came out again at 7:00. George was dressed as he had been when he came off the train, Ashley now in brown sweater and trousers of a fine khaki-and-white check pattern. Perhaps they were going out to eat. Dolly followed them as far as the Hollybush but no further. She had never in her life been in a pub.

The next morning — this morning — she was outside the flats early. What was the point in staying at home? Pup wasn't there and Harold ate nothing. It was cold and damp, not clear and not foggy either, the kind of day that makes everything look dirty.

Ashley Clare did not appear at all, though George did, very casually dressed for a dentist, Dolly thought, in a kind of anorak and Ashley's check trousers. Or perhaps they were *his* trousers and it was Ashley who had borrowed them last night, not George this morning. It made her feel rather uncomfortable. Nothing so far had shown her the intimate relation in which they stood to each other, but this did. Like sisters or hetero-sexual lovers, they wore each other's clothes. Poor Yvonne! Dolly felt certain now that the bond between them was unbreakable except through Ashley Clare's death.

She caught the No. 210 bus to Highgate, replenished her wine stocks from her favorite shop and walked home along the old railway line. The leaves were falling but the buddleias were still in flower. A butterfly lay dead on the path, its tiger's-eye wings spread wide. She climbed up out of the damp grassy gully, shooing Gingie, who hunted unknown things among the long stalks and seedling trees.

She put the doll back in the box, picked up the phone and dialed. A man's voice answered and she replaced the receiver. George went home sometimes, once a week maybe, Yvonne had said. Dolly had finished the day's bottle of St. Nicolas and after a moment's hesitation she opened one of those she had bought that morning.

Presently, from the temple, she fetched some of Pup's books. For the ceremony of the destruction of Ashley Clare, she had decided to ask Pup to evoke a god. Evocations of that kind, all the books said, should only be attempted by a proficient and experienced magician — but what was he if not that after that long training with the Golden Dawn?

The god she fixed on was Anubis, the

jackal-headed. There were lists and lists of gods in those books of his. She might have had Enlil or Marduk, the Dagda or Balder, Khol, Sin, Ruda, Wadd, Apollo, Teteshapi or a host of others, but there was a picture of Anubis, a man whose height and thinness somehow reminded her of Ashley Clare himself and whose dog face was not unlike that of the dog who had found the girl's body and her head. But more than that, Anubis was a god of death. The ancient Egyptians called him the Lord of the Mummy Wrappings. It was him who opened for the dead the roads to the Other Side.

Dolly took the books and the rest of the wine to bed with her. Muzzy by now, her head singing, she gazed at the picture of dog-headed Anubis, fearful of what she had to do but unable to see any other way. Pup came home at twelve. She heard him moving about with deliberate care, tip-toeing and closing doors gingerly so as not to wake her or Harold. Myra was sitting on the end of her bed and Edith under the center light, sewing. She could just see them, but when she tried to look more closely, they, though not their voices, were gone.

"If you want the honest truth, Doreen, you're turning into a real alcoholic, a wino."

"She's got to have some consolation, poor thing, with that disability of hers. We did everything we could, took her to specialists.

Nothing to be done, they all said that."

"Don't think I'm blaming you, Edith," Myra said. "All I'm saying is, we all have our troubles and we have to learn to live with them."

"That's true, that's very true."

They began talking to each other as if she wasn't there.

"Get out, the pair of you!" Dolly shouted. "Get out of my room!"

Pup, coming out of the bathroom, heard her and stared. He went cold down his spine as if someone had put an ice cube down the back of his neck. But he didn't go into her room or even knock on the door. He told himself she had been calling out in a dream.

19

Once Diarmit Bawne had gone, Conal felt grand. That was how he put it to himself.

"I feel grand, boy, grand!"

Like a schoolmaster, Diarmit had watched over him and ruled him and told him how to be. But in the end, Conal had been too much for him, refusing to wash or clean the place or go to bed at a regular hour, and he had the law on his side too. It was his room, he was the tenant, not Diarmit. If he said to get the hell out of here, Diarmit had to get the hell out.

"And take your rubbish with you!"

Diarmit had not done that, so one evening when it was too late for anyone to come and start demolishing the building, Conal had taken all the clothes that were not dark red and four plates and some cutlery and a teapot and a mug and stuffed them in one of the litter bins on the far side of the green. That would be a disappointment for the Dalmatian and the collie when they came scavenging in the morning, he thought, laughing. He laughed all the way back to the room.

And now Diarmit was really gone. Conal need not be conscientious or steady or a good citizen any more. Diarmit had kept on at him about getting a job and that was something else he could forget now. He could forget about getting up early and going out into the cold and worrying about his duty and the future. He was Conal Moore, who was wanted by the police for robbery and for murder.

These afternoons it began to get dark at four. Once it became dusk he felt safe. He went out and bought himself an electric knife sharpener. He sat on the floor in the middle of the room, sharpening his knives with the knife sharpener and testing the edges on his left hand. After a while the pads of his thumb and fingers were crisscrossed with cuts. He wiped the blood off on his trousers or the tail of his shirt which, being dark red, showed no marks.

Once or twice Diarmit tried to come back. He didn't knock on the door or call out but scrambled with his nails on the linoleum outside which was how Conal knew it was him. Like a mouse, so who else could it be?

Pup knew very little about Anubis, he had

heard of him and that was all. But he mugged it up. He read up about evocation ceremonies and realized it was hopeless trying to get that lot by heart. Presumably, if he had really done two or three nights a week training he would be able to recite evocations from memory in much the same way as a clergyman can recite the marriage service.

Dolly wanted it done for her birthday. She wanted a god evoked. Pup thought of someone — Dilip, say, or Andrea — asking him what was he going to give his sister for her birthday and his saying a god. Putting it like that made him see just how badly disturbed Dolly had become. She must have alcoholic poisoning, he thought vaguely with the hazy notions of someone who on the whole prefers a cup of tea to a double Scotch.

He had asked her if she'd like to go out or have a piece of jewelry or something to wear. At the time she had been wearing that red and green painted bit of tin and which, each time he saw it on her, made him wince. She had said no, she'd like them to do something in the temple, she'd like him to evoke Anubis for her.

It was going to be the last time, he was resolved on that. Afterwards, without telling her, he would quietly take the temple apart, so that the next time she went up there, she would find an ordinary, shabby, empty bedroom. And his alibis? He would think of something. The time might even be coming when he must tell the truth and let her make the best of it. She could hardly be worse than she was now, could she?

Yvonne had sent Dolly a card. She had happened to mention her birthday was coming and Yvonne had remembered and sent her a card. There was one from Pup and one from Harold with "Dad" on it in Pup's writing. Dolly bought a Tunis cake for herself and set it out on the tea table.

She had dressed with care. No one was coming and they were not going out but she dressed with greater care than usual in her new plum-colored velvet skirt and top with the plum and lilac blouse. There was a tradition among the women of the Yearman family that you dressed up on Christmas Day and for your own birthday. All the time she was getting ready, she could hear Edith telling Myra about it.

"No matter how busy I was, I could be up to my neck in it, I'd always find time to run upstairs and change into something nice."

"To be perfectly honest with you, I'd say life was too short for that kind of carry-on."

"It was short for us, wasn't it, dear?" said Edith.

Pup blew the dust off the elemental weapons. The cup was the one that would chiefly be used. He wondered to which Sephirah of the Tree of Life Anubis was attributed. Might as well say the fourth. He drew a circle on the floor with a four-sided figure inside it and hung up over the window a length of sky-blue material which Dolly had given him. On the altar he displayed the four fours of the tarot. He tied round his waist, over the golden robe, a sky-blue sash.

All the time he was doing these things he felt he was behaving in an insane way. He felt this more than he had ever done in the past and it affected him so strongly that from time to time he paused in his preparations and said aloud: "Are you mad? Are you quite crazy?"

He was glad he couldn't see himself, that there was no mirror in the temple. It was bad enough seeing Dolly, her face flushed as it usually was these days, her eyes bloodshot, yet dressed up as if for a party. He wondered how many bottles of wine she was getting through a week now, he wondered — as often, as daily — what he ought to do. Tell their father, get their father's help? That was a laugh. She was holding something in her hand, wrapped in tissue paper, and he supposed it was the present he had given her. It would be like Dolly to carry about with her wherever she went anything he had given her, though she had not seemed much to like the Hand of Fatima on a silver chain and he doubted if she would replace the tin talisman with it.

He lit the two blue candles on the altar and

filled the cup with wine Dolly had brought him in a glass. Before evoking a god the magician should cleanse his temple with a Banishing ritual and Pup had told Dolly this had been done, though in fact he had done nothing, he knew himself incapable now of getting up to any of this mumbo-jumbo while alone.

He turned towards Dolly, who was sitting on a floor cushion, and began the evocation, holding in his hands the cup of wine. The words he used would have shocked Crowley or Abremalin the Mage, for they were a hotch-potch and a mingling of every conjuring recipe, diabolic litany and summoning prescription Pup had ever absorbed into his consciousness. From lost mythologies he dredged up names and titles the world has long forgotten. His language was that of Dr. Dee, of Jacobean sorcery.

"I evoke thee, the Bornless One,
The terrible who dwellest in the Void
   Places,
Anubis, son of Nephthys,
Of the race of Asar-Un-Nefer, the
   resurrected Osiris,
Jackal-headed, Lord of the Mummy
   Wrappings,
Anubis Osirides, Lucifuge, Thantopher,
Thou who walkest in the Deeps,
And hath sight in thy feet,

Oh, Adonai, Gnomus, Salamandrae,
Begetter of Light and Transcender of
    Mortality . . ."

And so on.

Dolly watched and listened, rapt. She had
drunk a whole bottle of Valpolicella before
the ceremony began. Her head was throbbing
and she had a feeling of breathlessness and
tension. Now she wished she had not drunk
quite so much. She had selected Anubis from
a book of Pup's called *Interpretations of the
Book of the Dead* because of his attribute of
conducting souls to the Other Side but now
she asked herself if perhaps she had also
chosen him because of his freakishness, his
dog's head. She and the god had something
in common, they were both different, both
bearing a disfigurement that could not be
concealed.

She put up her hand to touch the nevus but
Myra's hand brushed it before hers could.
They had come to join her in the temple, she
could hear them whispering to each other,
though she could not decipher the words. And
she was reminded of Mrs. Fitter's seances.
There was the same feeling, as of impending
excitement, of suspense. Pup, restoring the
cup to the altar, was setting light to the
contents of a small bowl filled with pieces of
incense sticks. A powerful scent of burning
patchouli and sandalwood arose from it. He

blew out one of the candles. The burning bowl glowed red and a little thin smoke came off it. It was dark in the black-walled room now and dark with the darkness of a winter's night at nine o'clock out there beyond the blue blind.

The candle cast a soft beam on Pup in his golden robe but his face was in shadow. In the far corner to the left side of the window, Dolly could make out the dim forms of Myra and Edith, their white robes falling about them like the drapery on Greek statues. Pup entered the chalk circle, closing it where he had stepped in with the point of the elemental wand. He laid the wand across his feet and lifted the glowing bowl up high.

It was silent in the house. The two women had ceased to whisper. The traffic seemed to have stopped, though you could never hear much of it in the back here with nothing much behind but the old railway line.

"I adjure thee, Anubis, Osiris' son or haply son of Ra, come forth! Appear instanter, *venite, venite,* Lucifuge! Come forth and show thyself in thy immortal shape . . . !"

An absolute silence but for his voice. It had grown cold in the temple, nearly as cold as in the hall when Edith had been conjured. Gooseflesh was coming up on Dolly's arms and shoulders.

"Appear, Osirides, Lord of the Lower World, Guide of Souls, Bearer of the

Caduceus and Palms . . ."

Dolly had begun to tremble. "Pup . . ."

He did not hear her. At this stage he always enjoyed himself, he enjoyed the acting. You could understand what those old dabblers in the occult had got out of it, the names and the archaic language alone.

"Arise, appear, I command thee, incarnate Anubis, Conductor of the Dead, Funerary Prince, *fundador sepulcrorum,* come forth . . ."

The yellow fumes which had begun to rise from the square inside the circle now swelled towards the ceiling, hiding Pup from Dolly's sight, hiding the candle and the bowl of smoldering incense. It was the first uncoiling of this smoke which had made her cry out to him. But he was obscured now in thick acrid yellow, a fog that smelled of fire, and his words dwindled as if he were far distant from her.

And now a shape was forming in the dark smoke, rising up, standing there ceiling-tall, its tower of headdress wreathed in rings of yellow fume. The body was naked and glistening as if made from bronze and the face which thrust itself forward with elevated snout was the face of a dog.

Dolly screamed with all her might. She screamed as she had screamed at the seance when Myra appeared. She leapt to her feet, knocking over with a sweep of her arm the candle on the altar and hurling the little wax effigy into the square at the feet of the god. For a second she stood there, arms out, and then she plunged forward in a faint.

Pup had finished, had run out of epithets and titles when Dolly screamed. He had turned his back and set down the smoky basin and within a moment would have crossed to the door and switched the light on. He spun round when Dolly screamed but he wasn't quick enough to catch her as she fell.

The candle had got knocked over and gone out but in its fall had set light to whatever it was Dolly had had in her hands, something of cloth and wax that burned fiercely on the bare boards. He put the light on. With the help of the dagger he picked the burning object up and dropped it into the bowl.

Dolly opened her eyes. He knelt down beside her.

"Are you okay? What made you do that?"

She stared. She raised herself up and looked at what was in the bowl, still burning.

"You saw him?"

A cold finger seemed to touch his spine. "I saw nothing. There was nothing to see. I'm sorry, I shouldn't have done it, I'm a fool. I went too far."

She got up, casting looks about her. The light turned the temple back into a boxroom with unaccountably black walls and a blue rag pinned up at the window.

"Where is he now?"

"Come downstairs," he said gently. "I'll make you a hot drink. Are you all right? Shall I carry you? I bet I could."

She put out her hand and touched the bowl. "Good, that's good. Are you sure he's gone?"

It was useless to argue with her. "He's gone. I banished him. I promise you he's gone."

Pup was almost hysterical with self-disgust. He bundled Dolly out and banged the door. Downstairs he made tea for them both, hot strong Indian tea. Dolly sat silent, drinking it, both hands clasped round the cup. He thought of the beginning of it, the start of her trouble that was a good deal more now than mere strangeness. Surely that had been when, in adolescent folly, he had carried out that soul-selling ceremony on the old railway line. She had been normal before, or as normal as any woman could be with a thing like that on her face. But once he had introduced her to the occult, the blight had begun, the gnawing into her mind of evil. Was that then what the books really meant when they spoke of an invisible world entering the real world of a practitioner or follower of magic, an addict of magic? Was that what one must infer from the ancient writers when they talked of demons conjured up that afterwards could not be banished? Did they really mean a mind split off from reality — schizophrenia? These days Dolly seemed always to be accompanied by invisible companions; she saw things and heard voices. What had she seen just now in that room?

She must see a psychiatrist, she must have treatment. He took her to her bedroom. While she undressed he fetched from the bathroom cabinet a sleeping pill from a bottle that had been Myra's. He sat on the bed beside her and took her hand. He had this piece of business to get done and get done perfectly, he had to find someone he could trust to be left in charge of the new branch — when all that was over he'd find her a psychiatrist. And meanwhile he'd look after her, he wouldn't leave her alone too much, he'd stay in more in the evenings and he'd never have anything more to do with the occult.

The Seconal sledge-hammered her into eight hours' heavy sleep and when she awoke it was to an immediate recollection of how utterly the Ashley Clare effigy had been destroyed. If in the process of that destruction she had been vouchsafed a sight of the dread god, that was the price she must pay. It was proof, too, of Pup's marvelous magicianly powers.

Yvonne was coming in the afternoon. It would be the first time she had ever come without a reason — that is, a reason apart from just wanting to see Dolly. This time there was no green dress to be fitted or skirt hem turned up. Dolly went up to the temple and unpinned the blue blind from the window. She picked up the candle and put it back in the candlestick and she took hold of the bowl and examined its contents. The tweed and cotton and the hairs had been entirely consumed in the burning and the body had melted, so that all that now remained in the bowl was a twisted lump of gray wax with bits of joss stick embedded in it.

The doll she put away in the remnants box. She didn't want Yvonne to see it. When she had dusted the room and put a bottle of Asti in the fridge, she went upstairs and dressed herself very carefully for Yvonne, the soft dressmaker suit in blue-and-gray check Viyella, fuchsia-pink polyester blouse with the Princess of Wales stand-up neckline and bow tie, navy belt and navy pumps, grey ribbed tights. Her hair was longer than it had ever been, grown long because Yvonne's was. She looped it carefully across three-quarters of the nevus and fastened it above her ear with a pink slide. Myra and Edith whispered together in a corner of the bedroom. It was as if they had a secret, for they kept breaking off to look at her, and sometimes they giggled. She had never know them to giggle before.

Pup intended to get home early. He was going to stay in that night and the next and the next, until he was sure Dolly was better. Andrea cut his hair at 4:30, blew it dry, pouted when he said he had to get home to his sister. He drove her back to Mount Pleasant Gardens and saw for the first time Diarmit Bawne, who had come out of the house, down the steps, carrying a green and gold Harrods bag.

For a moment, as he parked the van, he thought Yvonne hadn't come. There was no green Porsche parked outside. But as he entered the hall there came to him a delicate floating nuage of musk and flowers. The relief was enormous, disproportionate somehow. But he told himself he wanted her friend to be there, he wanted her to have a friend.

They were sitting on the sofa, drinking Asti, Yvonne, naturally, on Dolly's left side. He was seized with a pang of compassion for his sister, so dowdy in her homemade clothes, the silly blouse that showed up her florid skin. Of course it was the contrast with Yvonne that highlighted it, Yvonne, who was a sprite, a pixie, a naiad, in a dress that was of wool yet filmy and lacy, pale as ivory, with a malachite necklace and thin silver bangles on her white arms.

Nymph, nymph, what are your beads?

Green glass, goblin, why do you stare at
   them?
Give them me — No.

What had made him recall that from some old
school anthology? He asked her how she was,
sat down and accepted a glass of their wine.

"My car's being serviced and I won't have
it till tomorrow. Dolly says you'll be awfully
kind and take me home. But you don't have
to, really you don't, I can phone for a taxi."

"Of course I'll take you home."

"We'll have another bottle of wine," Dolly
said.

She didn't see the quick glance that passed
between Pup and Yvonne. Pup shrugged.

"I'd rather have something to eat."

Dolly said rather huffily, "It's all ready for
you on the kitchen table. Don't I always have
your meal ready for you?"

He fetched a trayful of it into the living
room: cold Tandoori chicken wings, bridge
rolls, potato crisps, pickled gherkins, lemon
curd tarts, and pineapple-flavored yoghurt.
Yvonne accepted a potato crisp or two and
then she ate a tart and all the yoghurt. Dolly
opened a second bottle of Asti. She did it
quickly, she hurried. For some time she didn't
like being out there alone in the big old
kitchen after dark.

It was nearly 10:00 before Yvonne said she
ought to go. She said to Dolly on the door-

step: "George was going to be home for the weekend but he phoned and said he couldn't make it. He's going to stay at that flat and look after Ashley Clare."

"Look after him?"

"Didn't I tell you? He's ill. He's got a mysterious virus, he's quite ill."

20

Venus (or possibly Psyche or Helen) reclined on cushions, naked but for the obligatory wisp, and contemplated her beauty in a gilt-backed hand-mirror while a wrinkled crone — her face providing a contrast and, to non-immortals, a foreboding — crouched on the far side of the bed, holding in her outstretched hands a necklace of pearls. The painting was large, executed but for the flesh of the young beauty in rather dark oils. Its gilt frame sat opulently on the ivory watered silk with which the walls of Yvonne's bedroom were covered.

"George never liked it," Yvonne said.

"Well, he wouldn't, would he?" Pup sat up, bent over her and smoothed the thistledown hair back from her forehead. "She's too fat for modern taste, though. She's not half as beautiful as you."

"No one's ever said I was beautiful since my first husband died."

"We don't have to talk about him, do we? Or George. One's dead, poor chap, and the other one's no good to you, so let's forget them and talk about us. I think we ought to get up now and get dressed and then I ought to take you out to dinner."

Yvonne looked at her diamond watch on the bedside table and gave a little shriek. "Oh, look at the time! D'you know we've been in bed for seven hours!"

"And on a Sunday too."

"Peter, I want you to know I was never unfaithful before, not to either of my husbands. I promise you I won't mention them again but I just wanted you to know. I mean that I don't make a habit of this sort of thing. It really has to mean something to me. I won't say I was attracted to you that first time we met when poor Myra was alive, it was more like a huge emotional upheaval I felt. And that combined with your powers, Peter, like some kind of god or guru . . . ."

"I'd like you to call me Pup, please," said Pup, getting out of bed. "And I've never asked anyone that before." He began putting his clothes on. "But you'd better forget that god and guru stuff, it never was and it never will be. It's all in Dolly's head. Whatever she says, there's nothing I can do to split up George and this Ashley chap. Why bother anyway? You don't need George now."

She looked at him doubtfully and then she smiled.

George had not spent a night in his own room for a fortnight. Ashley Clare was a heavy smoker and the virus had affected his chest. Yvonne told Dolly this on the phone when she made an excuse for not coming to Manningtree Grove as she had promised. He lay in bed, too weak to move, his temperature rising each evening so that the doctor talked of having him in hospital for tests. All the time he was not at his dental practice, George was at his bedside.

Dolly was not surprised but still she felt a kind of awe. This had been done by Pup, who had not even known he was doing it. Pup had conjured up the god and the god had consumed Ashley Clare in his fire. His was not to be a quick death like Myra's but long drawn out, yet ultimately he would die. Just as they had said Myra had died of an air embolus so they would say his death was due to heart failure or an allergy to antibiotics. Only she would ever know Pup had brought it about by magic.

She was impatient for news but Yvonne no longer came or even rang up. Dolly knew perfectly well why this was. It was because she was tired of waiting. She had no real faith in Dolly or Pup; perhaps she even thought Dolly had never mentioned the matter to Pup and had done nothing about it. Instead of coming back to her, she saw that George was more devoted to Ashley Clare than ever.

Well, it was only a matter of time. Dolly missed Yvonne but she could understand how Yvonne felt, disillusioned, bitter perhaps. Once Ashley Clare was dead, she would come back, she would be grateful. George would return to her and the two of them with her and Pup would become eternal fast friends. She thought of them all going out together, in the Porsche perhaps or in George's Mercedes. They would go to restaurants in Hampstead. People would take her and Pup for husband and wife. Dolly went through Edith's things and found her wedding ring. It fitted the third finger of her left hand as neatly as it had fitted her mother's.

Seeing the ring, Edith said to Myra, "I'm glad to see her wearing that. It was hurtful to me not wearing my ring. I always wore my mother's wedding ring, on my right hand of course."

Dolly switched the ring over to her right hand. She sat at the sewing machine, stitching the long seams in the green cord dungarees she was making for Yvonne. Yvonne hadn't asked for them. She was making them on spec, for a surprise, but she knew Yvonne would be pleased. The two voices were whispering over in the corner by the remnants box, whisper, whisper, they had become close friends. They never spoke directly to Dolly any more.

"Candidly, Edith, no one in their senses would actually take Doreen for your son's wife."

"No, dear, I know."

"That disfigurement of hers really puts that kind of thing out of court, if I may be honest."

Dolly treadled furiously, trying to silence them with the sound of the machine. It was raining, dark outside at 4:30 as the winter solstice approached. The seam came to an end and she had to stop. Whisper, whisper. How was it they could read her thoughts? And read, too, the thoughts she had but never expressed on the exposed surfaces of her mind?

Myra said confidingly, "Peter's very clever, of course, I grant you that. It's not impossible he could do something for her."

"We did everything in our power. We took her to specialists, they all shook their heads, they all said there was nothing to be done."

"Not by medical science maybe, that's a different thing altogether. Why doesn't she ask him to use his powers to take away that birthmark?"

Dolly jumped up. She threw a cotton reel at them and they vanished. It had made her tremble a little, what Myra had said. She went out to the kitchen to fetch her frascati from the fridge. Nothing happened when she tried to switch the light on; the bulb had gone. The kitchen was dim, lit only by the blue gas pilot on top of the oven.

He was standing between the back door and the fridge, tall and glistening, his crested headdress reaching to the ceiling, his furred snout twitching and his muzzle bared in a snarl. Lord of the Cemetery, Anubis, jackal scavenger, bearing in his hands the caduceus and the palms. Dolly screamed. There was no one to hear her. She screamed and slammed the door on him and fled back to the living room where she lay screaming and beating the floor with her fists.

The footsteps sounded heavily above them, pacing up and down. It was unpleasant, inescapable, it made the room vibrate.

"It's worrying me," Andrea said. "I'm worried sick."

"You'll have to move," Pup said. "What else can you do? You've been up and asked him to stop and I've been up. I'll do anything you want but I don't know what to suggest."

Andrea looked at him. They were sitting on her neat bed eating eggs Benedict, which she had gone to infinite trouble to make for him.

"There is one thing you could do. Come with me to a doctor and tell him we think the boy upstairs is having a — well, a mental breakdown, and ask him to do something. He ought to be in a mental hospital, Peter, he ought to be having treatment."

"I don't think I could do that," Pup said slowly. He told himself that he had trouble enough of that kind at home without looking for it outside. "It's nothing to do with me."

"Who is it to do with, then? He's all on his own, he doesn't seem to have any family. I said mental breakdown but it's more than that, he's not sane, I'm sure of it, he's crazy. He thinks if he goes out in the daytime, workmen are going to come and demolish the house, he told me so, he believes it. And he says his name's Conal Moore. Three people in this house have told me Conal Moore was a big, tall, fair fellow who moved out last July twelvemonth and hasn't been back since."

"You want me to go with you and tell a doctor that? What doctor anyway?"

"I haven't got a doctor here yet but you must have. You must have a GP."

"You mean you want to have the poor guy — what do they call it — committed? You want him committed to a mental hospital?"

"It would be for his own good, Peter."

"You go to a doctor if you must," said Pup, "but you can count me out. If I were you, though, I'd find another place to live. It would be simpler."

She looked at him as if she wanted to say something but did not quite dare. He raised an eyebrow but the moment was past and she shook her head. She took their plates and began to de-mold a *crème brûlée*. Above them the footsteps marched wearily back and forth across the twelve-foot-square floor space.

Later, when he got home, Dolly asked him to put a new bulb in the kitchen light. He noticed she wouldn't go out there until the new bulb was in and the light switched on. She smelled of brandy this evening, not wine. There had been some brandy in the sideboard, he remembered, left over from the days of Myra.

Charity begins at home. Before he did anything about Diarmit Bawne he must do something about his own sister. He watched her creep fearfully into the brightly light kitchen and look wide-eyed about her. Without thinking of the implications, wanting only to bring her back to normalcy, he said: "By the way, George Colefax's friend has been taken into the Royal Free."

"Into hospital?"

He nodded. "He's got congestion of the lungs. He's quite seriously ill."

"How do you know?" she said sharply.

Which of them was she jealous of? Him or Yvonne? He lied smoothly, "I was doing a servicing job in the Suburb and I ran into Yvonne."

Her eyes and her very slightly trembling mouth were full of suspicion. He saw her keep glancing at him. At breakfast next morning she began on the subject again.

"I don't know anymore," he said, an edge now to his usually gentle voice. "Only that he's in his hospital and they're not happy with the electrocardiograph they did. They say he has a heart murmur."

She gave a sort of grunt, staring intently at him like one of those mothers who say they can tell their child's deceit by the way his eyes shine. Harold came to the table in his best suit but tieless. He accepted a cup of tea and scattered dry rustling cornflakes into his bowl, though making no attempt at first to eat them. The suit hung in folds on his small, now emaciated frame.

"Not another funeral, surely?" said Pup.

Harold shook his head. "Can you let me have a loan of a tie? Mine aren't up to much. Nothing flashy, mind."

Pup went upstairs and brought him down three ties, a navy patterned with white daisies, a dark gray with tiny fawn and pink squares, a cream and silver stripe with a brown chevron cutting across the center. Being Pup's, they were all of silk. Harold chose the dark gray.

"I shan't be in the shop today. I'm going up to town."

"Christmas shopping?" said Pup.

Harold, who had not smiled for weeks, now burst into a high-pitched cackle of laughter. The idea of him going Christmas shopping!

"I don't know about that, I don't know about that at all." Mirth shook him. As if his laughter had effected some kind of catharsis or liberation, he suddenly grabbed the sugar basin, sugared his cornflakes, poured milk on them, and began voraciously to eat. Pup said no more. He could tell his father didn't want to say where he was going or why. Probably, whatever it might be, it had something to do with the typewritten letter which had arrived for him two days before and which had thrown him, also at breakfast, into a minor excited panic.

After they had gone, Dolly phoned the Royal Free Hospital. It took her a while to find out which ward Ashley Clare was in. When they put her on to the staff nurse on duty, she said she was his sister.

"There's no change," the nurse said. "He's as well as can be expected."

Dolly had to be content with that. She tried to phone Yvonne but there was no reply. Since that evening in the kitchen she had not directly seen Anubis, not face to face, but she had glimpsed him out of the corner of her eye, the glitter of his headdress, the snakelike skin, or his dog's face had looked at her suddenly out of a darkening recess of the room. She could bear it, she set her teeth against the fear. He would stay until his work was done, she thought, but when Ashley Clare was dead he would depart.

She finished the green cord dungarees. The idea came to her of making a doll for Yvonne, a doll to match her white and gold bedroom, to sit on her bed and conceal a nightdress under its skirts. That night she dreamed of Anubis for the first time. He was performing his function of conducting the dead along the path to the underworld or Other Side. Edith and Myra followed him and Ronald Ridge and Mrs. Brewer with Fluffy in her arms, but ahead of them all, at the god's side, was Ashley Clare. And the path they walked along, leading into the Mistley tunnel, was the old railway line.

Pup came home at about eight in the evening. He kissed her cheek and she smelled Balmain's Ivoire on him. She heard Myra and Edith whispering and she jumped away from Pup as if, instead of French perfume, she had smelt a foul stench. He didn't seem to notice.

"I've got something interesting to tell you," he said.

She was instantly suspicious. "What sort of something?"

"Dad's written a book. It's a historical novel and it's going to be published. That's where he was going the other day, to see these publishers. They wrote to him to say they like the book, they want him to make some changes but they like it and they want him to do a sequel. How about that? He's going to retire and leave me a clear field."

"Oh," she said, thinking.

"He's over the moon. I left him in the pub, having a drink with Eileen Ridge to celebrate."

"So he's happy and successful," she said in a strange concentrated tone. "He's got what he wanted. Everything has come right for him."

"You could put it that way, yes."

She was silent. He suddenly felt, without knowing why, extremely uncomfortable. She was staring at him, her eyes slightly out of alignment, so that the left one seemed to be looking at something beyond or behind him. It made him turn round and look. She had been making a doll that looked exactly like Yvonne, with beige-blonde nylon hair and dressed all in bridal white. Why? he asked himself, what for?

She said, "Pup?"

"Yes, dear?"

"Could we go up to the temple?"

He shrugged. He was tired and he had a lot to think about. The color had come up into her face, a dark ugly flush.

"You can do anything," she said. "I know that now. You've got power, more than a doctor, more than anyone . . . So will you — will you . . ." Her hand went trembling up to her cheek. "Will you take this away?"

He was speechless. She held her hand there, covering the nevus.

"You could do a Pentagram ritual," she said. "Or an invocation. You could do it by degrees, it doesn't have to be all at once, you could . . ."

He shouted at her when of all times he should have been gentle. "I can't! You know I can't!"

She nodded, said in perfect faith, "You can do anything."

"Dolly, I can't. Listen to me." He came and sat beside her, taking her by the shoulders. "I'm sorry I shouted at you, I shouldn't have done that. I can't take away your birthmark, do you understand? I can't, it's impossible."

"You mean you won't."

"No, I don't mean that. Listen to me, I'd give everything I've got, I'd give years of my life to take it away if I could." He believed he was speaking the truth. "I'd do anything in the world for you but it's not in my power to do that."

She said slowly, heavily, "You killed Myra, you made yourself pass your driving test, you brought Dad happiness and success, you've got the business for your own, so why can't you do that for me?"

"I did not do those things. They happened. Don't you see? Myra dying was a coincidence. I passed my driving test because — well, because I can drive. Dad wrote his book himself, didn't he? How could magic make him a writer?"

"I don't understand what you're saying."

Desperately, forgetting the consequences, he said, "There's no such thing as magic, Dolly. There never was and there never will be. They were all crooks or mad or superstitious fools who wrote those books. It's all rubbish. You can't reverse the laws of nature with water and incense and stupid words, you can only deceive people. If I've deceived you, I'm sorry, I'm desperately sorry, but you've got to know sometime, it may as well be now. I was just a kid dressing up and pretending, don't you see?"

She didn't. He saw, to his horror, disbelief in her face and pain and resentment.

"Why did you keep on with it then? Why do you go to the Golden Dawn?"

"I was wrong," he said bitterly. "I was wrong and I'm sorry. I'll never do it again, though, that I can promise you. I'm going to see to it I never can do it again." He jumped up and went swiftly out of the room, closing the door behind him.

She sat there quite still. She could see herself in the small mirror that Myra had hung on the opposite wall and she turned her face aside. Pup's footsteps running up the stairs made a soft pounding through the house. The front door opened, closed, and she heard Harold cross the hall and go into the breakfast room.

"He doesn't mean it," Edith's voice said. "He'll calm down in a day or two."

Myra laughed. "The fact is, Edith, he's been seeing Yvonne Colefax, he's been in her house with her, I could smell that perfume she uses all over him. Well, she was bound to prefer him over Doreen, wasn't she? It stands to reason."

"He's upstairs now looking through his books to see what he can do for poor Dolly."

"Mind you," said Myra, "once that fellow is dead and George goes back to her, he'll put a stop to that. He won't want Peter there and Yvonne won't want Peter either. The sooner that happens the better for all concerned, I'd say."

"He's upstairs making holy water and studying high magic," Edith whispered.

At 9:30 Dolly picked up the phone. Yvonne answered after the second double ring. This time she did not say it was Dr. Colefax's residence but uttered a timid "Hello?"

"It's Dolly."

"Oh, Dolly, how are you?"

"I'm all right. I've made you something for a surprise. Well, two things. Something to wear and something else. Would you like to come and fetch them sometime?"

Yvonne did not reply immediately. Her voice sounded strained and awkward.

"I'm a bit busy at the moment actually, Dolly."

"I could come to you."

"Just let's leave it a bit, shall we? I mean, unless you think your brother would run them up to me sometime in the van. I tell you what, I'll ring you."

Dolly felt cold. She needed a glass of wine. As soon as she had rung off, she would brave the passage and the kitchen and fetch herself a fresh bottle of wine. But first . . .

"How is Ashley Clare? Is he — is he dead?"

"Dead?" echoed Yvonne shrilly. "No, of course he isn't dead. He's much better. He's coming out of hospital for Christmas and George is taking him to Morocco for a week to convalesce."

Dolly put the receiver back and left the room. There were no voices now, no shapes in the dark corners, nothing but herself alone, walking towards the kitchen and her wine. She had failed Yvonne and because of that Yvonne would never want to see her again.

21

The girl downstairs was a police-woman. Either that or a spy set on him by the builders. He was not sure which or she might be both, it hardly mattered. What was important was not to have too much to do with her. He must never allow himself to forget that he was wanted for murder, the police wanted him for murder, only as things stood they couldn't quite pin it on him.

The girl downstairs called him Diarmit, pronouncing it incorrectly. He supposed she did that because the name Diarmit Bawne was still under his bell at the front door. He had left it there deliberately to keep the police from knowing Conal Moore had come back. That she called him Diarmit proved she didn't know. She said she was called Andrea, an obvious invention, laughable when you thought about it.

"You ever go down on the old railway line?" he had asked her.

She shook her head. She said she had never heard of it, she didn't know there was an old railway line.

"There was a girl murdered down there a year and a half back," he said. "You want to be careful. He might strike again."

"I don't go there," she said. "I told you, I don't even know where it is." And he saw that he had frightened her.

But he must be careful to give her a wider berth now, not to get talking with her, he might say dangerous things. Before he said that about the girl being murdered, she had tried to persuade him that there was no fear of the house being pulled down. As if she would know! Sometimes he thought she was a bit mentally unbalanced. At Christmas, before she went off somewhere for the four days, she brought him a piece of cold roast turkey and four mince pies. He didn't eat them, though, he knew for a fact they had a truth drug in them which would make him reveal everything next time he saw her. He took them across the road by night and left them on the green for the Dalmatian and the collie to find in the morning. Truth drugs were harmless to dogs, who couldn't talk anyway.

The New Year was two days old when the builders came back and started pulling down a row of shops with mansion flats over them on the west side of the green. The shops had been boarded up for months. He felt very relieved to see the men so fully occupied over there because it meant they couldn't start here yet. For the first time in months he went out in daylight and the place he went to revisit was the old railway line and the Mistley tunnel, scene of Conal Moore's crime.

Coming home, he met Andrea in the hall and with her that police colleague of hers, the fair-haired cop who drove a van camouflaged to look like it came from a typewriter firm. He looked through them, he ignored them, not speaking a word, it was the only way.

"You see?" said Andrea. "Now don't you think we ought to do something?"

"He's harmless," said Pup. "It's no business of yours."

"Yours," not "ours." She noticed that. They went upstairs and Andrea unlocked the door of her room. Knowing he was coming home with her, she had left the room spick and span before she went out in the morning. The steel of the draining board, glimpsed through the canework of her new room divider, shone like a mirror. On the coffee table lay a large and glossy Haringey Public Library book of Audubon prints, open at a printing of Columbian humming birds. He felt uncomfortable and sad.

She began making coffee. Overhead the pacing had started. "I still think I ought to do something," she said. "I," he noticed, not "we." She looked at him. "Peter?"

"Mmm?"

"Mr. Manfred's opening a new salon in St. Alban's. He says if I'll go there he'll let me have one of the flats."

As the footsteps pounded, "That might be the answer," he said.

"Oh," she said. "It was just that I thought . . . Oh, well."

He knew what she thought. That there was a chance he might ask her to stay, to tell her they'd start going steady, get engaged.

"It wouldn't work out," he said gently. "Really. We've had a nice time but it wouldn't work."

She glanced at the bed where the cushions were arranged with perfect symmetry, as smooth and shiny as a mint humbugs. "Is it because I wouldn't — you know?"

"Oh, no."

"My mother says that, if you do, a boy doesn't want you afterwards but my girl friend at the salon says they only want you if you do. It's hard to know."

"It wouldn't have made any difference. Really."

Andrea poured two cups of coffee. "I'll tell Mr. Manfred in the morning that I'll go to St. Alban's. I think it could be quite soon."

"It'll be the best thing, you know," said Pup. "No more of that racket going on and you won't have to do anything about him."

"I wouldn't have anyway. Not on my own." She looked out of the window. It was snowing lightly, flakes melting on the glass and running down. She drew the curtains. "Is there someone else, Peter?"

"Yes," he said. "Yes, there is." He was tired of telling lies, he thought he might try never to tell any more.

Andrea looked as if she was waiting for him to go so that she could have a good cry. What could he do about that? He had never made her any promises or led her to believe that he felt any more for her than liking sometimes to be with her. She stood up and looked wanly at him. He hugged her and said goodbye and went downstairs out into the snowy evening. They were all gone now, Suzanne married, Philippa in Australia, Terri with a new boy friend. Caroline had never been more than a flash in the pan.

Fidelity now seemed extraordinarily attractive to him. He wondered if he could ever again fancy a girl who was not blonde, whose eyes were any shade but aquamarine or who weighed more than a featherlight seven stone. He got into the van, switched on the wipers and drove carefully through the driving sleet up to the Bishop's Avenue.

It took Dolly a while to believe, fully to realize. Like a trustful cripple she had gone

308

to her Lourdes and the miracle she knew must happen had not happened. There had been no surprise in hearing from Yvonne, the day after the conjuring of Anubis, that Ashley Clare was ill. She had expected that, known it already. And later on she had known he would die, it was simply a matter of time. That he was recovering, that he was better and would get well, was not only dismaying — for a while it was incredible.

She could not believe that Pup had failed. If the evocation had not worked, it was because he had not known what its purpose was or even of the existence of the little wax figure. It was she who had done it wrong, it was her fault. Gradually she was coming to understand that the evocation had not succeeded, that Ashley Clare was in truth recovering and that this was because she had made a mess of things.

Yvonne had promised to phone and Dolly waited almost hourly for that phone call. She disliked going out in case Yvonne phoned while she was out. The green cord dungarees hung on a hanger from the picture rail in the living room and the blonde doll in the white diaphanous dress sat on the mantelpiece between the ballet girl and Ashley Clare.

Dilip Raj phoned for Pup. Someone who said she was a friend of Caroline's sister phoned for Pup. Wendy Collins phoned. She didn't say what she wanted apart from asking

Dolly how she was. A bit later on she came to the house and behaved in an abstracted way as if she were listening or looking for someone who wasn't there. Dolly thought she had put on weight. She had never before seen Wendy's hair in such stiff curls; it looked like a wig.

"I love your sweet dolls," she said. "I've always liked dolls since I was a wee thing. I never had any time for other toys, only dolls."

"Pity you never had any children of your own," said Dolly.

Wendy tossed her head. "I've got plenty of time yet. Would you make me some of those?" She pointed at the dungarees.

It was the first time Dolly had felt like laughing for ages. But it wasn't for her to comment on what was suitable or unsuitable for potential customers.

"If you like."

Dolly wondered why she lingered for a good five minutes in the hall before leaving. The phone rang. It was Christopher Theofanou for Pup. Each time the phone rang, every single time, Dolly thought it must be Yvonne. Yet she was never really surprised, for in her heart she knew why Yvonne didn't phone, why she wanted no more to do with her. She recalled that breath of perfume she had smelt on Pup. Yvonne liked Pup better than ever. Now that she knew him personally, she had probably asked him herself to break up the friendship between her husband and Ashley Clare.

He might do it for her, Dolly thought, though he would do nothing for his own sister, who loved him like a mother.

"To be perfectly honest," Myra said to Edith, "he was just having Doreen on when he said he didn't believe in magic. Of course he believes in it, it's his life. He's still going to those meetings of his, isn't he?"

Edith said something Dolly couldn't catch.

"He's at the Golden Dawn now," said Myra. "It stands to reason he wouldn't waste all those years of study."

Pup didn't want to *kill,* that was the trouble. It had upset him, killing Myra, he really only wanted to do white magic. Not even to please Yvonne, not even to bring her husband back to her would he kill Ashley Clare. That, Dolly thought, must have been why Ashley Clare hadn't died, because Pup hadn't willed it. She sat by the living-room window, her first glass of wine from the second bottle of the evening in her hand. It was snowing lightly. She heard Harold let himself out of the house. He walked along the pavement under the bare branches of the ginkgo tree without looking up at the lighted window. Since becoming an author, he had taken to wearing a brown tweed hat.

He was never much comfort to her, yet she felt more alone when he had gone out. If

311

Ashley Clare didn't die, she would never see Yvonne again. She knew that for certain, she knew it as positively as she believed in Pup's spells. For promising to get her husband back and then failing, Yvonne would hate her forever.

During the night there was a frost and icicles hung in fringes from the eaves of houses in Manningtree Grove. In spite of the cold, Dolly got up very early and walked to the Archway and caught the No. 210 bus. She wore her old thick winter coat, one of the few garments she had that she had not made herself, and knee boots and a scarf round her head. She noticed people who had wrapped scarves yashmak-wise round their faces, and while she waited for the bus, she did the same with her scarf. Afterwards she felt just like anyone else, unscarred, unmarked, not set apart, and holding her head high, she looked others in the eye.

It was George Colefax she hoped to see emerge from the entrance to Arrowsmith Court, not Ashley Clare. She wanted only to check that they had returned from Morocco. Ashley Clare would still be convalescent, would hardly yet venture out early on an icy morning like this one.

She paced up and down the pavement, rubbing her hands together in their woollen gloves. People were knocking snow off the roofs and bonnets of cars. There was a silvery icing of hoarfrost on the branches of trees. The low sun had come just above the horizon, reminding Dolly of that lovely morning — years ago, it now seemed — when she and Pup had walked along the old railway line to cut the flowering hazel branch at sunrise.

Out of the swing doors at the entrance came Ashley Clare. Dolly was surprised. He was going to work, she was sure of that; so soon after his illness he was back at work and walking briskly down the hill towards the station. He wore a coat of white or natural-colored sheepskin, full-length and belted, a gray fur hat, and around his mouth and nose a scarf was tied just as she had tied hers. She followed him for a little way, then turned back and made for the bus stop at Jack Straw's. It seemed that he had made a complete recovery, was more fully restored to health than she had expected. She felt depressed and afraid. It was as if she was having to learn all over again that the magic had failed.

Because the sun had come up and the sky was blue, she walked home from Highgate along the old railway line. Until she walked there, it had been a white avenue of virgin snow, undisturbed, unprinted. Gingie, stalking hungry birds, showed up on the snow like a spoonful of marmalade on a white plate, and from the Mistley tunnel, feathers, discolored gray, still blew out from the inexhaustible mattress. Dolly had to go up the steps. She couldn't manage the slippery, snow-covered embankment.

As she let herself into the house she fancied she heard a woman's voice, and not Myra's or Edith's. The breakfast room door had been open when she went out but now it was shut. Eileen Ridge, she thought, and she seemed to know what she was about to hear.

"It's for the companionship, isn't it?" Edith's voice said.

"You could see that coming a mile off, to be frank," said Myra. "You could see that coming from the day of poor Ronald's funeral."

"She could do worse when all's said and done," said Edith.

Dolly hesitated and then opened the door. Myra's paints and brushes and dust sheets were gone. The two of them were sitting at the gate-leg table, reading together some sheets of manuscript. The woman was Wendy Collins and she was wearing the trouser suit Dolly had made her.

"Here's Dolly at last," she said. "We can tell her our news, Harry."

Dolly minded much less than she had about Myra. What it would mean for the future did not trouble her.

"If there's anything could put Doreen's nose out of joint, this will," Myra said and yet she was wrong. It had hardly touched her.

If Pup would be what he had once been, if Yvonne would come back and be her friend, nothing else was important. If that would happen she even felt Edith and Myra might go away and not come back. As she put the wine that she had bought into the fridge, she thought she saw the dog-faced god looking in through the window at her, but she stared hard and bravely at him and he vanished, he melted away with the snow and the icicles that the sun was now melting.

Suppose she were to try and do magic herself? In the past, she had felt too humble to attempt it. It had been Pup's province, the province of the male magus. Yet women could become adepts as well as men. If you believed, surely, if you had faith, and did all the right things, drew the circles and the pentagrams correctly, made the holy water, learned the words without mistakes . . . . And there was something psychic about her, something of the invisible world. Her ghosts, raised by Mrs. Fitter, had stayed with her and not departed as those others had. The god she picked out had come and still remained, waiting like a genie. There was more affinity with the occult in her than there was in Pup, the geomancer.

The books would instruct her as they had instructed him. She could work in the temple, wear the robe and use the elemental weapons. She went up the stairs. At about lunchtime

Harold had gone out and Wendy with him and they had not come back. The phone had not rung once all day. It was four in the afternoon, not dark yet, not quite dusk, but on the point of twilight, the sky and air dark blue, lights coming on everywhere, and the streets glistening with yellow light that gleamed on the half-melted snow. A bluish glimmer, reflected off the snow, filled the house.

At the foot of the top flight she switched a light on. It seemed to fill a little space and leave dark corners everywhere. Yet she was alone, there were no voices whispering and no half-glimpsed shapes. She crossed the landing and opened the temple door. A feeling of faintness came over her and she gasped, for the temple was gone and as if it had never been.

It was just a shabby little back bedroom. The walls were white, or whitish, and patchy, the floor was bare, and in the middle of the floor stood a rickety bamboo card table. The whole room rocked as she looked at it. She steadied herself, holding on to the doorknob, a singing in her head. For a moment she had a dreadful thought that she had imagined it all, the years of its existence and everything that had happened and been made to happen in it. Then she switched the light on.

The uncurtained window became a blue rectangle, patterned with a trellis of black branches. She saw what the bamboo table was. Once it had been the altar on which the elemental weapons had lain. Now the weapons were gone and the robe was gone from behind the door and the *tattwas* had disappeared from the walls. But its existence had not been in her imagination only. The black could still be seen through the rough whitewashing of the walls. There was a burn mark still on the floorboards where the wax image had caught fire in the bowl.

Pup had done it. He had meant what he said. On that very night when he had told her magic was nonsense, he had done it, on other nights too perhaps, when she thought he was out or asleep. He had fetched Myra's paints from the breakfast room and painted over the black of the walls. He had stripped the cloth covering from the altar and taken away the weapons to destroy them. Suddenly she remembered the books. What had he done with the books?

She ran from room to room, looking for them. They were nowhere on this top attic floor. She went down to his bedroom and searched it. Without qualms, without caring for his privacy, she threw open cupboard doors, rifled drawers, looked under the bed, even under the mattress.

They were nowhere. They were not in the house. He had burned them or sold them. She trailed away, down to the kitchen, down to her wine. She opened the bottle, poured the first glassful, with hands that shook. What use would they have been anyway? What use was anything with the temple itself gone?

She understood now that the days of magic and all that magic could do were over.

22

*P*up was very gentle with her and very kind. He came home every evening, though sometimes very late. She made a point of not asking him where he had been; she told herself that perhaps he still had to go to the Golden Dawn to complete a course or some such thing. She hardly saw Harold, and after that day when she had surprised them together, she never saw Wendy. Once she happened to overhear Mrs. Collins say: "Poor Dolly's gone downhill a lot, hasn't she? Miss Finlay saw her out shopping the other day talking to herself."

And Wendy who was out in the hall with her laughed. "The first sign of insanity, they used to say."

It was Pup who told her Wendy and their father intended to live in one of the flats over the new shop.

"Then there'll just be you and me here?"

He nodded. "That's right."

A house of their own, a house to themselves . . . "You could have one of the bigger rooms for a temple. You could start all over again."

"No, I couldn't, dear. I shall never start it again, I told you. It's nonsense, Dolly, ask any rational person."

She knew no rational people, she knew no one. "Did you burn the books?"

"I sold the lot for a pound to a dealer on Highgate Hill."

"What are people going to think?" she heard Edith whisper to Myra over by the sewing machine. "I feel quite awkward about it."

"What are people going to think of you?" Dolly said. "All those Golden Dawn people?" She brought the name out with a bitter edge. "What's Yvonne going to think?"

"I shan't tell people," he said lightly. "Why should I?"

Yvonne didn't know, then. Yvonne still waited, expecting Dolly — or Pup through Dolly — to get her husband back.

"Hope deferred," said Edith sententiously, "maketh the heart sick."

Yvonne's heart was sick and sore and therefore she kept away from Dolly, hating her for her failure. Dolly came to a decision. The doll she would keep in reserve but the

320

dungarees should be sent to Yvonne by the means she herself had suggested. She bought dark green tissue paper and wrapping paper patterned all over with ivy leaves and wrapped up the dungarees and asked Pup to take them to Shelley Drive.

"If you're up that way," she said, kissing him goodbye.

"I expect I shall be," he said.

It was very late when he got home that night but Dolly was still up, drinking Yugoslav Riesling. He brought her a note from Yvonne. "Dolly," it began, the name written diagonally across the top and underlined, "the dungarees are super, a perfect fit, and I am thrilled. Thank you so much. You must let me know what I owe you, at least for the material. Yours, Yvonne."

Nothing about when she would see her, nothing about getting in touch. That bit about paying for the material hurt. Dolly thought Yvonne had meant it to hurt. Had she mentioned payment only to remind Dolly of that much greater service she had offered to pay for but which had never been performed? But what most pained Dolly was the way the letter opened and the way it ended, cold as ice and standoffish, no "dear" and "love" this time.

Once more there clung to Pup the scent of Ivoire. Of course, she knew he had been up to Yvonne's, she had asked him to go there, of course he had very likely shaken hands with Yvonne, and yet her imagination and her reasoning told her that secretly Pup and Yvonne had become friends. Lonely without her husband, Yvonne had turned to Pup and unless George went back to her . . .

"To be perfectly honest, Edith," Myra whispered, using the same phrases she had once used to Dolly in life, "to be perfectly honest, I can't say it doesn't look as if they've got a serious thing going because, frankly, it does."

Back in the summer, when the subject had first been raised, Dolly had wanted the world rid of Ashley Clare for Yvonne's sake. Now she wanted it for her own. Remembering the heart murmur Pup said he had, she worked in quite a precise and scientific way on the doll next morning, plunging not pins but two long tapestry needles into the region where its heart might be supposed to be. It seemed impossible to her that such vehemence of will and such concentrated malice could be expended without result, yet she had achieved nothing. Because she dared not ask Pup and could not ask Yvonne, she went over to Arrowsmith Court herself on the bus and waited outside for hours and in vain. It was only on her third visit that she saw Ashley Clare. At 9:00 in the evening he came out of the flats and got into George Colefax's Mercedes.

On the way back, perhaps because a woman sitting behind her mentioned to her companion that she lived in Camden Town, Dolly remembered those minutes on the platform when she had put up her hands and been prepared to push a woman over the edge and out of life.

"I used to wear that emerald shade a lot," said Myra, coming to sit beside her while Edith squeezed up on the edge of the seat.

"It's a difficult color to match and a difficult color to wear," Edith said.

Dolly swatted them away but they were waiting for her at the bus stop. "You don't know everything," she said to them. "You said Pup was doing magic when he wasn't, he was breaking up the temple." She shouted out, "You said Ashley Clare would die!"

A man coming down the hill said, "Here, steady on, love. Real little piss artist you are."

Under the light he saw her face, her cheek, and she saw him look away embarrassed. He thought she was drunk. The funny thing was it was the first evening she could remember when she hadn't had a drink. Her body craved it. She went up the steps on to the Archway bridge and Hornsey Lane. Standing on the bridge, close by one of the yellow-painted, concrete lamp standards, Anubis pointed his dog snout at the smoky purple sky. She looked away and looked again and he was gone, melted into the ironwork. In Manningtree Grove she met Miss Finlay, scuttling home from the Adonai Spiritists, but she did not acknowledge Miss Finlay's timid greeting. She passed on, her head averted, scolding Myra who kept touching her and whispering. The wine, after the first tumblerful, drove Myra and Edith temporarily away.

"I'm leaving," the policewoman said. "I'm moving out." He saw her give him a cunning look, seeing how he would take it. "I've come up to say goodbye."

He wondered whether to believe her. You could never really trust those people.

"I'm moving to St. Alban's," she said. "I've got a flat there."

An unlikely story. "Who'll be moving in then?"

She said she didn't know. She was going in an hour or so and she had all this stuff left over, tins of food and jam and some potatoes, scouring powder and washing-up liquid, and she wondered if he'd like to have it. It seemed a pity to throw it away.

"You can leave it with me," he said and he smiled, pulling the wool over her eyes. They still thought they could drug him. If you looked closely at those tins you'd see minute pin holes they'd pushed the hypodermic through. The potatoes too. They must think him daft if they reckoned on him eating that jam.

"Well, I'll say goodbye then, Diarmit."

That angered him and told him a lot. "My name's Conal Moore, I'll thank you to call me by my name."

She shrugged. "Goodbye."

After she had gone and it got dark he took the tins and the potatoes and the jam across the street to the green and divided them among the three litter bins. Someone had been up and searched the room in his absence, he was sure of it. The Harrods bag containing the knives was lying a little further from the bed than it had been. He could smell that girl in the room. Cautiously he sniffed the scouring powder, the washing-up liquid, then the scouring powder again. It made him sneeze. He sneezed twenty times or more and his nose started to run. They were trying to poison him now. He opened the window and put his head out into the frosty February night.

After a time his head cleared a little and he began to understand what they were doing. They had tried to make him say he was Diarmit Bawne, for Diarmit Bawne was a witness and could tell the whole truth about Conal Moore. Hadn't he helped the police before? That responsible hard-working citizen had helped the police before, had them here in Conal's room, talked to them, asked them to keep in touch. They'd tried that on with persuasion and drugs, sending that woman to disarm him, but they had failed. No one should make him say he was who he was not. But he would have to get out of here, he was in grave danger here.

He must get out before the new policeman moved in downstairs. Carefully he scattered scouring powder, a very thin, almost invisible, film of it, on to the surface of the Harrods bag, on to the heap of red clothes, on to the draining board and around the knob of the cupboard door. Then he put out the light and crept downstairs with the tin of powder and the plastic container of liquid. These he deposited in one of the house dustbins in the side entrance. Returning, he removed from under his bell by the front door the piece of card with "Diarmit Bawne" on it to reveal the old one that said "C. Moore."

Slowly he went back upstairs, allowing them plenty of time for their searching. But when he came into the room he found everything undisturbed and the scattered powder lying as he had left it, like a slight fall of virgin snow.

Pup and Yvonne stood on the Chinese bridge, looking down at the red fish in the dark water. It was one of those mild days that sometimes occur at the start of Lent and it was the eve of Pup's twenty-first birthday.

"So it looks," said Yvonne in the voice that had never grown up, "it looks as if he won't live very long. Poor Ashley! I never thought the time would come when I'd say poor Ashley."

"What is it exactly that's wrong with him?"

"Something with his heart. He can't work anymore, he's had to give that up. He could just drop down dead in the street, George said. I've never seen George so depressed."

"And if he dies," Pup said in a low voice, "George will come back here? Come back for good?"

"I don't know. I suppose. Let's go in, I'm getting cold."

Pup put his arm round her and they walked back to the house. He was very much in love; he was, as he had never been before, ill with love. With Yvonne, primarily and absolutely with Yvonne, but also with everything she represented and everything that formed the matrix of her, with Ivoire perfume and Cacharel clothes, red lacquer bridge and swimming pool, house and car and breath of affluence. For wasn't Yvonne herself those things and those things Yvonne?

They sat on the white fur rug in front of the log fire that Yvonne's cleaner had built and lit and maintained. Yvonne's fingernails were painted a pearl color and she wore a pearl ring. Pup kissed her hand and her wrist.

"I love you. I don't want to lose

you to George."

"Ashley might live for years," she said. "Isn't it funny? It's not very long since I asked Dolly to get you to split them up. And now I only want them kept together. Could you have?"

"Split them up? Of course not. Yvonne?"

"Yes, darling?"

"I wish you still saw Dolly."

"It's a bit embarrassing, isn't it? You know, you and me. After what I told her about George. And besides — you mustn't be hurt."

"I won't be hurt."

"She's so strange. I'm afraid of her."

"She's harmless," said Pup. "She loves us — I mean us two — more than anyone in the world. She'd do anything to make us happy. At least give her a ring sometime, would you? To please me?"

"Shall I tell her about us?"

He looked into her eyes. They were the only eyes he had ever seen that actually reminded him of jewels, large, uncut, water-washed gems. "There isn't much to tell, is there? Only that I love you and you say you love me — and your husband's coming back."

Yvonne, having rehearsed what she would say, tried to phone Dolly next morning. Dolly was out, buying her wine. She tried again in the evening and Dolly, machining the seams of a dress for herself, heard the phone but let it ring. She thought it was Wendy Collins, who had already phoned twice that day. Yvonne gave up, postponing her call until the next day.

She could only have been in time, she could only have talked to Dolly in time, if she had phoned before 7:30, and no one does that.

The Yvonne doll and the Ashley Clare doll sat side by side sedately on the mantelpiece. Dolly looked at them with a constriction in her throat. What she had to do frightened her and if there had been another way she would have taken it. There was no other way, she had tried the other possible means and this was all that remained.

It was a blue morning, bright and with a tearing wind. She wrapped up warm, once more tying the scarf to hide half her face. The confidence this gave her she needed. Myra and Edith meant to go with her, there was no escaping them. Myra's greenness awaited her in the hall by the front door, a misty mass of emerald green, and as she approached it to open the door, her hands held out in front of her, she recalled another occasion when her hands had reached towards greenness. She seemed to see that shocked face looking at her, the aghast eyes, full comprehension of what she had been about to do distorting a pleasant, kindly face into a mask of shock.

The green mist melted away and for a while there was no whispering. Dolly walked along through the driving wind to the bus stop down below the Archway. It was more than likely, of course, that she would not see him. She was rather late. Perhaps she should postpone it till tomorrow. But what was the point of putting off and putting off while Yvonne's disappointment in her grew and Yvonne began more and more to hate her? The bus came and still, as it drew to a stop, she considered postponement, going home, leaving it for a day or a week even. But she got on the bus and paid her fare to the driver and found herself a seat where she could sit with her right cheek against the glass.

Edith and Myra had got on the bus with her and they chattered to each other in a fretful, scared kind of way. The bus was going down Hampstead Lane, already under the overhanging trees of Kenwood, before she could make out what they were saying. They wanted her to stop, they wanted her to stop now and go back.

"I'm on the bus, I can't go back," she said to them.

A man sitting in front of her looked round and at the empty seat beside her. Dolly was embarrassed because the man was not psychic and couldn't hear them. She held her hand over her mouth. While she was dressing she had put on Pup's talisman, put it on over her dress which was rust red and matched it, but now, to feel the comfort of it closer to her,

330

she undid the top button and slipped the talisman in against her skin. The whispering had not stopped but it had become very faint. No one, whatever they might say about magic, whatever Pup might say, was going to convince her the talisman was not fraught with power and charged with protection.

The wind caught her as she stepped off the bus. It caught one passenger after another, tore them off the bus and sent them half-running, holding on to hats and scarves. A regatta of tiny clouds was racing across the blue sky. London lay down there in the bowl beneath the heights, all bright and glittering in the smokeless, fogless, clean air.

It had been precisely 8:30 when he had come out last time, just after 8:30 that morning when she had followed him into the train and plucked the hairs from his coat collar. The time now was twenty-five past. She had no clear idea yet of what she would do when she saw him, how she would act, certain only of one thing, that she would follow him and stick to him, all day if necessary, for the rest of her life if necessary, until she had done what had to be done. After all, what else was there for her to do?

George Colefax's Mercedes stood in the car park, the nearest vehicle to the flats' entrance. A girl came out of the swing doors, then a couple, then, walking languidly in spite of the cold, a man in a long white sheepskin coat. It was Ashley Clare.

He glanced into the car as he passed it. He turned up the collar of his coat and pushed his hands into his pockets. She saw his face closer to and more clearly than she had ever done. It looked dark and drawn with deep lines running from the nostrils to the corners of the mouth, it looked very middle-aged. There was a sallow pallor about that face as if there were no blood under the skin to give it color.

He passed within a yard of Dolly. She let him get a little ahead and then she followed him down the hill, down steep, winding Heath Street where the ramparts of walls and tall houses did something to shelter the narrow defile from the wind. He walked with his shoulders hunched and his head dipped as if the cold pained him. At the bookstall outside Hampstead tube station she expected him to stop and buy a paper so that he could do the crossword as he had before, but instead he went straight into the station and, holding out his season ticket, turned left for the lift. Neither of the ticket machines was working. Dolly had to join the queue to buy a ticket, but Ashley Clare had not gone down. The green metal doors had already closed before he reached the lift which must have contained its requisite maximum of thirty passengers.

The station was crowded this morning. Unlike last time there was for some reason a great crush of people. Ashley Clare and Dolly were among the first to get into the lift and Myra and Edith got in with them. Dolly couldn't see the greenness or smell the lemony scent, nor could she decipher their words but their whispering had become intense and shrill.

In the passage at the bottom of the lift a gale was blowing as strongly as aboveground, only here the wind was warm and with a metallic smell. The crowd went hard along the passage and over the bridge above the line like a herd of animals starting to stampede. Once or twice Dolly lost sight of the white sheepskin coat ahead of her and then, as they went down the steps, it was gone altogether.

It was a train northward bound for Golders Green that was making the hot wind. Dolly and almost everyone else took the left-hand turn for the line that went down into the center of London. It was a nasty moment for Dolly when she thought she saw the bun-faced woman in the brown coat who, that evening at Camden Town, had seen her hands flexed to push. She was standing reading a poster for a new film. Dolly gazed. The woman turned and looked at her and of course it was not the same one at all, not in the least like, only the coat was similar.

Dolly walked along the platform, looking for Ashley Clare. Last time she had made a mistake, she had picked the wrong person, which in the circumstances had hardly mattered. But what if her hands had not drawn back? What if she had pushed? There would be no other man here wearing white sheepskin, she thought, and then she looked up and saw him. He too had been reading a film poster and now he was looking at her, studying her so intently, that she wondered for a moment if, once upon a time, Myra had told George and George had told him of her stepdaughter with the birthmark or if Yvonne had told George . . . But it was more likely that with the arrogance of the handsome unblemished he was merely staring at the nevus itself. She returned the look so savagely, hating him with a personal hatred now, that he moved his eyes, turned his head, and, with his hands still in his pockets, walked towards the edge of the platform.

Once more the waiting passengers had formed themselves into huddled groups at points where they guessed the doors would be. Instead of doing the same, Ashley Clare had stationed himself between two such groups and he stood there with his head bowed, very close to the edge. But a fresh surge of people had come on to the platform from the next lift and he was joined by a man on one side of him and a woman on the other. Dolly moved herself in behind him. She looked up at his hair above the coat collar and thought it seemed grayer than before. Edith and Myra were chattering away urgently now, they sounded nearly hysterical.

The train would come in from the left. Already the warm wind had begun to blow. There were two people standing very close behind Dolly now and they seemed very tall people. She was surrounded by tall people, a man at least six feet two on her left, a girl stilted up on immense heels on her right. She felt small, hidden, squashed. She heard someone say over her head that there had been a breakdown and a train left out, that was why there was such a crowd, the whole platform packed. Hemmed in, towered over — or so it felt — she moved her hands. The cream woolly gloves she wore were almost exactly the same color as the sheepskin. One of his hairs, a dark one, such as she had used in the making of the useless wax image, fell from the back of his head to alight on the pale knitted back of her glove. She looked at it, clinging there, and Myra and Edith's frenzied shouting roared around her.

The train came out of the tunnel and through a gap between sheepskin and the tall man's herringbone tweed she could see the driver's face, young and pink. Before he was lost to view she saw his mouth open and screaming, for by then she had pushed.

He might have given a cry as he went over. How could she tell when, as the crowd went back like a wave, a sound rose from it that was a mingling of screams and gasps and dreadful moans? She cried out with them and the wave drew her back with it. An impersonal, inhuman voice arrested movement and made temporary silence.

"There has been an accident. I repeat, there has been an accident. Please keep calm and don't panic . . ."

A woman standing beside Dolly, a stranger, began to weep.

23

The man who had moved in downstairs came under immediate suspicion. Conal had seen him only in the distance, the dark hair, the blank meaningless face, the blue jeans. He heard his voice too, with the false English accent they had taught him while he was away training to be a police spy. Could he be Diarmit Bawne? For a moment the fog cleared and Conal knew he was himself Diarmit, it was his mind that had done this to him. But it was only for a moment. The fog rolled back and he was Conal again. That evening, he thought, the man downstairs would come up and knock on the door, introduce himself by some outlandish name and offer Conal food or ask him to make less noise. Conal was very careful to make no noise and at 7:00, when Diarmit had not appeared, he went out.

He had no doubt the room would be searched in his absence. Diarmit had a key and would have no need to pick the lock as the so-called Andrea had done. This time he had not scattered any scouring powder. What was the point? He knew they would search and he was tired, he hardly cared any more. Most of the energy and high spirits essential to Conal Moore had subsided and he felt himself becoming as slow and steady and *dead* as Diarmit had been. He tramped the silent streets with nothing to do and nowhere to go, half afraid to go back.

But at last he had to. He fully expected the man who was to be inside the room, waiting there to speak to him and urge him to give himself up. Find a priest to confess to, tell it all to Kathleen, then go to the police. But it was worse than that, more sinister than that, for the room was empty and reeking of Diarmit and the girl, her perfume and Diarmit's stinking clothes.

They had taken the knives. He couldn't see the Harrods bag anywhere. In a burst of panic that renewed his strength, he threw open doors and drawers, pulled the pile of red clothes apart, scrabbled under the bed, pulling out papers, old carriers, and, at last, *the* carrier. He fell asleep on the bed from the exhaustion of it.

When he awoke in the deep middle of the night, he saw chaos around him. They had searched without caution, without caring if he knew. Drawers were tumbled on to the floor, their contents scattered, clothes lay everywhere and in the middle of the room, as a signal to him, he supposed, that all was now known, on top of a pile of newspapers and carrier bags lay the cleaver and the two knives.

It was then that he knew he must get out and defend himself against them. Once the morning came he must get out, taking his property with him, to find himself a refuge. The electric knife sharpener made scarcely any sound. He sat cross-legged on the floor, sharpening the knives and testing them on his left hand until the fingertips were all scored across and bloody. If Diarmit heard the faint noise and came up, he would be ready for him, but Diarmit did not come.

It was in a state very like a trance that Dolly walked back up the steep hill. And for almost the first time since Myra died she found herself in silence. Myra and Edith had whispered together, making a sound like the shrill twittering of frightened birds, then sighed, then gasped, then gone. She knew she would never hear them again or smell the lemon of her mother or see the green that was Myra. They had gone and left her in utter silence.

She hardly noticed the wind. The bus came after she had waited twenty minutes for it.

For a stupid moment she thought the bus driver had a dog's face but she closed her eyes and opened them and saw a brown man, an Indian, with an aquiline nose. A deadly silence enclosed her on the bus. She put up her hand and felt the hard edges of the talisman through her dress and it made her easier, it brought her a little life.

There was no need to hurry home. She could not have hurried if she had wanted to. The news would not reach Yvonne until the evening or perhaps even tomorrow if she saw no paper and had to wait for George to tell her. Dolly got off the bus in Highgate village and walked slowly, buffeted by the wind, down the hill to Holmesdale Road where she made her way on to the old railway line.

Spring catkins were appearing on the birch trees and the willows. By the time the summer came, she and Pup would be on their own in their own house and George and Yvonne happy again in their own house. Tomorrow, if she hadn't heard from Yvonne, she would send her the blonde bridal doll by Pup. It was wonderfully peaceful without Myra and Edith. Dolly thought she would drink a bottle of wine when she got home, though it was so early. Enough wine would kill the day for her until Yvonne phoned.

She touched the talisman. Feathers were flying out of the mouth of the Mistley tunnel like snow blown from a drift. Dolly walked through the tunnel and went up the steps on the other side.

Harold was at home. She could hear the clatter of his typewriter from the breakfast room. In the kitchen she opened a bottle of burgundy and drank a glassful down at a gulp. She took the bottle with her into the living room and began drinking the wine steadily, not bothering to make it last. There was another bottle where that one had come from; in the wineshops there was an infinite number of bottles waiting for her to come and buy. The typewriter rattled away on the other side of the wall. She missed Edith and Myra. Often she had hated them and tried to drive them away, but now that they had gone back to their abode on the Other Side, she wanted their voices back again, their comments on what she had done, their judgment.

She fetched the other bottle and drew the cork. Her hands were shaking. She realized that tremors had been passing through her whole body ever since she came back into the house. It was a strange thing to happen because she was happy, now Ashley Clare was dead she was as content with her life as she ever could be.

Wendy Collins arrived in her car to take Harold out somewhere. Dolly thought of when she and Pup would be alone, of turning the dining room into a temple, of George and Yvonne coming. Her thoughts buzzed in her head like a skep full of bees. Harold and Wendy went arm in arm down the path and got into Wendy's car. Dolly thought she might sleep, it was many nights since she had slept well. The dolls on the mantelpiece seemed to be watching her, their eyes following her, swiveling in their padded rag faces.

She sat down at the sewing machine but her hands were too unsteady to hold her work. Half the bottle of burgundy remained. She slopped some of it into the glass, spilling red drops, a little red pond of it, on to Myra's haircord. The dolls put their heads on one side and stared, Ashley Clare and Yvonne began to shake their heads and roll their embroidered eyes. Dolly finished the wine and got up, holding on to the furniture to help her across the room. She saw her face and the masking red nevus in Myra's mirror and as she looked at it with misted, distorting eyes, she saw another face appear behind her, its dog snout peer over her left shoulder.

She closed the door and turned the key in the lock, shutting Anubis in with the dolls. It was impossible to walk upstairs, so she crawled from tread to tread, crawled across the landing, climbed on to her bed and slept.

The wine stains on the carpet looked like spots of spilled blood. Dolly moved the sewing machine table a foot or two to hide them. She had slept for ten hours, turning day into night, and now, primed with aspirin — she had taken six — she felt weak and shaky and somehow disembodied. Harold was still out or had gone out again, Pup had neither come nor phoned. Or she supposed he had not phoned. She had been dead to sound or any change or disturbance of her surroundings.

She could feel the presence of the dog-faced god but she could not see him. She walked about the house, turning the light on as she entered a room and off as she left it. It was as if she were getting her bearings, taking a view of the new life that was opening ahead of her. All the time as she walked she could hear, or perhaps only feel by means of soft vibrations, some creature always padding a little way behind her. When she looked to see, there was nothing there. It was a couple of days since she had eaten anything more than a couple of biscuits or two but she did not feel like eating now. She took a bottle of white wine, Sauterne, out of the fridge, drew the cork and sipped it slowly straight from the bottle. It made her feel queasy and weak-kneed but she went on drinking it.

Still Pup did not come. Once she would have believed him to be at the Golden Dawn but she could hardly think that now. Once, before the Golden Dawn days, she would have worried, imagining him mugged or run over. He had grown too self-sufficient, indeed too great and powerful, for her to feel those things now.

Harold was back. She heard Wendy leave him and the smack of their good-night kiss. Night had become day for her. She would sit up through it, sit in the living room with her last bottle of wine, waiting for Pup to come.

Very early in the morning, Saturday morning, Conal began moving his stuff out. He started before it was light. There was a lot of stuff belonging to Diarmit Bawne: a gray duffel coat, a raincoat, blue jeans and light shirts that had to be washed and ironed. There were tins of food and bottles of sauce, a colored blanket that looked as if it had been made out of wool by some woman, an ashtray with a shamrock leaf painted on it. All this he left behind for its rightful owner. Into the place where he would withstand their siege he took his red clothes and the knife sharpener and the Harrods bag with the knives and the cleaver in it. He walked through the cold dark morning, carrying his possessions, down the muddy steps to the platform of the old station.

He had to make three journeys. When he had got everything that was Conal Moore's and left everything that was Diarmit Bawne's, he opened the room door and left it propped wide open with one of Diarmit's tins of Campbell's soup. Diarmit would not have been capable of writing them a note, he could write his own name and that was about all. Conal could write, he was an educated man, but he did not choose to do so. Why bother with them? Why make their job easier for them?

They would guess where he was anyway. When they came he would be ready for them. The dawn had come, it was almost sunrise, the sun was showing in pale yellow bars above a ridge of black roofs and the black feather-iness of tree branches. He humped his stuff along the platform and into the tunnel. The mattress had dwindled in the eighteen months that had passed but it was still a mattress and it was still possible to stand it up on its side and curve it round into a windbreak or defen-sive barrier. He had brought a blanket from the bed and the dark red anorak that Conal had bought third or fourth hand in the Mind shop. The knives and the cleaver were what were important, his weapons. The sight of them, sharp and shining, laid out carefully, each parallel to the others, on a thick pad of damp newspaper, comforted him and made him feel safer. Any policeman or woman, any spy, who came near him had better look out, that was all.

Conal Moore had always been a brave boy, a daredevil, a wild fellow. He sat down behind the barricade on a mound of wet newspaper, the blanket tented round him, ready for anything.

At 9:00 in the morning Pup came home. Dolly, waking up on the living-room sofa, heard him go straight upstairs. She just had time to put her shoes on, run her fingers through her hair, stretch, before he came running down again and was in the room with her.

She hoped to avoid having to explain, she hoped he would simply think she was up and dressed early for a Saturday. But he was not even looking at her. He was looking at the dolls on the mantelpiece.

"Don't you think we'd better put them away now?" he said gently. "Well, the — the man, anyway. Not in very good taste." He hesitated. "You do — know?" She remained still, saying nothing. He picked the dolls off the shelf. "I tried to phone you a good many times yesterday."

She said indifferently, "I was out a lot yesterday," and with a show of insouciance, "What should I know?"

"You didn't see an evening newspaper?"

She shook her head, waiting for the pleasant news that was no news to be broken.

He opened the lid of the remnants box and slipped the dolls inside. She thought he looked suddenly much older, far older than his years, and content in a strained kind of way. He must be happy for Yvonne, relieved for Yvonne getting her husband back. She

346

laid her hand on his sleeve.

"It's been quite a shock," he said. "Yesterday morning — well, twenty-four hours ago now, George Colefax fell on to the line at Hampstead in front of the incoming train."

24

After he had gone, she found the photograph Yvonne had sent her and looked at it. For some reason — because George Colefax had spoken of Ashley Clare as a beautiful boy? — she had taken the man smoking the cigar for George and the slimmer handsomer one for Ashley Clare. She had been wrong, just as she had been wrong that evening on the platform at Camden Town, only then it hadn't mattered, it hadn't been too late and beyond remedy.

Yvonne's husband was dead. She had murdered him. Since Pup told her, her head had been full of a rushing, roaring sound and full, too, of thick mist. She sat where he had left her, quite still, staring, afraid to move lest any movement she might make should bring down fresh disaster on them all.

The thought came to her that she would

never see anyone again, no one would ever again see her or speak to her. There was even no sound of Harold in the house this morning. Pup had gone without saying when he would come back. Yvonne hated her. She was left alone for the rest of her life — or alone but for a single companion and even he had deserted her since, just before Pup came, she had for a moment seen the shadow of his dog's head appear on the wall.

It was more than twenty-four hours, much more, since she had taken her clothes off. The rust-red dress was crumpled and it seemed to her that it smelled of sweat and pain. Without getting up, without drawing the curtains, she began unbuttoning it. But before she had reached the waist she was aware of loss, of something — more than everything else — being wrong, of a terrible lack. Both her hands went to her neck, her breasts, searching.

The talisman was gone.

She cried out, a useless cry, since there was no one to hear her and no one to come. Was it because she and the talisman had been parted that this horror had happened? But no, it had been with her then, she had felt it against her skin. If she were not to lose everything, to lose her own self as well, she must find the talisman, she must not permit it to be lost, to wander the world ownerless.

Feverishly she began to search the house.

"I suppose," Yvonne said, holding on to the Pup very tight, her head on his shoulder, "I suppose what happened to poor George was like they say in the papers, the balance of his mind was disturbed. The policeman said to me it would just be made out to be accidental at the inquest but what I think is he meant to do it, don't you?"

"It seems an odd way to do it," said Pup, "and an odd place to choose."

Yvonne shivered. "If your mind's unbalanced you don't think of things like that. It was quick. You see, he told me he couldn't live without Ashley and the chances were Ashley'd be dead in a year. I think he must have been feeling very sort of low and he got down on that platform and despair came over him and he jumped. But we don't have to tell them that at the inquest, do we?"

"Of course we don't."

"Poor George. I was very fond of him once, you know. I do feel quite upset. It's awful to have been a widow twice when you're only twenty-five."

"Twenty-seven," said Pup gently. "I think you and I should get married quite soon, don't you?"

"Oh, yes, please," said Yvonne, putting up her lips for a kiss.

Pup kissed her. He saw no reason why they shouldn't be very happy. He wanted a large family. George hadn't made a will but that was of no consequence since Yvonne was his sole heir. Above her downy golden head, Pup surveyed what he could see of the house that would soon be his and took in a corner of Kashmiri rug, a segment of Chippendale cabinet, a scarlet shimmer of Chinese bridge beyond the window in the green grounds. Sometime or other he had promised to go down to Arrowsmith Court and fetch home the Mercedes. It wasn't bad, he thought, to have got everything you wanted by the time you were twenty-one, a flourishing business, a successful career, an apparently attractive appearance, a beautiful wife, and a million pounds' worth of house just off the Bishop's Avenue.

Dolly would say he had got it through selling his soul to the devil. In which case, like poor old Faustus, he would presumably be expected to pay some sort of awful price for it. Pup couldn't think of any awful price that might be exacted from him and he laughed aloud, it was all such nonsense.

"I know," said Yvonne, snuggling up. "I feel happy too. Aren't we awful?"

Amid the rushing in her brain and the swirling mists, Dolly's memory was clear. She could remember she was still wearing the talisman when she left the station, still wearing it on the bus and when she walked down Southwood Lane, across the Archway Road and up on to the old railway line. She thought she had still been wearing it when she passed over the bridge at Stanhope Road and came down into the valley, but that she could not quite remember.

It was a bland day, white-skied and color-less. She put on her coat, and as she came to the front door, she saw the shadow of Anubis on Myra's biscuit-colored wall and now his face was neither friendly nor indifferent but twisted into a snarl. She wouldn't look. She thought she would forever be afraid to look behind her. Out in the air it was better. She shook her hair down to cover her cheek. There were a few people about going Saturday morning shopping and they all had the heads of dogs set on the shoulders of their coats or sweaters. Sometimes if she looked away and looked back quickly they became people again, staring back with hostility. She walked back as far as the bridge at Stanhope Road. She was sure she had still had the talisman before she reached there.

Perhaps because it was so wet underfoot and the tree branches dripped dampness, there was no one else on the old railway line. If no one had been along, or no observant person, since she had, the talisman might still be there. She walked slowly, her head bent and her eyes down, and presently she picked herself a long thin wand of poplar with which to probe the grass. With a wand very like this, cut from a tree very near here, Pup had done so many wonderful magical things. The talisman was all that was left from that time and she must find it.

In the wider valley, searching was slower. She could not remember exactly where she had walked the day before. Against the grass the green of it would not show and the red part was very small. She peered from side to side, her head moving rhythmically. A feather, borne on a light breath of breeze, fluttered down and fell at her feet, and suddenly the memory came back to her, the feather recalling it, how on the morning before she had felt the talisman on her skin as she entered the Mistley tunnel.

So she had lost it somewhere between here and home. It was darkish inside the tunnel but no grass grew there, the ground was bare, dark and damp. A feather touched her face as lightly as Myra's spirit fingers used to touch it.

Someone had heaved the mattress up on to its side. Dolly did not think it had been like that yesterday. Was it possible that she could remember just at this point a slippery touch as the thong of the talisman had come unfastened and slid down through her clothes? In the twilight of the tunnel, mud and feathers underfoot, she moved towards the mattress, the wand in her hands like a diviner's rod.

And then she saw him, just the shape of him in the gloom, not his dog's head nor his glistening body, and in his outstretched hands not the caduceus and the palms but two bright knives that caught what little light there was.

He had waited for her, knowing she was bound to come. She had known she must be caught by him sooner or later. Everything that had happened to them had inexorably led to this end, and as they closed together with the knives between them, each gave an equal cry of fear.

The publishers hope that this Large Print Book has brought you pleasurable reading. Each title is designed to make the text as easy to see as possible. G. K. Hall Large Print Books are available from your library and your local bookstore. Or you can receive information on upcoming and current Large Print Books by mail and order directly from the publisher. Just send your name and address to:

G. K. Hall & Co.
70 Lincoln Street
Boston, Mass. 02111

or call, toll-free:

1–800–343–2806

A note on the text
Large print edition designed by
Bernadette Strickland
Composed in 16 pt Times Roman
on a Mergenthaler Linotron 202
by Modern Graphics, Inc.